STOLEN
WOMAN

Praise for Stolen Woman:

"Travel with these characters, and like them,
be changed by this reality and this fight."
-Origin Coffee & Tea,
all profits given toward rescuing the trafficked.

"You will want to read this!"
-Joe Olachea II, Pastor Lakes Community Chapel,
Board Member at America's Keswick

"I'm on pins and needles to see how this story
- with all its plots, tensions, and layers-will end!"
-Shawne Ebersole, Association of Baptists, Bangladesh

"This is a book you can't afford *not* to read. God can use
one person—each reader—to make a difference.
And the place to start is right here . . . inside these pages."
-Susie Shellenberger, Editor, SUSIE Magazine

"In Kimberly Rae's novel *Stolen Woman*, she juxtaposes the natural
beauty of Kolkata, India, with the insidious evil slithering under
darkness on street corners where women are sold to the highest bidder.
Rae's message of hope and the education the novel provides should
open our eyes to an issue which can no longer be ignored
and needs everyone's efforts to eradicate."
-Chapter 61 Ministries/Truckers Against Trafficking

"My hope is that many more will be awakened by *Stolen Woman* and
resolve to sacrifice much to bring redemption to the broken, poor
and oppressed. I am thankful for this beautifully written
voice in the fight for freedom."
- Chad Salstrom, Co-founder Origin Coffee & Tea

"...as well written as Karen Kingsbury and others I have read!
Wow! What a message. I couldn't put it down."
-Kim Olachea, Educator & Seminar Speaker

". . . exceedingly well written."
Jeannie Lockerbie Stephenson,
Author of On Duty in Bangladesh,

"I was intrigued from the beginning. Excitement, adventure, suspense and romance awaited on every page and chapter. Exactly the kind of book I like. It is certainly a book that is hard to put down....
I can NOT wait until part 2 is out!!!"
Laura, Blue Ladybug Mamas,
theblueladybug.com

"*Stolen Woman* contains many twists and turns that totally kept me guessing. Right when I thought I had it figured out, I was wrong. This book which is full of mystery and suspense also contains a great message of hope and redemption for those who seem like they are in hopeless situations. I could also personally identify with the message that no matter how bad we mess things up, God can turn our mistakes into something good. The book also contains a surprise element, which I thought was very sweet."
Cari Jean, HubPages, Faith's
Mom's blog, CariJean.com

"Kimberly Rae offers a rare inside look at the lives of young Indian women held captive in brothels. You'll undoubtedly get caught up in the suspense, romance and battle between good and evil in a red light district. And, you'll likely come away with a deeper understanding of Christ's call to the Church to be His heart and hands to offer hope to the broken-hearted and freedom to the those sitting in darkness."
Dawn Herzog Jewell, Author of
Escaping the Devil's Bedroom

"I read it in a total of 6 hours! It was SO hard to put down! I was sucked into the culture of India, Asha's romance, and her riskiness of rescuing a friend!...I highly recommend this book to anyone!"
Mary Beth Shaw, Blue Ladybug Mamas

What Readers Are Saying:

WOW!!! It was awesome! I don't know how I'll get through work today as I was up to the wee hours of the morning because I couldn't put it down! Can't wait for #2!   *Amanda*

AMAZING! .... loved reading every second of it, and can't wait for the second book!   *Laura*

I thoroughly enjoyed Stolen Woman. The characters were well developed, the setting was colorful and exotic and the authors descriptive language made the settings come alive. I enjoyed the undertone of humor that ran throughout. Once I started reading it I just couldn't put it down and I can't wait for Kimberly Rae's next book to come out.   *Robin*

I loved it!!!!!!! ... really drew me in to the characters and I can't wait to read the next book.   *Melissa*

I read it in one day. I can hardly wait for the next two to come out!   *Kathy*

This novel turned out to be even better than expected. I could hardly put the book down, between the suspense, the romance, the adventure. The author did a fantastic job of opening my eyes to the truth and terror of human trafficking, and yet gave me hope and ignited a passion to fight against it, all while truly delighting my reading senses. It's an absolutely fabulous book! If you enjoy Christian romance novels, this is the perfect book for you! I can't wait for the 2nd book in the series to publish!   *Laura*

...my new favorite author!!!   *Becky*

The book was intriguing in every way...the love story, the risks, the history of other parts of the world and the in your face realization that young girls and women everywhere are precious to our Creator and deserve to be treated as such! Kudos...can't wait for book 2 :)   *Beverly*

Read it cover to cover in one day and LOVED IT! It tore at my heart with every page!   *Kayla*

Just wanted to say that Stolen Woman was like, the best book I've ever read! I'm so psyched about the next one!   *Alison, teen*

... amazing and very touching!   *Stephanie*

I couldn't put this book down. The story is compelling, the subject is moving and the characters are vibrant. I fell in love with the characters and saw myself and people I love in the pages of this book. I can't wait for the next book! *JD*

...can't wait to read the next one. *Stacy*

This amazing book is an intriguing page-turner that will grab your attention from the first paragraph to the last... Stolen Woman contains all the qualities that make up a good read: suspense, intrigue, romance, characters that are likeable and interesting, and also a bigger purpose. ...I highly recommend this fast-paced novel to anyone who enjoys Christian romance or suspense. I can't wait for the sequel to come out! *Sue*

I will tell everyone I know they need to read this book. *Karen*

I am thoroughly enjoying the book! *Joe*

Love the book. *Chase, teen*

I loved this book! Kimberly did an amazing job creating her characters and setting. I very quickly got lost in the story and could easily picture the people and places that were being described. The story flowed so smoothly that I felt like I was right there experiencing and feeling all of the emotions that the characters were experiencing! I admit that my family was neglected as I read this book because I couldn't put it down. I have been waiting eagerly for the next book in the series, and I am already making plans to clear my schedule so that I can read it without interruption! *Amy*

Combining action and adventure with a fascinating culture and entertaining characters, this book will leave you wanting more ... *Melissa*

...love, love, love the book. *Stacy*

Kimberly Rae has a keen eye for the everyday perspective in life. She painted a vivid picture of a culture I knew nothing about. With humor and a great style of writing, she created characters you can't help but care for and cherish. A book well written and worth reading! *Christine*

I found it immensely riveting both in its plot and characters *Charae*

...can't wait for the second book *Hope*

Half way through the first chapter, I was already wanting the next book in the series. It is hard to believe this is her first novel! Very well written. I would recommend this book to anyone. Will be first in line for the next installment. *Jo*

Excellent piece of Christian fiction by a very gifted author! *Bethany*

Stayed up all night tonight to finish the book; it was truly inspiring and well written. I'm so glad I read it, by far one of the best books. *Megan*

…a strong story and creates memorable characters you'll want to hear more about. Definitely worth reading!! *Amy*

Stolen Woman is one of the best books I have read in a long time! For me the best part of reading a fiction book is when you can actually FEEL the emotions of the characters in your heart/soul. That's what Stolen Woman did for me. I appreciate how the author tastefully presents the horrific subject human trafficking, and that she has included an underlying love story (which I was not expecting). …I can't wait for the next one! *Katie*

It is great!!!!!!!!!!!! *Alayjah, teen*

I thought this book might be depressing, but was very pleasantly surprised. I don't read many books, but at the end of every chapter, I had to keep reading. I read it in 2 days!!! I normally take 2 months to read a book. You will not regret buying this book, and you will recommend it to your friends! *Brian*

I would love nothing more than to read this to my Sunday school girls. *Angie*

I started Stolen Woman…and I had about 4 chapter[s] left last night but I stayed up to read them all. When I told my uncle about it, he said, "you stayed up all night reading?" I told him it was just that good. *Saraya*

…compelling, compassionate and encouraging. I've recommended this to my book club. Although I finished the book a few weeks ago, the story lingers with me. *Cindy*

What a fascinating book! I couldn't put it down. *Janette*

I enjoy reading Christian romances, but it is not very often that I absolutely love one. Loved your book!...this book is everything a Christian novel should be. *Kristen*

…your book has changed my life. *Meghan, teen*

STOLEN WOMAN

KIMBERLY RAE

*For the women
who have not yet been given hope.*

Character Pronunciation Guide:

Asha—pronounced Ah-shah

Rani—pronounced like the English name Ronny

Milo—pronounced Mee-low

Didi—pronounced Dee-dee, means "Big Sister"

Dada—pronounced Dah-dah, means "Big Brother"

Mashi—pronounced Mah-shee, means "Auntie"

PROLOGUE

$\mathcal{A}$sha shivered despite the intense heat. Why had she never considered the brutal fact that she, too, might get caught? Stolen. Sold. Bartered over like one of the pieces of blood-dripping meat in this filthy market.

Someone was following her.

Back home she would not have noticed, but weeks in India had taught her to be wary. All the noise and clamor along the busy Kolkata street could not distract from the shadow that appeared, then retreated whenever she turned to find its source.

The person following her was not very good at the game of stealth. That fact, however, did not make the predator any less dangerous. Who was it? And why was she the target?

Slipping around the nearest corner, a whisper of wind teasing her shawl out behind her, Asha dodged a wandering goat, then turned quickly down an alley to the left hoping to lose whoever was on her trail.

She was already late. But better to make Rani wait than to put her in even more danger.

If that were possible.

Could there be any danger worse than what her friend had already experienced? Asha could not stop her body from trembling. She flattened a shaking hand against the wall. Edging forward inch by inch, she angled her head to glimpse around the corner without revealing her face.

Was he gone?

She desperately wanted to remain where she was, clinging to the remote feeling of safety that curled around her in the small, dark corner where she hid. But how could she stay, avoiding risk, knowing that doing so would abandon a friend to the evil of the night while she remained untouched?

Asha's whole body cringed. What a bad choice of words to think.

Mark had warned her about this. Mark. Just the thought of his lean, contoured face, muscles tensed along his jaw as he tried to convince her to keep away from the very street she was now traveling, gave Asha a sharp pain near her heart.

She should have listened. Should have asked for his advice . . . his help.

Why had she been so stubborn?

"God, help me," she whispered. Summoning all her courage, she stood and stepped back into the alley, casting a wary gaze around before continuing toward the rendezvous point.

Was that Rani waiting beside the mounds of colored spices for sale?

A sudden glimpse of a following shadow stopped Asha cold. Her heartbeat shot up and she broke out in a cold sweat. She had not lost her predator after all.

A quick, desperate look left and right revealed several narrow, shadowed pathways through shanties and market stalls.

Should she run, leaving Rani to think she had not come? Should she meet Rani and tell her they must go separate ways? Surely the public arena of the open marketplace would protect them as they spoke.

However, Asha knew with certainty that once they separated the predator would follow Rani, forgetting about her.

Tears stung her eyes. She took a deep breath.

She would run.

Turning to the left, she quickly chose the closest path. Three steps would carry her, and hopefully the person following after her, into a different section of the market, away from Rani's watchful eyes.

One step. Two. Asha took one glance back at her friend, her eyes full of regret, when Rani saw her. Rani's eyes lit up in recognition. She smiled.

Asha's spirit groaned in defeat. Now what could she do?

She could not keep the fear and confusion from her features. She could tell the moment Rani saw them, too. It was as if Rani's face immediately transformed from a woman holding on to a shred of hope to a child terrified of the monsters under her bed.

Or worse.

I'm so sorry. Asha wanted to say it out loud but could not get her lips to move.

When the shadow came closer then stopped only a few feet away, she closed her eyes, wishing all of it away. Wishing she could go back to that morning and change the choices that had brought her here into this web of danger and fear.

No, she would have to go farther back than that. Before meeting Rani. Before meeting Mark. Even before her arrival in India.

She would have to go back over six weeks ago, to the day of her flight. To the moments before she left home, when she kept an important truth from her parents. To the first time she decided it was okay to deceive in order to do good.

That first deceit had begun a pattern, a trail that had led her to this moment, this foolish choice to do things on her own without help.

A choice that might destroy her and the friend she wanted so desperately to save.

Waiting for the follower to approach, grab her, and possibly cart her off to a lifetime of slavery, Asha's mind took her away from the marketplace and back, flashing scenes across her closed eyelids, rewinding through the choices she had made.

Back to the beginning.

To the day she left for India . . .

Part One

He has sent me (Jesus) to heal the brokenhearted,

To proclaim liberty to the captives . . .

To set at liberty those who are oppressed.

Luke 4:18

CHAPTER ONE

"*This* is ridiculous. You've got to stop crying," Asha muttered to herself. She wiped long, slender fingers across her cheeks as she glanced toward the couple across the aisle, then to the rather staid businessman sitting to her left. No one else on the flight to Atlanta was crying.

Of course not. I wouldn't be either if I was only going to Atlanta. If the passengers knew it was her first time leaving her small hometown in North Carolina, if they knew how significant this trip was for her, they would certainly excuse her tears.

"We will miss you, honey," Maryanne Rogers had said as she hugged her at the airport. Asha could still smell a faint hint of her mother's vanilla and cranberry lotion on her clothes. "I know you won't be able to call because of the bad phone connection there at the orphanage, but send us an e-mail when you can."

The seat-belt light overhead went off but Asha had no desire to stand up and stretch her legs. On the contrary, she felt like curling into a ball and giving in to the fears that had plagued her since she boarded the plane just hours earlier.

She reached down into the pocket of her carry-on and pulled out the brochure from the mission orphanage nestled deep in the heart of Kolkata, India. The dark green tri-fold, old and worn, still displayed the old-style spelling of the city in its heading: "Come to Calcutta and Make a Difference."

"This is Lloyd Stephens." Asha had shown the brochure to her college roommate, Amy, just a week earlier before the summer break began. "He's the missionary who came last semester and spoke in my cultural anthropology class."

"He looks really old," Amy had commented about the white-haired, slightly stooped-over man in the photo.

"He's the first of three generations of missionaries there." Asha opened the brochure to show more pictures. "Here are some of the orphans. You should have seen the pictures he showed, Amy. They pulled at my heart till I thought it would burst right out."

"They're cute."

Asha had not been thinking how cute the thin, brown-skinned children were. She had been considering how, had she not been adopted, she could have been one of the children in those photographs.

She had found a tack and pegged the brochure onto a cork board hanging over a desk in their room. "And now I get to spend my whole summer there, helping orphans and making a difference."

"Yeah." Amy left the desk and flopped onto her bed, ignoring the clothes piled on the floor next to an open, empty suitcase. "I bet your parents aren't as excited as you are."

The day Asha had received an e-mail from Lloyd Stephens inviting her to spend her summer in India, she had rushed to the phone, thrilled to tell her parents about the opportunity. Their response had been far from enthusiastic.

"You've only got two months for your summer break from college," her father had reminded her with his unfailing sense of logic. "Spending your entire summer in India would take away any chance for rest and vacation. I fear you would begin your senior year exhausted and worn down."

"How did you convince them to let you go?" Amy asked, interrupting her thoughts. Amy picked up a yellow cotton shirt from the pile, balled it up and tossed it into the suitcase.

"It's no wonder all your clothes are wrinkled," Asha said. "I didn't convince them. I had to wait while they prayed about it."

Amy chuckled and threw another shirt in. "That's right. I remember listening to you on the phone, pleading like a kid in a toy store, giving them all your arguments how it would be a great way to find out if God was really calling you into missions or not, and how it would be good to go see your birth culture and all that."

"That was a risk." Asha knelt and began sorting the pile of clothing. "It's been years since I've said a word about how much I want to go to Bangladesh and see where I was born and somehow find my birth family."

"Why? You were adopted as a baby. You don't even remember anything from over there."

Asha sighed. Amy wouldn't understand. "Lots of reasons," she said, folding a shirt, thinking of the opposite side of the world. India was right next to Bangladesh, and Lloyd Stephen's orphanage in Kolkata stood near the border between the two countries. So close.

Amy grinned when her pink tossed shirt landed on Asha's neatly folded pile. "The only argument you didn't tell your parents was your best one, how you could use a few months away from James, too."

"No." Asha looked at the photos tacked to the cork board. "I didn't want them to think I was running away."

"Why not?" Amy said from the bed. "That reason might have worked right away and you wouldn't have had to wait for weeks until they decided."

Asha noticed the photo of James on the board was partially hidden behind her proudly displayed plane tickets. "Well, in the end they did say I could go, and I can't wait. These last weeks of the semester have really dragged."

"Are you kidding?" Amy sat up. She reached over to lift the entire pile of clothing and, with a grunt, dumped it into the suitcase. "You've researched Indian culture, packed, unpacked and repacked, like, three times, and you've missed all the end of the year fun studying that squiggly language." She zipped the suitcase closed. "There, that's done." She crossed her arms and leaned her back against the side of the bed. "Were you really that excited about going, or were you just avoiding James?"

Asha unzipped the suitcase, opened it, and resumed folding the clothes. "Both. James and I didn't exactly have a pleasant conversation last week."

"Did you tell him you needed some space, like a few thousand miles?"

Amy was laughing but Asha did not join her. "Something like that." She had tried to explain that eight weeks away would give her some breathing room—the perfect opportunity to decipher how she really felt about him.

Asha's hands stilled on a crumpled dress as she looked back up at the photo on the wall. Stocky and muscular, James' every inch showed off the wrestler he was, even down—or rather up—to his shaved head.

"That boy is more opinionated and emotional than any guy I've ever met," Amy said. "When he cares about something, he gets all fired up about it." She cocked her head. "I guess in that way at least, y'all are two peas in a pod."

Asha nodded. She admired James' passion for God, and she was flattered by his ardent attention toward her. Lately though...

"He says he knows it's God's will that we be together," Asha said, smoothing the wrinkles from the dress before folding it and placing it back into the suitcase.

"If it is God's will, then God can tell you, too," Amy responded.

"That's what I said." Asha folded a slip, then started matching pairs of socks. "He wasn't happy to hear that."

"Well, next week you'll be on a plane to India and you can forget everything else." She waved Asha's hands away from the suitcase. "Would you stop already? This is my pile of dirty clothes! I'm going to wash them all as soon as I get home."

Asha smiled at the memory. That week had passed and now she really was on a plane flying away from James, away from college, and on her way to Kolkata, a city where over fifty percent of the population was not Indian, but Bengali. Her own people.

She looked out the airplane window as a shiver ran down her spine. For the first time in her life, she would be like the average person. For two whole months she would not stand out as the only dark brown-skinned person in a sea of white faces.

Asha had never experienced being part of the majority population and felt a heady exhilaration just imagining it. Best of all, her years of learning Bengali, the language of her birth, were going to finally be worth it. She had studied off and on since high school so she could talk with her family if she ever did find them, but now she would get to use it over the summer, for Bengali was one of the major spoken languages in Kolkata. Asha envisioned walking off the plane and conversing easily with a taxi driver, or a rickshaw driver, or whoever would be waiting for her.

Reality brought Asha harshly back to the present. No one from the orphanage had responded to her e-mails for over a week. The elder Mr. Stephens had warned her that the internet connection often went down, sometimes for days, so she assumed that was why she had received nothing from them about her itinerary. Asha had been unable to make arrangements about who would be picking her up, or how she would get to the orphanage.

Good thing I didn't tell Mom and Dad about that little glitch. Asha bit her lip. *They'd have never let me on this plane.*

But the trip was too important to let hesitancy or even guilt stand in the way. She had sent several e-mails with her flight itinerary and arrival times. Surely someone would get them sometime during her nearly fourteen-hour flight from Atlanta to Dubai, her overnight layover, or her four-hour flight from Dubai to Kolkata.

The plane dipped toward a landing in Atlanta, shifting the cabin pressure and Asha's thoughts. Stuffing the brochure back into her carry-on, Asha sat up straighter and lifted her chin. She kept up a competent presence through the landing, transit, and as she settled onto her next plane. As the great bird rose into the air, however, the reality of a fourteen-hour flight with no stops weighed down over her like a heavy jacket on a humid day.

She had never been very far from home before. This was a rather overwhelming way to start!

As the sky all around her turned dark, the lights on the plane dimmed. When the stewardess handed her a small blue blanket and a child-sized pillow, Asha gave up on looking confident, scrunched against the window, curled into a ball, and tried to sleep.

Tomorrow she would be in India.

Would anyone be waiting for her?

CHAPTER TWO

None of the pictures in the *National Geographic* magazines she had devoured, nor the travel books she had read, nor even the missionaries she had talked to—nothing could have prepared Asha for her first moments in India.

It was not just the sights: the incredible number of people going in every direction, the bamboo scaffolding crawling up foreign-looking buildings, the rickshaws being hand-pulled along the road, the chickens clucking and pecking around her feet.

Her sense of sight was only one part. India was a land to affect all the senses.

Like her ears. Asha had been unprepared for the noise. Horns blaring, birds calling, even a goat—or a sheep?—bleating somewhere. All around her, people were talking. Asha tried to listen, tried to make out what they were saying, but it was all too fast. She could not catch even one word.

And the smells. Even while her taste buds watered toward the tempting aromas from a small restaurant across the street, another part of her recoiled at the dank smell of piled garbage and what was likely sewage edging the road at her feet.

Overriding everything else, nothing could have prepared Asha for all the feelings that assaulted her the moment she stepped off the airplane and was fully, finally, in India.

For a moment she thought of Alice in Wonderland, when Alice steps through the hole and finds herself in an entirely new world.

But this was Asha's world; a world where she looked like she belonged.

Asha felt for a moment as if she'd been cloned, dressed in saris of a hundred different colors, and scattered out as far as the eye could see. Dark chocolate skin. Black, silky, straight hair. Dark eyes. Everyone around her looked like her.

She felt as if she had come home, but to a place she had never been before.

Standing just outside the airport, bags in hand, it occurred to her: no one was there to meet her. Her e-mails must not have made it through, which meant no one even knew she was here.

All her independence, all her abilities of quick thinking and good ideas failed her in this world. Asha did not know the first thing about how to take care of herself here. What to do.

Mentally, she kicked herself for her stubbornness. She had figured she would just make do, figure out a way, like she always did.

Asha found a pay phone, but realized with a frown that she could not use it because she had not exchanged any money into *rupees* yet. She tried to ask several people if she could borrow their cell phones, but no one seemed to be able to understand her at all.

Asha carted her luggage back into the airport, ignoring the men who had been following her since she got there, to "help" her with her baggage, she presumed.

Once safely back inside, she set her suitcase on the floor near a wall, then flopped down on it. It was more comfortable than the airport chairs anyway.

Though the middle of the afternoon in India, it was the middle of the night back home in North Carolina. Her body kept reminding her it was past time for her to be in bed.

Asha tried to muster up some determination through the fog of jet-lag that kept begging for rest. Sleep was the last thing available to her, so she might as well try to accomplish something.

Sending up a quick, silent cry for help, Asha again tried approaching several people to ask where she could exchange some money.

"Kibhabe poribawrton poisha?" she asked in Bengali.

Each response was unnervingly similar. When approached, people initially looked at her with recognition, likely because she looked completely Bengali. But once she spoke, the friendly look morphed into one of confusion. She knew she was speaking Bengali. She had practiced for weeks. But everyone was looking at her as if she were spouting Chinese.

Were the people here not mostly Bengali after all? Maybe the internet statistics had been wrong. Maybe they only spoke Hindi.

Not to be deterred, Asha whipped out her Hindi phrasebook. Unable to find any phrases about exchanging money, she tried saying "Can you please help me?" instead.

"Kya aap meri madad karenge?"

Same response.

She tried her Bengali phrase again. Nothing but confused stares.

Now Asha was starting to take it personally. Why was this not working?

She even approached several arriving tourists—easy to spot because of their white skin, t-shirts, and backpacks—to ask if any of them had cell phones she could use. No help there; none of their phones were set up to work internationally.

Thoroughly dejected, Asha once again sat on her suitcase and tried not to give in to tears. Was she going to be stuck in this airport forever?

It was at that precise moment that a man approached her from the side. He was white, probably in his mid-forties, and dressed in pants and a button-down shirt despite the heat.

Asha noticed that he was not looking in confusion at signs, or taking pictures, or using a phrasebook.

He was definitely not a tourist.

The man's grin was wide and friendly as he sat down in a chair near her suitcase. Asha squirmed a little; she was not used to being approached by men old enough to be her father.

Then again, she was desperate. She needed help, and he was the only option.

Before she had a chance to ask him, however, he chuckled, a deep, belly chuckle that made his ample middle jiggle.

"I have lived here all my life," the man started in, talking casually as if he had known her forever. "I thought I'd seen it all."

Then he laughed. "But I have never, ever in my life seen a native Indian woman trying to talk to people in Bengali with a southern accent!" He slapped a hand on his knee, delighted. "Southern as it gets, like honey dripping off a honeycomb. My dear little lady, nobody will be able to understand a word you say," he informed her bluntly.

Asha sank down on her suitcase. So it was her accent that was the problem. Asha did not even know she had an accent, much less that she had carried it over into her language learning.

Now that she thought about it, though, she realized that she had never actually listened to anyone speaking Bengali. She had only learned from books, reading Bengali and then pronouncing it the way that made sense to her.

She looked over at the stranger. "Not a word?"

The man shook his head with a laugh. "Not even one."

"Oh, this is just terrible—after all that work, after coming all this way!"

She had been speaking to herself, but the stranger, his mirth softened by her misery, kindly offered his help.

"Here." He held out his cell phone. "Do you know the number of the person who is supposed to pick you up?"

Asha grabbed the phone. "Yes. Oh, bless your heart. Thank you." Everything would be all right after all. She would call Lloyd Stephens' son, John Stephens, the missionary in charge of picking up visitors. He would come get her, and then he would take care of everything from there.

Letting out a relieved breath, she opened the cell phone and started dialing.

Frowning, she turned to the man. "Nothing's happening," she said. "Is it not turned on?"

The man took the phone back and looked it over. "Shoot," he said. "The battery's dead. Oh, is my son ever going to give me what for about that. His flight is already delayed. I bet he's trying to call me this very minute to tell me his plans, and here I am with a dead phone."

Asha hated the rude thoughts that came to her mind, but her disappointment was keen.

"Oh well." The man stuffed his phone into his back pocket, shrugged as if it did not matter, then smiled at her. "I'll just have to guess at when my son's coming in, and you'll just have to find another phone."

Her look must have communicated her feelings sufficiently, for he decided to offer more helpful information. "Look." He pointed. "There's a phone booth right over there. I'll watch your stuff and you go call your ride."

"I can't." By this point, Asha did not even care how pathetic she sounded. "I haven't exchanged any money yet, and even if I found the place to do it, apparently nobody can understand me at all, so it wouldn't do any good anyway."

The man chuckled again. He obviously was not having a lousy day. "God works in mysterious ways, little lady. You never know when a barricade on one road is just God holding you back so you notice the even better road He has laid out for you."

Though glad to hear he was a man of faith, Asha had to admit she was more encouraged by the money he held out than his words.

"This is enough for a couple of calls," he said. "Don't worry about your bags. I'll guard them with my life."

This time she returned his smile, tossed out a quick "Thanks!" and rushed to the pay phone.

Five minutes later, she was back.

"What's the status?" the man asked.

"Nothing. Not even a voice mail." Her day had not gotten better after all. "Mr. Stephens told me that this was the number for his son, John Stephens, the missionary who was in charge of picking people up. What am I supposed to do now?"

The man looked at her oddly. "John Stephens?"

"Do you know him?" Asha brightened. "He's a missionary here in Kolkata."

The man burst out laughing.

Asha frowned. "What's so funny?"

The man was laughing still, slapping his hand to his thigh. "You can't get a hold of this guy because his phone battery is dead!"

"What?"

"This is my number," he finally got out. "I'm John Stephens, son of the Mr. Lloyd Stephens you've been in contact with."

When Asha just stared at him, mouth agape, he held out his hand for an introductory shake. "You must be the girl coming for the summer," he said. "We had no idea you were coming today! And I had no idea you were Indian instead of American."

"Well, I am American," Asha corrected him, trying to cover her feelings of embarrassment. "I was born in Bangladesh, actually, but adopted when I was a baby."

"Ah," the newly introduced John Stephens said. "That's why you've been learning Bengali."

Asha could see the laughter in his eyes. "And that's why your Bengali is completely incomprehensible. I'm guessing wherever you came from in America, there weren't many Bangladeshi people to tell you that your language has 'Southerner' written all over it."

Asha did not have anything nice to say, so she did not say anything at all.

Mr. Stephens did not seem to notice. "What a fortunate thing that my son's flight was delayed. If he had come in on time, we would have gone back to the compound and you, little lady, would have been on your own."

Asha gulped. She should be thanking this man, who really was rescuing her, instead of feeling irritated with him for his teasing.

She took a deep breath, then let it out again. "When do you think your son's plane will get in?"

That was all the opening John Stephens needed. He began talking and kept talking. The one-sided conversation was a relief to Asha. As the fatigue of jet-lag closed in on her, she marveled that sitting next to her was the man who would have come to pick her up had he known she was coming. Asha guessed God decided to bail her out after all, despite herself.

Thanks, Lord. Asha sent a small smile upward, then toward the man who would be her boss for the summer.

Perhaps things were not so bad after all.

CHAPTER THREE

Deep in the bowels of a garment factory in Bangladesh, a short-statured, large man with greasy black hair and one long fingernail on the pinkie finger of his left hand, surveyed the morning's arrivals with interest. One hundred and seventy-four girls trudged by as the first rays of morning light pierced through the few grimy windows of the three-story building. The girls were tall or short, thin or plump, intelligent or foolish; it mattered not. The only factor of importance, the reason they became one large herd of flesh under his ownership, was their shared desperation. That sense of need, of hungry young siblings or a parent's debt, kept them pedaling at rusty sewing machines twelve hours a day. By noon, their faces and backs would show why such places were called sweatshops, but he never stayed that long.

"There." He gestured toward the last arrivals. The assistant at his side, known only as "the boy" simply because the man had no desire to bother learning his name, followed his gaze.

"You want me to lock the door now, *Sahib*?" the boy asked.

The man liked the respectful term and also liked that the boy did not know his own name was Gar, and thus could never reveal it. "No, don't lock them in yet. There are still ten girls coming." He counted them every morning. Any girl who was late had to pay—or more accurately was not paid—for half her work that day. Keeping the girls submissive was a difficult job, which is why he came each morning to make an example of any who wandered in after starting time or slacked in their work that first hour. Once fear settled each into a position of full productivity, he left the boy with the chore of overseeing the factory throughout the hot afternoon.

Gar pulled a limp handkerchief from his right pocket and wiped his face. He gestured again toward three women, one older and two younger, who had passed them and found places at the button station. "See those three, the woman and two girls sewing buttons?"

The boy looked and nodded. "They are new. None of them ever worked before. Their fingers blistered and bled on the cloth so we shifted them from the machines to something easier for awhile."

Gar grunted. He loved the boy's fear of him, but hated the whine in his voice whenever he was questioned. "New, huh? That one is old to start working for the first time."

"They used to be rich. The woman was married to your partner, and you—"

"Ah, yes." Gar indulged in a victorious smile. "So they are his family. The taller daughter is pretty, don't you think?"

The boy's glance was quick. He lowered his eyes back to the ground, as he should. He was only allowed to look at the chosen ones. "She is, *Sahib*. Very pretty. Are the daughters to be the next victims?"

Gar winced. "Don't call them victims." He wiped his face again. The building already felt like an oven. One day he would leave this place. He was already developing connections in Kolkata, people who paid more for one transaction than the factory produced in a week. He would work with them, learn from them, then overtake them. "Call them the chosen ones. You must treat the chosen as special, make them feel they are above this work and deserve better. With this family, it should be easy to do."

33

Gar let his eyes wander over the new family. The mother's mouth was lined with bitterness, but the sag of her face and shoulders showed a despairing acceptance. The smaller daughter looked merely bored. How fortunate that the daughter with the most beauty was also clearly the most discontent. Her eyes lifted to scan the building; her gaze landed on exits or windows; her sighs reached his ears.

"She is ripe for the plucking," Gar whispered, pocketing his handkerchief.

"*Sahib?*"

"The taller one," he said to the boy. "She is the one."

CHAPTER FOUR

CMark draped one leg over his fifty-pound bag, leaned back in the uncomfortable airport chair, and glanced out the window at the kaleidoscope of colors rushing by. Women in bright sari dresses chattered in small groups as they scurried across the street. Yellow taxis, windows down in the heat, honked impatiently. Men in wrap-around *lungis* pulled rickshaws by hand, their feet hardened and calloused after years of running bare on India's streets.

Mark smiled. He loved India. Always had.

He had never understood why, when he and his family had packed up and flown across the ocean to visit churches in America and talk about the work, people in churches so often looked on him with pity. They would comment about how wonderful it must be for him to come to America and enjoy ice cream and fast food and amusement parks, as if he had been living in a cage overseas and was finally getting a taste of freedom.

He never spoke up to say that India was his home and America was the foreign country to him. Oh, he had mentioned it once or twice when he was a boy, but at the blank looks he had gotten in response, he gave up trying to explain.

Even at seminary, where he had just completed his training in linguistics, Bible exposition, and Teaching English as a Second

Language, whenever he had wistfully spoken of returning home to Kolkata, the response, or rather lack of response, always stopped him. Seemed even his Bible-college friends assumed he should feel a sense of self-sacrifice in regards to India.

Mark chuckled. One missionary student had stated passionately, "You're just not missionary material, Mark. Not for India, at least. It's never been a sacrifice for you, living there." At Mark's confused look he had expounded, "You need to go somewhere else, some country where you will feel the alienation and discomfort and suffering that keeps a missionary on his knees before God."

Mark shook his head, remembering. The guy had been right that Mark felt no sense of sacrifice in giving his life to India. The rest he disagreed with. "Going to a place that will keep me miserable just for the sake of being miserable shouldn't be the goal," he had responded. "That's no different than the Hindus putting huge fish hooks into their flesh, or beating themselves with whips to get the gods' attention."

God did not work that way, Mark was certain. "Suffering, if it's not directed by God, is just another attempt to attain spirituality by works."

"I think the real question," offered another classmate, who had come in and decided to join the conversation, "is whether or not you're willing to go somewhere else if that's what God wants."

"I am," Mark had said with sincerity. "That's one of the reasons I'm here at seminary, to search the will of God for my future: where He wants me to go, what He wants me to do."

The passionate student—Mark could not remember his name—had reluctantly concluded, "Okay, that's good. Just be sure you check and re-check that you keep following God's will and not your own heart."

Mark had almost laughed at that. This guy obviously did not know him; Mark had never been known for following his heart.

Following the heart was dangerous.

He had tried not to trust his reason either. That had proved more difficult. Reason told him that India was the only logical place for him. He was fluent in both Hindi and Bengali, had grown up more familiar with Indian culture than American culture, and there was already an established work with specific needs ideally suited to his gifts.

Why would he consider anyplace else?

Thankfully, by the end of his years at seminary, God had shown clearly that Mark should, indeed, return to serve in India. And he was more than glad to obey.

A smooth voice came over the loudspeakers, announcing that Mark's flight from Amritsar to Kolkata had been canceled. Sighing, Mark slung his backpack over one shoulder, tilted his very full suitcase up onto its wheels, and headed back to the ticket counter to ask if another flight to Kolkata was available that day.

No one knew. The man with the schedule had gone.

"Where did he go?" Mark asked.

He was just gone, came the answer.

Mark could not help but smile. He was back in India, all right.

Should he stay in the airport, hoping another flight would become available, or should he give up and head for a hotel for the night?

Finding another hard bench, Mark sat down yet again and grabbed a power bar out of his backpack. At least he would not starve.

"Sorry, Dad," he said aloud in English as he tore off the wrapper and took a bite. "Delayed again."

Mark wished there was some way he could contact his father. He had tried calling his cell phone several times, but had no response. He tried sending an e-mail to another missionary, who could then call his dad, then remembered that the internet had been down there for over a week.

"I hope you're not as bored as I am," Mark mumbled. Then he smiled. His father would likely make ten new friends while waiting for Mark at the airport.

Sometimes Mark wished he had his father's lack of inhibition when it came to people. Then again, when his father would speak before thinking, and later have to apologize to some poor visiting missionary he had teased into tears, Mark was thankful for his own reserved nature.

Not that he could take credit for it. It was not that he did it on purpose, waiting before he spoke. Most of the time he could not think of anything to say, and the waiting was not waiting for the exact right thing, but just something to say at all.

Mark walked a few feet to toss his empty power bar wrapper into the trash.

Sometimes he was tempted to envy his father's natural gift of talking to anyone and everyone about the Savior he loved so much. But then his grandfather, who was more in nature like Mark, would remind him that had God made them all to do one work, none of the other needs would be met.

Which carried much truth. Mark's father had little time and no interest in the work so fulfilling to Mark: translating resources and materials for the national pastors to use in their churches, traveling and talking to the national pastors to find out what their needs were and how he could help, strategizing about the changing culture and the complexities that inevitably came with it.

Mark thrived on problem solving, analyzing, critiquing.

Not a good quality when stuck in an airport yet again, with no option of solving the present problem because the man with the schedule is "just gone."

Weary from days of travel and hours of sitting, Mark rose, shouldered his backpack, grabbed his suitcase, and began the walk back to the ticket counter for the third time.

It was going to be a long day. He wondered what his dad was doing right now, and if he was nearly as frustrated as Mark felt.

Probably not. His dad enjoyed the adventure of things going awry.

With a quick swing of the arm, Mark flattened a mosquito against the bare skin near his wrist, then brushed it off. As he waited in the now long line of passengers who suddenly needed their tickets changed to a non-cancelled flight, Mark's thoughts traveled to wonder about the visitor coming to work with the missionaries for the summer. His dad had given him little information, just stating she was coming to help at the orphanage, and was interested in missions.

The line inched forward and Mark inched forward with it. He hoped this new person coming had been well prepped for India. He wondered if he would be responsible for showing her around, a job he rarely enjoyed.

Hopefully she would not be the kind who squealed about bugs, or hated the rain, or refused to wear the modest national clothes, like the girl who had visited two years earlier.

When Mark's turn came up at the ticket counter, however, all thoughts of the new girl were abandoned.

No more time for musings. There was a problem to be solved.

CHAPTER FIVE

"Mark! Over here!"

Mark turned toward the voice to see his father waving, a huge grin on his face.

Lifting a hand in reply, Mark swiftly crossed the airport lobby toward the enthusiastic hug he knew would be waiting for him.

He was not disappointed. His dad hugged him, slapped him on the back several times, then hugged him again.

"Glad to see me?" Mark said with a smile.

John Stephens laughed. "Just a little. Course I should be mad at you for making me spend the whole day yesterday at this airport waiting for you," he joked. "I finally gave up and left. Wasn't sure you'd be coming in today either."

"I tried to call you at least twenty times," Mark said as his dad grabbed his suitcase and they started toward the car. "I even tried—"

"Well, my phone battery died," John Stephens interrupted offhandedly, as if that pertinent fact held little significance.

"Dad, you've got to keep your phone charged." Mark started in on a conversation they had already had several times before. "What if your car broke down, or you needed help, or—"

"Well, I plugged it in to charge it up last night, but then I forgot to bring it with me today. It's still in the kitchen

40

charging." He laughed at himself, then threw his hand to the side in a gesture of impatience with such details. "But you're here now and that's what matters. Only how about you hold off on the lectures for at least the first hour or two."

Mark grinned. He loved his dad, quirks and all. "Sorry, Dad. I just feel bad you had to spend a whole day in the airport."

"Aw, don't worry about that. I ended up having a great time," he said, to which Mark again grinned. He figured as much.

"I helped out this cute little Bengali woman. She is—" John Stephens stopped himself, smiling. "Well, I'll just let you meet her and see for yourself."

Mark looked over at his father. Meet her himself? "A-a woman?"

"A beautiful woman," his father said with a grin in Mark's direction. "She's already fallen in love with the orphanage kids, and they've taken to her like she's the cat's meow. The missionaries like her already, I can tell. I think you'll like her, too."

Stunned was too inconsequential a word for what Mark felt at that moment. Ever since his mother had died of dengue fever, Mark's father had not so much as mentioned the possibility of another woman.

What was going on? Surely his father was not that impulsive. Or was he?

"Dad?" Mark asked tentatively. He had been gone a long time. Perhaps his father's feelings had changed.

Mark was not quite sure how he felt about that.

John Stephens kept up a stream of conversation as crisp and rapid as his steps as they pressed through the crowd toward the parking lot. Mark had not really listened, catching only snatches of information about the various families on the compound and what was new in the different ministries they were involved in.

John talked as he drove, honking regularly. Though normal, Mark found it unnerving after being gone for so long, particularly as it was combined with driving on the left side of the road, dodging various goats, sheep, and other wandering livestock, and swerving to avoid getting hit by large and unforgiving buses, the bullies of the transport playground.

Not to mention his father's nerve-wracking habit of turning to look at him at the most inopportune times, like just then as a rickshaw full of live chickens was pulling out into the street.

"Dad, watch out!"

John Stephens did not grimace, did not even halt his commentary as he swerved, barely avoiding the rickshaw, chuckling as dozens of chickens flapped and squawked their indignation.

When the welcome sight of the compound came into view, Mark let his breath out in a sigh of relief. Maybe he would just take rickshaws for awhile until he got used to the traffic again.

Or I could just stop riding with dad. That would probably fix half the problem.

The guard opened the gate with a wave, and as Mark had hoped, his beloved grandparents, Lloyd and Eleanor Stephens, sat on the porch of their small house, waiting to welcome him home. For a rare moment, Mark's reserved nature was set aside. He jumped from the vehicle and ran to their open arms, reaching out to hug them both at the same time.

"It is very good to have you back," the senior Mr. Stephens said in his unassuming way, guiding his wife back to her rocking chair with a gentle hand. Mark had always loved watching the two of them interact. She, lively and sweet, adored him, and he treated her as a precious, fragile treasure. Someday he wanted to have a marriage like that.

Mark's father turned a full circle, as if looking for someone. "I thought she would be here," he said.

Mark's eyes narrowed. They had been on the compound for less than five minutes, and already he was looking for her?

"Just who is this woman?" Mark asked. "How old is she?"

Eleanor Stephens supplied the information. "Her name is Asha. She is maybe twenty, a college girl."

"A college girl?" Mark spit out. "A—a—college girl?"

When no one responded, Mark walked around to look his father in the face. "You brought a girl my age, one you'd just met, back home with you? Dad, what are you thinking? I mean, I'm okay with you wanting to date again, if that's what you want, but—a college girl? A twenty-year-old?"

Mark's father finally looked at him. His face filled with shock. "You think I want to date this girl? Why in the world would I do that? She's your age, for goodness sake!"

Mark was stumped. "Well then why—"

Hearing a small sound, Mark and his father both turned to see Mark's grandfather expelling his breath in a wheeze. Mark realized he was laughing.

"I'm sorry," his grandfather said, trying to stop, which only resulted in a coughing spell. "Who exactly do you think this girl is?"

"Well, Dad said he had a great time at the airport yesterday, and he met some woman and brought her home and everybody loves her," Mark sputtered. "What am I supposed to think?"

Mark's father looked at him in astonishment. Then his belly shook. A laugh rumbled upward, into his throat, then out his mouth in one big guffaw.

He bent over laughing until Mark's patience was worn thin.

Mark looked at his grandmother, hoping for an ally. "Would someone please let me in on the big joke?"

Ever obliging, the elder Mrs. Stephens responded, "The young lady in question is our new visitor, here to work in the orphanage for the summer. Her plane arrived most fortuitously at the airport yesterday, as your father was waiting for you. They spent the afternoon at the airport waiting in case you arrived, and then he brought her back here."

Mark's head was swimming. "The short-termer? You didn't know when she was coming?"

"Well, we knew she was coming sometime, but the internet had been out for awhile, you know," his father said, somewhat recovered, wiping his damp face with his hand. "And son, pretty as she is, I don't think she's my type. Now whether she's your type . . ."

Knitting his brows together, he turned to look around once more. "So where is she then?"

"She is at the orphanage, of course," Eleanor Stephens answered. "The children—"

"Mark!"

All four porch occupants turned. Mark saw Ruth, his favorite "auntie," rushing toward him. Older than him by a decade, though shorter by at least a foot, Ruth was the older sister Mark had never had.

"*Mashi!*" he called, using the Bengali term for aunt while approaching her with a glad smile, ready to ask if her health had improved. The distress on her face stopped him.

"*Mashi*, what's wrong?" This was not the greeting he had expected.

"Mark," Ruth said, breathless after her rush across the compound. She tossed her thick, waist-length braid over her shoulder. "I'm so glad you're here. You will know what to do."

Mark's eyebrows rose. "What to do about what?"

"Having trouble with the new girl already?" John Stephens said with a finger wag. "Is she causing you trouble trying to talk to the orphans in Bengali with that southern accent of hers?" He chuckled.

Ruth ignored him and looked to Mark. "This morning, I was feeling unwell. The new missionary was liking the boys and girls so much, I thought it is okay to ask her to watch them while they are playing. I tell her if she has trouble or problems, she can come inside to be asking for me," she said, nervousness obstructing her usually good English.

"Don't fret, dear," Mrs. Stephens said. "You didn't do anything wrong. We all know that."

Ruth swallowed, nodded, and continued her story. "I told her the children would not be understanding her Bengali talking. It is most bad. So she could be speaking in the English, and Milo could translate for her." At this point she did look at John Stephens. "You know him, the boy with only one foot, who uses a crutch. He has been learning the English and it is quite good, yes?"

Mark's father nodded absently.

Lloyd Stephens looked keenly at his son, John. "Knowing Milo's reputation since he came here, we can guess the rest."

Again, Mark's father nodded. "I'm guessing our youngest escape artist somehow got loose, and our newest recruit panicked and went after him."

Ruth gave a little sob. "I did not know until after she has gone away," she said. "The children, they are running to me. They say she ran out to chase him. So I go out too, and I look all around, many streets. I do not see them so I come back, hoping they have returned, but still they are not here!"

"Oh boy." Mr. Stephens whistled. "This is bad."

Mark sat down. What a drama.

What had the girl been thinking, running off like that? She didn't know anything about the area. She couldn't speak the language. What a foolhardy, impulsive thing to do.

"Do you think she's okay?" John Stephens asked, to no one in particular.

There was no answer.

And unfortunately, Mark thought with a disturbed frown, there was no way for any of them to find out.

CHAPTER SIX

Well, this is a fine mess you've gotten yourself into, Asha chided herself. What had she been thinking? She hadn't been thinking, really. The boy had charmed her with his adorable dimples and his quick smile. She had fallen for the whole act.

When young Milo told her his father was a rickshaw driver, poor and practically starving, who had given his son up to the orphanage so he could have enough to eat, Asha's heart had melted. The poor boy.

"Poor boy, my foot," she said with a scowl, hobbling by now. Her new sandals had not been broken in yet and she could feel a blister forming on the side of her left heel. How far had the kid gone? A mile?

Just then Asha stepped into a puddle. Mud splattered her new salwar kameez outfit. "Rrrrg" she let out, forgetting about the puddle and stomping her foot, bringing even more mud to her lovely green outfit, and tears of frustration to her eyes.

Asha considered just stopping and standing right where she was. "Let the little manipulator run off and get lost. It will teach him a lesson." Then her face paled as she realized the truth. Milo would not lose his way. He knew exactly where he was going.

But she was lost already. She could not get back to the compound at this point even if she could catch the boy.

Hurrying to catch up, Asha was beyond relief when she turned one last corner and saw her young charge sitting, grinning as if he owned the world, on a concrete slab at the edge of a busy intersection. He turned as she came into view and motioned for her to come over.

"Enjoy your victory while you can," Asha said. "What in the world do you think you are doing?" she hurled out once she had stood still long enough to catch her breath. "Why have you dragged me halfway across Kolkata to end up on the side of the road in front of an ice cream store, just sitting here as if you were waiting for someone to come out and offer you some?"

Asha could hear her words tumbling over themselves. Taking several deep breaths in a vain attempt to calm herself, she then said, slowly enough for him to understand, "Why-are-we-here?"

Milo smiled up at her, as calm and at ease as if nothing in the world was amiss. As if he had no idea the trouble she was going to be in when they got back. Or did not care.

"This is my home, Asha *Didi*," he said, his hands sweeping the view like a proud owner. "This place I lived here."

"Here?" Asha was confused. "Here, where?" She could see no shacks, no homes. Only stores and restaurants and a few market stalls. There were some boys begging in the median of the road. In another direction she saw a man and a boy napping on the sidewalk.

"Here." Milo pointed down to where he sat comfortably. "Just here."

"You lived on the street?" Asha was dumbfounded. She looked around her again with new eyes, imagining this young boy spending his days and nights in this busy, dirty part of the city. Had he had a blanket to sleep on? Did he get cold at night?

Her eyes pricked with tears, but then a cold wave washed over her. *Wait a minute. He told me a big story about his dad the rickshaw driver, too. Maybe this is just another trick to get something out of me.*

"I thought you said your father was a rickshaw driver." Asha eyed him with suspicion. "So why do you live on the street?"

47

Milo shrugged. "It is true," he said. "But he only gets enough *rupee* for feeding us. Not for house. He stays with other rickshaw driver men. I stay here."

"Why do you not stay with him?" Asha was genuinely interested now. She forgot her desperate desire to be back on the secure compound and sat beside the boy.

Milo shrugged again. "In this place, I can get the good food," he said with the smile of one quite comfortable in his own skin.

"What do you mean?" Asha asked. She gasped. "You don't mean you steal food from people, do you?"

He waved a hand as if shooing her away. "No way, American person. I no steal. I no need for stealing."

Then he did something completely unexpected. He took off the one shoe he had, took off his shirt and belt, roughed-up his hair, and rubbed some dirt onto his face.

All ready, but for what Asha could not fathom, he then looked her way and grinned ear to ear.

"You watch, Asha *Didi*. I show you."

Speechless, Asha remained motionless on the slab of concrete as Milo, who suddenly began hobbling as if in pain, slowly approached the ice cream shop. A pair of girls in shorts and tank tops exited the shop, so enthralled with the scenery they were obviously tourists. They took pictures and pointed and checked their guide books.

Until they noticed little Milo.

He had tugged on the edge of the blonde one's shirt. Asha could see he played his part perfectly. His face looked mournful and he held out his hand pathetically, then rubbed his flat stomach, looking for all the world like he had not had a bite to eat in days.

Asha almost laughed. If begging was an art, this boy was a master.

The two pale-skinned foreigners cooed over him in pity, then motioned for him to wait while they went back inside.

Milo looked back at Asha and winked.

Soon the tourists were back, this time with an ice cream cone which they gave the little beggar boy. His smile was like the sun bursting through the clouds, and the two women giggled and took his picture and then moved on, talking and gesturing and looking back to see if Milo was enjoying his treat.

He was. Thoroughly.

Milo waited until they were out of sight then proudly made his way back, deftly using his crutch and one foot. He sat down next to Asha again with a satisfied sigh.

"Ah, Asha *Didi*," he said with relish. "What you think? No money? No problem! I eat ice cream anyway."

It was as if the world had tilted upon its axis, and knocked over not only Asha herself, but all her preconceived ideas about what she expected to find in India. She could not quite figure out how to right it again.

Poverty she was ready for. People in need, yes.

But she had not expected to encounter a little boy at home on the busy and dangerous streets of Kolkata, not only smart enough to get by, but crafty enough to get more than just what he needed. What he wanted, too.

Her head was reeling.

Perhaps slightly hysterical after her ordeal, or perhaps because it really was funny how helpless she had assumed him to be when she was the one really helpless, Asha started laughing and could not stop.

At first, Milo laughed with the new lady, but then as she continued, holding her stomach and leaning over, he watched until he became concerned. Was she okay?

Should he find an adult to slap her? Once, watching television from outside an appliance store window, he had seen that done on an American cowboy film. The girl had gone a little crazy and the man slapped her and it fixed her, just like that. Ever since then Milo had watched Americans, waiting to see someone do it in real life.

He was disappointed when she quieted down before he had the chance to think on it further. But then she smiled and said, "Milo, you are a wonder."

Milo did not know what a wonder was, but she was smiling, so he was happy. He liked the new *Didi*. He liked that she looked like him and did not have see-through skin like the other foreigners did. He liked that she was not angry with him.

So for the next hour, Milo showed Asha his world.

Milo introduced Asha to his friends, the boys she had seen begging along the median. He even showed her his special hideout, the place he went when the monsoon rains flooded the streets and the beggars had a hard time finding a place to sleep that was dry.

Asha had to give him credit; he had done well with the little life had given him. Milo told her that he and his father had come to the city when a drought wiped out their crop back in his village. His mother and baby sister were still there, living with other family members.

"Why did you come instead of staying home?" Asha wanted to know.

Milo tapped the stump of his right leg with his crutch. "This I had since I was born. No work for me. But in the city, the tourists, they feel sorry for boy with only one foot. So I am better for being worse, yes? I get the good food."

Asha shook her head. She had always assumed people begged because they did not want to work for their food and wanted a free hand. This boy had few options, but he made the best of what he had and what he could do.

Would everything be this topsy-turvy? Would all her experiences in India be the opposite of what she expected them to be?

After her tour Asha sat for awhile, watching the busy intersection and enjoying Milo's camaraderie with the other boys.

Eventually, reluctantly, Asha said it was time to get back.

Her feet ached. Her whole body screamed for a rest on something other than concrete. How did people sleep all night on such an unforgiving surface?

Milo slowly put on his one shoe and started to put on his shirt. She knew he was not ready to go back yet, but she also knew the missionaries would probably be frantic by now. She felt a stab of guilt; she had been enjoying her adventure so much, she had forgotten about them and how they must be feeling.

"Hey, should we take a taxi?" Maybe that would cheer the boy up.

"Taxis do not take beggars," Milo said with practicality.

Asha wanted to point out that she was not a beggar, but then reality hit her like a splash of cold water. She had no money with her. She was dirty, her outfit splattered in mud. And she was sitting on the side of the road with a street kid.

She sure looked like a beggar.

Asha wondered for a fleeting moment what James would think if he saw her in such a state. He always said a woman should never appear in public at less than her best. Imagining his face would have made her laugh had her situation not been so dire.

Asha shook herself free of her thoughts. They were not really in such bad shape, she decided. It would be a long walk back, and her feet did hurt, but Milo knew the way, so all was well enough.

"I'm sorry, Milo," she said, standing up, attempting without success to brush some of the dirt off her salwar kameez. "I don't have any money for a taxi. We will have to walk. Are you feeling okay? Does your foot hurt?"

Immediately, Asha realized she had said the wrong thing. Milo's chin jutted out in pride.

"I may be beggar, but I no—" he then said a word in his language. She had no idea what it meant, but assumed he was letting her know he was no wimp.

Not like her. Asha felt like a wimp and would have had no trouble saying so at that moment. She wanted nothing more than a nice, air-conditioned ride back to the compound, a long soak in a bathtub, and a soft bed.

Dwelling on the thought of a long, hot bath, Asha almost did not notice when Milo's mood changed. His grin came back, this time full of mischief. He began edging away from her.

"I show you, Asha *Didi*," he said. "I show you I better on one foot than you on two feet. We race, and I will be inside gate before you!"

And off he went. Like a streak, he disappeared before Asha could get out, "Wait! Milo! I don't know the way back!"

She ran to catch up, turning in the direction she saw him go first. He was nowhere to be seen. Frantically, she ran down one alley, then another, looking in panic for a boy with a crutch.

After twenty minutes, Asha gave up.

On top of everything else, now she was even more lost than before. She could not find her way back even to Milo's intersection, much less the compound. How would anyone ever find her?

Asha tried talking to a few street vendors, but no one could understand her.

"This can't be happening to me," she muttered. "Not on my second day here." She had wanted to experience the real India, but not this way.

"God," she whimpered, her voice tremulous, "I need help." Asha did not care if the vendors around her were listening. No one could understand her anyway. "I didn't mean for this to happen, God. You know I wasn't trying to create the big mess I'm in. I really, really do not want to spend the night outside in this city. I know Milo was fine here, but I'm not. I can't talk to anybody. I don't know where to go."

A tear slipped out. Weary beyond words, Asha slumped down right there on the side of the road next to a stall filled with mangoes. Their sweet smell tantalized her, making her stomach growl with hunger. She wanted to get up, move away, sit near a stall that sold something she did not want. But she was just too tired.

There was nothing she could do but wait. She had no money. No phone. Not even her mostly useless phrase book. She was utterly helpless.

"God, please help them find me. Please." Asha leaned her head against the dirty wooden post barely holding up the mango stand, and tried unsuccessfully to relax.

CHAPTER SEVEN

"The noise in this place is making me insane."

Rani looked across the table at her younger sister and shrugged. "A hundred sewing machines running in a closed building—what did you expect?"

"Expect?" Her sister's eyes shot sparks. "I expected to be at school, not in a factory. I expected to be buying new clothes for myself." She pricked a finger with the needle and whined, shaking the finger. "Not making them for foreigners."

Her voice broke and Rani kept her eyes down on the button in her hands to avoid seeing her sister's tears, again.

"Hush, Padmamalini," their mother warned, "and get back to work. None of us want to be here, but this is where we are. Crying will only make things worse."

Rani sighed, then stiffened when she saw a shadow approaching from the side. "Shh." She kicked her sister under the table. "He's coming. Do you want a whip to your back?"

The shadow stopped. "You've done well at this station," a voice said. "I'm moving you to a better position."

Rani looked up just long enough to see if the words were meant for her. Her quick glance took in the young man the factory owner called "the boy." His features were attractive and his smile held just enough shyness in it to be appealing. Dark brown eyes looked at her with pleasure, but a boyish kind, not the lustful way the owner looked over her every morning.

Did he mean it? Rani looked over where Padmamalini sucked the finger she had pricked, then across to her mother. "Will all of us go?"

The boy moved to stand at her side. "Would that please you?"

She hesitated. "Yes." Why would he care what she wanted? "I would like us to remain together."

She heard kindness in his voice. "Then it will be so." He stepped back. "But first I shall take you and explain the job, then the others may join you."

Rani stood slowly, feeling the same apprehension she sensed in her mother's hunched posture. They had seen girls singled out before. The girls disappeared for an hour or longer, and always returned stone-faced or crying. No one spoke of it, but the story in their silence made Rani tremble with fear every morning when the massive factory owner ignored others and stared at her.

"I…I…" What could she say? He was in charge, and if they lost this job, they would be on the streets hungry and forced to beg or worse. "Where are we going?"

"Over to that empty table under the window." He gestured across the huge open room to a table holding a newer sewing machine. Whoever worked there would have the benefit of natural light. Rani blinked her own burning eyes. It seemed too good to be true.

"Follow me," the man said and led the way, but halfway across the room he moved to walk at her side. "My name is Khan. I know what happened to you and your family, and I want to help you." He looked around. "You don't belong in a place like this." He held out a pink plastic chair for her to sit at the rust-free machine and showed her how to pedal with her right foot to generate power for the machine, then how to gently nudge the cloth with both hands under the leaping needle. Another worker had shown her all these things the day they arrived, but Rani wordlessly followed his instructions, aware how he leaned close to direct her hands.

He whispered near her ear, "I know someone who can get you a better job with much more pay." Rani shivered. "Out of all the girls, I have chosen to tell you only. You must keep it a secret from everyone. I don't want to lose my job. Okay?"

Habit bobbed her head to the left in agreement, but instinct curled her fingers with fear. Her foot stilled on the pedal and the needle slowed to a stop.

"I understand your hesitation," Khan said. Could he read her mind? "Take some time to think about it. A few days if you need to." He looked around the room and Rani saw his gaze stop at the spot where the owner stood each morning. Her machine sat less than three meters away. She swallowed and moved her foot up and down, directing a swatch of bright yellow cloth under the needle's quickening dance.

He spoke behind her one more time. "But do not wait too long." His eyes were still focused away from her, as if he saw the owner watching her from his spot like a huge Bengal tiger at the edge of a village, choosing its target. "Sometimes delay can be…unfortunate."

She stared as Khan strode away from her table, forgetting to ask him how her mother and sister were to join her if there were no other empty machines nearby. She felt their gazes on her but she did not look their way. Her own eyes would show too much. He had said to tell no one. Did he mean not even her family? Was he warning her about the owner's intentions, trying to rescue her from him before it was too late?

How was it possible that out of all the girls there, he had chosen her?

A better job would mean more money for her mother and sister. Maybe she could even save enough for Padmamalini to go back to school. Rani missed school also, but that did not matter. She was older and could work harder. Besides, he had not offered the job to her thirteen-year-old sister.

She looked around the huge open room. Khan walked between the rows of tables and machines. Not one girl's eyes lifted from her work as he passed; Rani was the only one in the building daring a glance at anything beyond her own machine.

Khan's face turned and his eyes met hers. He smiled. Rani took a deep breath in and made her decision. She would find a way to meet Khan in secret, to ask him more questions. If what he offered was a good job, a safe job, she would accept it. She would take the chance at a better life, for herself and for her family.

CHAPTER EIGHT

When the gate creaked open and a small, dark-skinned boy with only one foot hurried in, Mark's entire family and Ruth all turned toward him expectantly.

The grin of triumph on Milo's face died. John Stephens and Ruth rushed toward the boy, asking questions.

Mark, trying to keep a cool head when everyone about him was losing theirs, took Milo by the hand, guided him to sit next to his grandmother on the porch, then demanded—politely—that he tell them what happened.

Milo's eyes were round with fear. He swiftly explained in his native language, with Ruth translating because his village dialect was not one any of the missionaries had learned, ending with profuse reassurances that the *Didi* would be there soon. They were racing and he won. It was no problem. She was fine.

Mark knelt down until he was eye level with the boy. "The *Didi* just came here from America," he told the boy in Bengali. "She does not know how to come back. She does not know the way."

With every word, Milo's eyes grew more horrified. He obviously had not thought about that.

Mark had a sinking feeling in the pit of his stomach. This was worse than he had thought.

Milo's eyes swept from one missionary to another. Ruth started lecturing him in his language, berating him for running off and causing so much trouble.

John Stephens intervened. "Okay, everybody calm down," he said. "Ruth, please take Milo back to the orphanage and get him cleaned up."

"You won't beat me, will you?" Milo asked with fear.

"No, son," Mr. Stephens said with a sigh. "We won't beat you. But you must learn that we have rules here, and if you want to stay, you must live by our rules. You cannot go sneaking off anytime you want."

After Milo was taken inside, head hanging low, Mr. Stephens turned to Mark.

"Well, my son, I was hoping to have some time to sit and talk with you today. Guess we can do that on a rickshaw just as easily as here on the porch. How about you and I go looking for that girl? I know where the boy stays when he's on the streets. She shouldn't be far from there."

"Not if she has any sense," Mark said. Surely she would have known to stay there, wouldn't she? Of course, if she had used common sense, she would never have run off in the first place. Mark sighed. It was going to be a long summer if this short-termer's first two days here had been any indication. "Sure, Dad," he conceded with a frown. "Let's go find this girl."

Forty-five minutes later, after riding in several circles to sweep the area near where Milo lived, John Stephens pointed toward a dark-skinned young woman sitting on the edge of the street. "That's her," he said. Huddled next to the rotting leg of a market stall filled with mangoes, their visitor for the summer looked completely lost and forlorn.

Mark felt his heart constrict with what must have been compassion, for a large part of the frustration he had felt seemed to evaporate at the sight of her. His next feeling was genuine sympathy, for his father, never one to miss an opportunity to tease, practically leaped from the rickshaw, his booming laugh announcing his presence.

Her head shot up in recognition of the voice. Mark saw her eyes light up in relief, and then perhaps he imagined it, but it seemed like her eyes filled with tears. She was certainly embarrassed at her present circumstances, and his father's laughter was far from helping.

"Well, well, well," Mr. Stephens boomed jovially. "We found you at last! I see your southern-accented Bengali hasn't served you very well in this here marketplace," he teased with a fake John Wayne drawl that made Mark cringe.

"I was starting to think you were going to have to spend the night out here if we didn't find you soon." John Stephens sat beside her and looked down into her face. Her obvious misery brought out his tender side. "You must have had a lousy time of it, I'd guess."

The sudden sympathy brought tears again to Asha's eyes. She had been terrified they would never find her, and she would indeed be spending the night out on the street.

"Did the little boy make it back okay?" she asked, chin trembling. She had so many questions, and she wanted to say she was sorry, but she knew if she tried to voice anything else she would burst into tears and humiliate herself even more.

Mr. Stephens patted her shoulder. "Don't you worry about that little guy. He could find his way back blindfolded. He's escaped several times before, usually by climbing the ladder to the water storage tin and then jumping over the wall from there. I have to give him credit for being smart enough to utilize the new teacher's ignorance to his advantage in this case. Smart as a whip, that one." He chuckled.

Asha winced at his use of the word ignorance. Not that it wasn't appropriate. It was just so far distant from the competent impression she had hoped to make her first week in India.

Her mortification increased when she saw a young, very stern, very good-looking man climb down from the rickshaw and start walking toward her. The slight facial resemblance to Mr.

Stephens announced that this must be his son, Mark, back home from seminary.

She hadn't expected him to be so attractive. Or so solemn. Apparently the facial resemblance was as far as the family genetics went.

Could things get any worse? This had already been the most humiliating day of her life.

As the son approached, Mr. Stephens jumped up to introduce him. "Little lady, this young man here is my son, Mark." He proudly put a hand on his son's back, then chuckled. "Now son," he said with mock sternness, "don't you go all sour on this poor girl. We spent a lot longer waiting for you at the airport yesterday than you and I spent looking for her today. And no harm done now that she's found."

Mr. Stephens hailed a second rickshaw driver and gave him some instructions before turning to Asha again. "Let's get while the getting's good," he said. "As we can't possibly all fit into one rickshaw, and I am by far the largest, thanks to my mother's amazing cooking, I'll take this rickshaw alone. Mark, you ride with our little lady here in the other rickshaw. You two can get acquainted that way."

At the extremely uncomfortable looks on both Asha and Mark's faces, Mr. Stephens let out a laugh as he climbed into the rickshaw. He leaned his head out and called, "Make sure you get her home, Mark. Don't let her run off again!"

As Mr. Stephens rode off in his rickshaw, still laughing, Asha shut her eyes for a moment, wishing she could open them to find that all of this had only been a dream.

But reality was waiting for her when she opened them again in the form of Mark Stephens, who was probably fluent in Bengali, and who looked like he never did anything impulsively no matter how important it may have seemed at the moment.

Asha sighed. "I'm sorry for all the trouble I caused. I hate it that you had to spend your first day back looking for me. But I really was trying to do the right thing."

She would have added a small smile to her almost-apology, but when he just continued to stand there staring at her, defensiveness kicked in. She stood, wanting to stomp her foot, but then she remembered the earlier encounter with the puddle and decided not to risk it. "How was I supposed to know the boy knew his way around the city? And had escaped before! If you'd been left alone with a bunch of children while you were exhausted and still feeling jet-lagged, what would you have done?"

As the long moments stretched and he continued to stare, Asha took a step toward him and huffed, "Hello. My name is Asha. I was born in Bangladesh, but was adopted by an American family. I grew up in North Carolina, where I apparently obtained an accent." She heard the sarcasm in her voice. "I have no memory of Bangladesh, if you're wondering, but I have been studying Bengali on my own. I was looking forward to using it here in Kolkata . . ."

All this time, nothing had changed in Mark's expression except a slight raising of the eyebrows. Asha heard herself rambling—she always rambled when she was nervous, and he was making her very, very nervous—and decided it was his own fault for just standing there like a totem pole.

"I was going to use my Bengali here," she repeated. Then her shoulders slumped. "But apparently all of it was for nothing. Maybe I shouldn't have come at all." Her words trailed off into silence. Asha felt all the energy leave her, like a deflating balloon. Her knees gave way, and she sat down again, hard, on the side of the road.

She had made no sound, but the action seemed to knock Mr. Stephen's son out of his reverie.

"You think you shouldn't have come because the Bengali you studied in America needs some work to be understandable?" he asked.

Asha sighed a deep, deep sigh. Had he not heard what she was trying to say? Did she have to spell out that she was feeling vulnerable and ashamed? That this was harder than she'd expected? That she really hadn't planned on making a complete fool of herself her very first week in India?

"I don't really mean I shouldn't have come—I—"

"So you only came so you could use your Bengali?" Mark interrupted, his voice still confused.

Did the man not listen? "No, that's not what I meant."

"Look," Mark said with a reasonable tone that was already getting on Asha's nerves. "It's okay to figure out that you came for lesser reasons than you initially thought. People come out here for all kinds of different reasons. We have short-termers come because they want to do something exciting, or they want to experience a new culture. People come trying to impress God, or to impress others at their church. Some people think they're coming because they feel 'called,' but often the truth is that they just felt a lot of emotion from watching a missionary slide show or some pictures of helpless-looking orphans."

The fact that she herself had felt a great deal of emotion from the orphanage pictures only made Asha's frustration mount. "I came out here because God wanted me to come here!"

"Maybe." He shrugged. "But are you sure it was God calling and not your own heart, wanting to rescue the poor, poor children of India?"

Tears were coming. Asha could feel them. But they weren't sad tears; they were anger in liquid form.

"Excuse me?" Who did this guy think he was? "Are you the pure motives guru or something? Are you here just because God called you, or are you here because this is where you're from, where you're most comfortable?" Asha heard the unforgiving tone in her voice, but was on a roll. She stood up to face him head on. "Let me guess, you think you have India all figured out because you grew up here, and you're certain you can do a better job at ministry than anybody coming from America with their emotional, new-missionary ideals, right?"

Mark's eyebrows raised, then raised higher. When Asha stopped long enough to notice that everyone within ten feet of them was staring, she felt her face flame. As impossible as it had seemed, this horrid day had become even worse.

Mark almost smiled. "Well, that was a very thorough, if perhaps incorrect, assessment of a person you have just met." He motioned toward the still-waiting rickshaw, complete with staring rickshaw driver. "Shall we continue this conversation on the way back, perhaps? Then you can condemn me all you like, but without the audience."

She could feel the patronizing undercurrent to his words, but this time her emotions had little energy left for a tart response. He was right. She had judged him unfairly, considering she did not know him at all. But he had judged her first.

Now you sound like a two-year-old, Asha reprimanded her own thoughts, climbing wearily into the rickshaw. Mark stepped up and sat down beside her, the small rickshaw confining them to an uncomfortably small space.

After a full minute of riding in silence, Mark let out a frustrated breath. He turned to face her. "Can we start over? We're both jet-lagged and tired. It's been a long day for both of us. Can we pretend that the conversation back there never happened and start from here?"

Asha looked sideways at him, wary. He sounded genuine.

Then he smiled, and for a moment Asha forgot to breathe. His smile transformed his chiseled features and lit up his eyes. For several seconds, all Asha could think was, *Wow.*

Shaking her head to clear her mind of the fog of fatigue, Asha offered a tentative smile and held out her hand to shake his. "Hi, I'm Asha. It's nice to meet you, Mark," she said.

He took her hand in his for only a moment, then released it. "Asha, I'm Mark. And it is nice to meet you, too."

Asha had a hard time believing he sincerely meant that statement, as she certainly would not have been happy to meet herself in the state she was in just moments ago, but as it was the only pleasant moment of the past several hours, she clung to it.

By the time they arrived back at the mission compound, the only thing Asha could think about was sleep. Never mind that it was only six o'clock and time for supper. She excused herself from the missionary group and their concerned questions, apologized for causing so much trouble, and dragged herself to her room.

Surely tomorrow will be better.

Tomorrow would be better, wouldn't it?

Nothing in the world was more appealing than the bed waiting for her when Asha got to her room.

She fell down upon it without bothering to undress, and within minutes was fast asleep.

It had indeed been a long day.

CHAPTER NINE

The early morning sunshine did not succeed in waking Asha, but a rooster crowing just outside the window did.

How did a rooster get into the yard? Asha's head felt numb.

She opened her eyes. Concrete block walls. Screened windows. Cheerful pea-green curtains floating softly in the morning breeze.

This was not her bedroom. Not her house, tucked on a hill at the edge of the Blue Ridge Mountains . . .

Asha sat up with a start. In a flash, memories of the previous day brought her fully awake. India. A little boy with only one foot. Rickshaws and street vendors. A stall filled with mangoes. Getting lost . . . meeting Mark . . .

With a moan, Asha flopped back down onto her pillow. Jet-lag, though dragging her down with fatigue all throughout the day before, had awakened her at ten p.m. and kept her awake until far past midnight.

She had hoped to sleep in. Only the iron bars—burglar bars, as the missionaries called them—fastened in criss-cross shapes across the window kept Asha from throwing something at the zealous rooster, its annoying, loud vigil continuing.

"Don't you have a snooze button or something?" she yelled at the animal.

What time was it? Asha shifted, her muscles stiff. She wished she had brought her favorite pillow that squished in all the right places. And she wished she had brought the picture of her family that remained hanging on her bedroom wall back home.

It's only been three days. Asha rolled over. *You're not allowed to feel homesick yet.*

Maybe the internet would come back on that day, and she would be able to let her parents know she had arrived. Asha thought of how she would describe India. And how she would not describe any of the events of yesterday.

As the rooster crowed yet again, Asha gave up any hope of getting more sleep. Might as well get dressed and face the day. The first thing to do was remove the mud-crusted outfit she had slept in, and take a shower.

Later, as she dried off Asha made a mental note to thank whoever had set up the room she was staying in. Not only welcoming and brightly decorated, it was equipped with an array of practical, helpful items especially for short-termers and guests—the most helpful being a wardrobe full of salwar kameez outfits to wear. Asha had seen pictures of the standard Indian outfit, along with the more dressy saris, but had never worn either before yesterday.

She opened the large wooden wardrobe, wondering why there was no closet in the room, and pulled out a deep red outfit, admiring the intricate gold embroidery covering the blouse.

Yesterday, just trying on one of the outfits had proved an exercise in humility. It had taken three attempts before Asha had finally secured the large, balloon-style pants in all the right places. Thankfully, today it was easier.

Over the pants went the loose top, billowing down over her hips, the hem stopping just below her knees.

Asha held up yet another piece of the same material, also embroidered in gold. Yesterday, having no idea what the extra part was for, she had carried that piece of the outfit to Ruth, who informed her that it was called an *orna*. Asha said thank you, but what was it for?

Ruth had laughed and pulled her inside. "The pants are your underwear, to keep your legs covered," she informed Asha as she showed her how to drape the *orna* over her shoulders in several different ways. "And the shawl is an extra covering for modesty."

Now standing in front of the full-length mirror in her room, Asha flung the several yards of today's *orna* over one shoulder, then another. She draped it over her head and marveled at how genuinely Indian she looked.

No one would believe I grew up in the hills of North Carolina.

"Southern accent included." Asha smiled at her reflection, the new day giving her a measure of acceptance of facts that had been so daunting two days ago.

Now dressed, Asha turned her attention to the wicker bedside table, on which was an album covered in homemade paper, detailed with intricate leaf patterns. Previously, Asha had been too tired to do more than glance through its pages, but today, with a missionary team meeting scheduled for ten a.m. in the Main Room, Asha sat at the small writing desk and focused on its contents.

The pages contained photographs of the missionaries on the compound, accompanied with names and facts about each. Beyond that, Asha found a list of common phrases in Hindi and Bengali, followed by helpful cultural information, a map of the city, and finally a map of the compound.

Page four presented the Stephens family: Lloyd and Eleanor, John and Susan, and Mark.

Judging from the photo of Mark, Asha guessed the album to be at least ten years old. A lanky teen with sandy blond hair and a self-conscious grin stood between two sets of smiling faces.

Asha concluded that the woman standing to Mark's left, her hand on his shoulder, must be Mark's mother. She wondered when Susan Stephens had died, and how long she had been sick beforehand.

Asha flipped through the following pages, then looked over the map of the compound. The buildings were situated in a U shape. In the center stood the Main Building, the largest on the compound, though still only one story. The main room of the building, a large concrete square in the center, spread out like fingers into five much smaller adjoining rooms. Asha's was the farthest on the right, the pinkie finger of the hand, across from the kitchen in the thumb spot.

Nearly every part of the building, the walls, floor and ceiling, were made of concrete, due to the weather she had been told. The tropical heat inspired quick mold growth and decay, and the yearly threat of cyclones made having one large building of concrete a smart choice, and at times a necessity for survival.

Asha looked out the window to where the elder Stephens' home stood to the right of the Main Building, then back at the map to see whose house was next to theirs. It was the Miller's. They were church planters.

Stacy Richardson's house was next. Asha turned back a few pages to note that Stacy was a nurse. She traveled the area doing free clinics, along with a nurse and doctor team, the Andersens, whose house stood to the left of the Main Building.

John Stephens' place and then the orphanage finished out the U to the left.

Picturing the compound in her mind, Asha visualized the playground out behind the orphanage, and then one more small frame of a building that she had been told was to be Mark's house once it was finished. Until then, as he and several Bengali carpenters worked on it, he would stay with his grandparents.

Thus prepared, but with a 3x5 card covered in names tucked secretly in her bag just in case, Asha headed outside toward the playground. She had discovered that the orphan children did not come out to play until after breakfast and Bible time, giving her a perfect spot on her favorite swing for time alone with God early each morning.

As ten o'clock approached, Asha nervously walked back to the Main Building, pen and spiral notebook in hand, wondering how her very first missionary meeting would go.

It was boring.

After trying to appear interested as the missionaries discussed everything from the new tax laws to whether or not to trim the trees along the walkway around the compound, Asha could no longer hide her disappointment.

John Stephens began talking about how several items had gone missing from the storage shed, and they needed to pay attention to whether things were merely being misplaced, or someone was stealing. Asha hid a yawn, and noticed Mark getting up to get a drink. He had been quiet throughout the meeting so far. She wondered if he was as bored as she was.

Asha looked down at the doodles she had swirled on her notebook and did not notice Mark's subtle move to sit behind her.

"Not exactly what you were expecting?"

He had leaned forward to whisper near her ear, startling Asha. She turned her head. "Does it show?"

"All over you."

Peripheral vision told her he was grinning.

Asha smiled with chagrin. When he scooted his chair up next to her, she murmured, "I just figured, this being a missionary meeting, y'all would be talking about really important stuff. You know, like helping poor people or evangelizing remote tribes or something."

"There aren't that many remote tribes here in the city."

Asha rolled her eyes. "You know what I mean."

"I know. We're supposed to wear little halos and quote Bible verses whenever we stub our toes, too."

She looked over to see if she had insulted him. His face was deadpan, but then he winked.

She smiled back in his direction, then leaned to ask if everybody on the compound had a wardrobe instead of a closet, and why, but then her head shot forward when she heard her name being called.

John Stephens was reading over the meeting's agenda. Her name was on it?

"We need to talk about what our newest, and may I say most adventurous, missionary guest will be doing while she's here with us this summer. Besides chasing children all over the city, that is."

Eleanor Stephens, pointedly ignoring both her son's comment and Asha's flustered face, leaned forward toward Asha. "Tell us, dear, what you were hoping to do while you are here with us."

Asha felt all the eyes in the room on her. She checked her shawl to see if it was still in the right place on her shoulders. Fingering the embroidered edge, Asha tried to communicate her desires in coming to India. She wanted to work with the orphan children. She wanted to help. Most of all, she wanted to make a difference, to do something that mattered.

"And to see if perhaps God wants me in missions in the future."

She felt rather than saw Mark's surprised glance.

For the next twenty minutes, she was the topic of discussion. "It's decided, then," Mr. Stephens concluded. "Asha will help Ruth with the orphan children, overseeing playtime in the morning and evening, and whatever else she needs help with."

"And during the children's naptime," Ruth added. "I will help Asha with her Bengali."

Asha was thrilled. "Oh, that would be wonderful! Thank you!"

The chords of Handel's Messiah suddenly filled the room. Mr. Stephens pulled a phone from his pocket and excused himself. Ruth smiled at Asha and began to speak, but her voice was cut off by a violent fit of coughing. She leaned forward, covering her mouth as the deep, rattling sound continued for a full minute.

Asha was no doctor, but even she could tell there was something very wrong with that cough. Dr. Elijah Andersen took Ruth's arm and gently led her from the room.

When Ruth was out of sight, Mrs. Andersen, the nurse, looked over at Asha. "Ruth has TB—tuberculosis. We're treating it as best we can, but she has gotten a great deal worse in the past few weeks. The truth is, we had planned much more ministry activity for your time here, but with Ruth being ill, the way you could help us best would be to remain available in case you are needed. And Ruth will probably need more help from you than she will ask for."

Asha's response was immediate. "I'll be happy to help any way I can."

"Thank you," the elder Mr. Stephens said, suddenly looking very old. "God sent you at just the right time. We did not know she would deteriorate so rapidly. Your being here will be a great help."

Deteriorate? "But isn't TB treatable?"

"Most of the time it is."

Before Asha could ask what that meant, John Stephens picked that moment to return to the room. He looked around and asked, "Why all the long faces? Did somebody die or something?"

When the silence continued, Mr. Stephens sat down with a shrug, picked up the agenda, and continued his meeting. "Now, did anybody tell our short-termer who is in charge of her?"

In charge of her? Asha forgot about Ruth for a moment. "I thought you were the one who took care of the short-termers."

"Up until today, you were right." Mr. Stephens stood up and approached a large wall map of the area. He pointed to a spot that meant nothing to Asha. "But tomorrow I'll be leaving for a whole month for this area here. There are churches that will be sending national missionaries out to survey the area and see where to plant new works. I don't want to miss that! The Andersens and Stacy are going, too, to set up temporary clinics in the areas we survey."

He grinned down at her. "Don't take it personally. Besides, I have just the right person picked out for you."

Asha gulped, and she heard a gulp from behind her. He would not—

"Mark, my son, I bequeath to you this lovely young woman. You're in charge of everything concerning her." He ignored Asha's attempt to disappear behind her hand, and smacked his son on the back. "Being in charge of a woman for a few weeks will do you good, my boy. Good practice for marriage someday!"

Asha did not look up from behind her hand. She heard a few muffled coughs, as if people were trying not to laugh. How mortifying!

"John . . ." Eleanor Stephens' tone was reprimanding.

John bent to kiss his mother on the cheek. "Don't worry, Mother," he said, all cheerful affection. "I promise I didn't do this to set them up, really. I didn't find out about this trip till after we knew the girl was coming, and I would have asked Ruth, but she seems to not be feeling too good lately. Besides, who better to show her around than Mark, who just got back and doesn't have set responsibilities yet? It's just practical."

By then Asha had slouched down as far as humanly possible in her chair. Eleanor Stephen's voice drifted toward her.

"Asha, dear, did you know that the internet finally came back on early this morning? If you'd like, you may use the phone cord in the kitchen to send your parents a message."

Asha flashed one grateful look toward Mrs. Stephens, then fled the room.

Mark watched her go. He turned toward his father, trying to contain his emotions. "Dad, for one, that was totally embarrassing. For another, I came back here to work with national pastors. There are a lot of important things I have been training to do, and none of them include taking a pretty girl shopping or showing her around so she can take pictures."

"So you admit she's pretty?"

Mark groaned audibly. "Never mind, Dad." He left the room and his desire to try to reason with his father. After stopping by in the kitchen to set the phone cord where Asha would be able to see it, he crossed the compound, talking with his Heavenly Father as he went.

"Lord, could this possibly be from You?" Mark was baffled. "I don't see how. But whether it is or not, help me to have the right attitude so I can honor You."

Mark went to his own room in his grandparents' house, opened his computer, and went to work readjusting the spreadsheet he had made of his plans for the summer.

Seemed all his own ideas had suddenly been shelved.

CHAPTER TEN

Asha leaned her body against the closed door of her room, trying to calm down. She wanted to throw herself on the bed and not show her face for the rest of the day, but instead she asked God to give her strength to go back out there, and tried not to ask Him why on earth He sent her to the same continent as Mr. John Stephens, missionary comedian.

Wishing for a breeze to cool her flaming face, Asha crossed the room and pressed her face against the window screen. A hundred tiny squares of screen wire made indentations into her cheek.

No breeze. She thought of taking a cool shower, but then decided she had better send an e-mail while she had the chance. Who knew when the internet would go out again, and for how long?

Giving herself a mental pep-talk about how the missionaries were surely used to John Stephens and his comments, and they likely did not take any of them to heart—unlike herself—Asha grabbed her computer, opened the door, and tried to sneak into the kitchen without drawing any more unwanted attention.

Once in the kitchen doorway, she glanced back to where Mark had been sitting. He was gone. Poor guy. Had he run away too?

On the kitchen counter she found the phone cord stretched out so it was obvious, and next to it a post-it note, written in a man's tight handwriting:

> *Sorry about my dad embarrassing you like that, and I'm sorry you're stuck with me for a boss. I have no idea how to do this, so please let me know what you need. I'll come over after the meeting. Mark*

Asha was impressed. Maybe having Mark for a boss would be better than his father, at least.

Plugging in the phone line, Asha tried to put the entire situation out of her mind. Why was it that she seemed to be trying to forget nearly every experience since her arrival?

Pulling up her Yahoo page transported Asha back to her own world, a world that suddenly seemed so much simpler, so much more comfortable. She checked a few news stories and looked at what the weather was like back in Weaverville before opening her Inbox to the messages waiting for her.

Her parents had written twice, their messages encouraging and full of the tidbits of daily happenings that she had already begun to miss.

Amy, her best friend from college, had written with a reminder to buy her a cool Indian outfit, preferably black.

And there were five messages from James, all questioning and insistent. Why hadn't she e-mailed to let everyone know she got there safely? How was she adjusting to the native culture? What ministries had she begun involvement in? James ended each e-mail assuring her that God was pleased with the sacrifices she was making on His behalf.

Asha sighed as she clicked out of his last message. She had not made any sacrifices on God's behalf yet. Did that mean God was displeased with her?

James certainly would be.

Opening a new e-mail page, Asha typed a quick note to her parents, telling them about her trip, first impressions of India, the other missionaries, and how much she liked wearing Indian clothes. She told them how Christopher Columbus had been looking for a sea-route to India when he accidentally discovered America and that was why he called the Native Americans "Indians." She typed on about the orphans, particularly Milo, but left out the fiasco of yesterday's adventure chasing him. She also skipped mentioning her arrival fiasco, and the fiasco that had just happened in the room next door.

Asha hoped fervently there would be at least a few days in the next two months that would not fit under the "fiasco" word.

She paused before hitting the send button. Should she e-mail James? What would she say?

Feeling slightly cowardly, Asha pursed her lips, inserted James' address below her parents, along with Amy's and several others who had promised to pray for her, and hit SEND.

That done, Asha left the computer and its connections behind, and headed for the door. India was waiting, and she was not going to let three days of fiascos, or a very unwilling new boss, however unnerving, get her down. She would get out there and experience India in all its glory, and maybe have something exciting—or at least pleasant—to write about next time the internet worked.

Flinging the screen door open and taking a deep breath of India air, Asha looked down the porch steps to see Mark standing there. Had he been waiting for her?

Having decided to make the best of the situation they had both been thrust into, she smiled brightly. Besides, she was finally feeling the effects of jet-lag starting to wane, and the small burst of energy that filled her felt good. Maybe he would take her on a tour of the city. Or shopping.

Once face-to-face, she stood looking up at him expectantly. "Well, boss, where do we start?"

Mark had been waiting outside, trying to decide how best to begin the short-termer orientation that was now his responsibility.

He had taken a few short-term visitors out around the city, showing them the sights and generally helping out where he could. But this was different. He had never wanted to be in charge of the short-termers, and he especially did not want to be responsible for this one.

The fact that his father seemed to think it all a good joke rankled on his nerves. The added fact that he found the new visitor distractingly attractive was not helping either.

Well, he would just have to do the best he could. Maybe after this summer his father would see him as an adult, and not just the missionary kid to call when there was a hole to fill.

Mark mentally searched through his options of what to do first with Asha. Should he begin with a tour of the city? Take her shopping? Go over the rules? Find out more about her personally?

Definitely not the last one, Mark decided quickly. He did not want her to get the wrong idea.

He did not want to take her shopping, having never enjoyed that particular pastime.

The rules. The rules would be a good place to start. Perhaps if he laid them out clearly, she would not need any more rescuing, or at least would not go running off alone anymore.

It was at that moment the screen door opened and the women in question emerged. She bounced down the stairs and looked up at him with a smile, asking, "Well, boss, where do we start?"

Her smile was drawing his attention to her mouth. She was not wearing any lipstick, but she did not need any. Her lips were full and red.

Mark's brows furrowed. This was not going to work. He had not spent years preparing to return to India, only to get sidelined by a woman who would only be around for a few weeks.

"Rules."

Asha's face turned quizzical. What had gotten him all peeved? Was he still upset about being assigned as her overseer?

"We'll start with the rules."

Asha almost laughed, but his face told her he was serious. No shopping? No ride in a rickshaw to see the sights? She might have known he would start with the boring stuff. With an air of martyrdom, Asha tromped back toward the building, sat on a rickety chair on the porch, and sighed. "Okay, let me have it."

She saw Mark roll his eyes and heard him give an answering sigh of his own before joining her on the porch. "I didn't ask for this responsibility, you know."

Bristling at the idea of being a "responsibility," Asha's retort was sharp. "And I didn't ask for a personal babysitter."

His mouth tipped to one side. "You sure could have used one yesterday."

Embarrassment and irritation shot Asha out of the chair and across the porch to the railing on the other side. Would her whole time in India be tainted by that one incident?

She felt a hand on her arm. "Sorry. That was unnecessary," Mark said. "Look, I'll try to make this quick, and only tell you the rules that I think will apply to you as a short-termer. For one, all of the missionaries decided years ago to adopt the national dress . . ." He looked at her warily, obviously bracing himself for her objections, and she could tell she surprised him by twirling around in her red salwar kameez then striking a pose.

"Check." She smiled. "I've wanted to wear one of these all my life, but there weren't exactly many to pick from at our nearest mall, which was forty-five minutes away anyway."

Mark nodded slowly. "Um . . . okay." He swept a hand around the compound. "The next rule would be, because we all live together like this, we've made it a policy to get the team's approval before beginning any new ministry or changing an existing one."

"Or trimming the trees along the walkway." Asha's good mood had come back. "So I'm not allowed to invite every kid in Kolkata into the compound for a Bible club without asking first. Got it."

"Okay. Third, since you don't know the language, you should probably have someone with you whenever you leave the compound."

Asha frowned. "But at the meeting today they said I could go to the market three times a week to practice using my Bengali."

She watched Mark swat a pesky mosquito. "Yeah. I wish they hadn't done that."

"You're not going to take that opportunity away from me, are you?" She scooted closer and leaned toward him. "I've been studying for years. And Ruth says my Bengali words are good; it's just my accent that needs work. And how will I ever improve it if I'm never out there hearing it?"

Mark responded, his face still solemn. "I'd feel a lot better if someone went with you. You could get lost out there."

"Not if I go to a common market each time. The rickshaw drivers know the way." Asha pulled out a notebook. "And I could have Ruth write down the mission address here in Bengali and Hindi so a driver could read it, just in case."

His eyebrows came together. "What if you got mugged? Or a protest started on the street you were on?" But finally, her pleading eyes won and he conceded, at least partway. "What if Ruth went with you once a week, and the other two times you could go on your own?"

Asha nearly hugged him with relief. "Sure." Ruth could help her when people talked too fast, or she could not think of how to say something. "I would like that, actually."

"But you need to be careful when you're out on your own. Carry your purse close to you at all times. Don't pull out a wad of money where people can see it . . ."

Mark continued his string of advice, and Asha glanced at him in between writing instructions in her notebook. *You worry too much,* Asha wanted to say. She tried not to take it personally, wondering if his caution was a subconscious attempt to make up for his father's complete lack of reserve. Or maybe he became this way after losing his mother.

Summoning some forbearance, Asha smiled. "Thanks for all that." She flipped her notebook closed. "Anything else?"

Mark sat silently. Was he thinking? Daydreaming? Asha hoped no more rules would come to his mind. She was aching to get off the compound.

"One more thing."

Asha fidgeted.

She could tell he noticed, but continued undeterred. "Until your stomach adapts, you shouldn't eat any of the food sold by the vendors in the road-side stalls. And you should never, ever drink the water. Take bottled water everywhere you go."

Asha's forbearance left and irritation flew in to take its place. "Not try any of the food?" Her disappointment was keen. "Should I avoid touching anything, too, to make sure I don't get contaminated? Maybe you'd prefer it if I shut myself in my room the whole two months."

"I'm not trying to take away all your fun." Mark's tone was weary. "But you wouldn't be having much fun if you ate some bad *samosas* and ended up sick for a week. Then you wouldn't be able to help in the orphanage."

"Right. I get it," Asha huffed. *So that's it. You just want to make sure I'm able to keep working.*

"I didn't make up all these rules right before you came, just to stifle you," he said.

"That doesn't make them feel any less stifling."

Mark sighed. Was nothing going to be easy with this woman? "So you came here to have a great fun time and not have to be stifled." He ran a hand through his hair. This was not going anywhere pleasant. "Why didn't you just admit to everybody that you wanted a vacation in India and skip the whole missionary thing?"

Asha stood and marched toward Mark. They stood, bodies facing, at the top of the porch steps under an overhang painted with a cheerful "Welcome" sign.

"I came here on a missions trip to do something that mattered," she sputtered. "I just didn't expect it to be so . . . so . . ."

"So not about you?"

Asha blinked. She opened her mouth to respond, but no words came out. Her body wilted. Mark glanced to the right and saw Ruth approaching.

The Indian woman looked from one to the other with a puzzled frown.

"If my new friend is going to have her first Bengali lesson today, it must be now while the children sleep for napping time."

Mark had a hand leaning against the post, a relaxed posture, except for the clenching of his jaw. "Looks like you've just been given an escape route."

He saw her blink back frustrated tears. "I think I'll take it." Her voice rang with sarcasm. "Though it will be an imposition on my *vacation*."

Her shawl had slipped. Flinging it back over her shoulder, she left the porch, not looking back.

Ruth and Mark watched until Asha disappeared into the building housing the orphans.

"Mark." Ruth's voice was stern. "I've never seen you act this way. I've never heard you raise your voice at anyone, especially not a guest. You have so much frustration." She looked over him like a mother would. "What did they teach you at that seminary?"

"It isn't the seminary." Mark blew out a frustrated breath. "It's the girl."

Ruth's expression did not change as she processed his words. Then, as if some sort of understanding dawned, she smiled. "I see."

That was the end of it. She walked away, humming. Mark wished he understood whatever Ruth figured out that made her so happy. Maybe she could tell him why he felt so mixed up. Asha was a nice enough person. Why did she frustrate him so much? Why did he keep blurting out things he later regretted?

Mark gave up. No sense thinking about it. Or her. That woman was a problem he had no hope of solving.

CHAPTER ELEVEN

All was dark when Rani awoke. The bus must have stopped, but where were the station lights, or even the light of the moon?

She shifted. Springs underneath emitted muted sounds like several old ladies moaning. She was not on a bus seat, but… Rani moved her hands around and down, over bare mattress and hard steel framing. It was a bed, a far from luxurious one. She leaned sideways and explored further. Her touch found holes in the mattress and particles from inside the mattress scattered around her. With a shiver, she lifted her hands and felt through the air until she encountered a concrete wall. Its rough surface would have broken through her skin had her hands not developed calluses at the factory.

Where was she? Rani searched her memories but could recall nothing past saying goodbye to Khan at the station and then thinking the rocking motion of the bus would surely lull her to sleep. It must have, but why had no one roused her once the bus reached her destination?

Rani yawned and curled up in the center of the bed, too afraid of whatever had eaten through the mattress to set foot on the floor. It occurred to her that she should find the door and leave the room, but she was somehow too exhausted to care enough to sit up now that she had laid down. She would rest, just a bit, then she would find someone and get some answers.

A shuffling of clawed feet under the bed sent a lightning bolt of adrenaline through her body. She had to get up, make noise, scare whatever it was away.

But she was so tired, and…

Before she finished her thought, Rani was asleep.

Pretty firelight. The yellows and reds of the fire were a comforting sight, and the crackling of the wood a comforting sound. Rani turned her head and now, with the illumination from the fire, could see she was in a very small room, still alone, with only the bed, the fire, and the mattress particles and a few chewed-off portions of her sari as furnishings.

Who had built the fire? It was small, for cooking obviously, but with no window in the room, the smoke quickly filled the air and her lungs. Rani coughed and used the edge of her sari to cover her mouth, until she noticed the ragged edges where it had been chewed on as she slept. She dropped the material and wiped her mouth with a shaking hand.

Near the corner farthest from the bed, which was not far at all, a door opened and to Rani's complete surprise, a child entered. She held a small pot of some kind. Ignoring Rani, she set the pot on top of the pile of burning sticks and used a non-burning stick next to the pile, which Rani had not noticed until then, to stir whatever was inside.

"Who are you?" Rani asked, sitting up and using her hands to smooth down her hair. "Where am I?"

The girl continued stirring, not acknowledging Rani's presence.

Rani slid her legs from under her and gingerly touched them to the floor. Any disgusting creatures would have fled from the fire and smoke, but just in case, she gave the room a thorough looking over before sliding to her knees to sit next to the girl, stifling another yawn as she did so. "I don't know why I'm so tired."

"It's the drugs."

The girl had not moved and Rani was not sure she had actually spoken. "What did you say?"

The child finally looked at her. Her features were older than her slight frame had implied. She might be nine or ten years old rather than the six or seven Rani had assumed. She seemed to be devoid of natural childish curiosity. "I said it's the drugs making you tired," the child said, her voice bored or resigned, as if she had mentioned the weather or the price of a cup of *chai*.

"Drugs? What do you mean?" It felt foolish to tremble near this waif of a girl who was clearly unconcerned, but Rani could not stop herself. Her insides shook as if cold even as the fire singed the hair on her arms. "Where are we? Do you know who brought me here?"

"You are in Kolkata, India. In Sonagachi." The girl's words were clipped, informative, and uninterested. "The madam brought you here from the station. You were given drugs before you got on the bus."

Rani stared at the child's hand on the stick, stirring, stirring. The firelight took on a hazy glow. Her thoughts seemed all muddled or mushed or—

She shook her head. "Nobody gave me drugs. I came to the station with Khan. He had my ticket. We didn't even drink a cup of tea before I left."

"But he gave you food, didn't he?" She still did not look up.

"Um…yes." Rani thought back. "He gave me a *samosa* for a snack since the ride was long. It was kind of him."

The girl snorted. It took minutes of watching the stick circle around and around before Rani concluded why. "The *samosa*. It was drugged?" Impossible. Khan was helping her, rescuing her. "But…why?"

Whatever was in the pot gurgled and a hissing steam rose above it. The girl pulled the pot from the fire and placed it near Rani's knees on the floor. "Eat. It's not much, but it's all there is tonight."

Rani looked down at the mush of little rice and much broth. "Who are you?" she whispered.

"My name is Dapika," the girl said, rising. "There is no reason to tell you more. By tomorrow you will forget everything that happened here."

"Forget?" Rani reached out to keep the girl from leaving. "Do you live here? Are you a maid, too? You're so young. Is your mother a maid?"

The child, Dapika, looked at the fire. "No woman here is a maid. My mother...works...here. I take care of her, and others like you."

"Am I going to be taken soon to where I will work?" Rani asked. She pushed the pot away and tried to stand, but her legs would not hold her up. "What is happening to me?" she pleaded.

Dapika sighed, picked up the cooled pot and placed it in Rani's lap. "Eat it. All of it."

Rani stared at the food, then the girl, tears now in her eyes. "Is this drugged, too?"

Dapika's eyes were not void of compassion. "You will be glad for the drugs. You will work here, but you will never be a maid. There will be no fancy house or abundance of money, or any money at all. Whatever you were promised was a lie."

"Dapika?" a voice slurred.

The girl spoke toward the door. "Coming, Mother." She touched Rani's arm. "Eat the food. You will want to forget."

Rani watched through tears as the girl stood and her bare feet carried her from the room. In the silence she left behind, Rani looked down at the food, saw her own tears fall into the pot, and thought of her mother. Her voice was both a whisper and a cry. "What have I done?"

CHAPTER TWELVE

Asha's days melded into a routine. She spent time with the orphan children, teaching a little in English with Ruth translating, overseeing playtime, and helping with evening meals. She studied Bengali daily with Ruth, and was progressing well. They went to the market together, where Asha practiced listening and speaking. Then the two times each week when she went by herself, she took notes and talked the next day with Ruth about what she had heard.

One week passed. Then two. She was progressing more quickly than anyone expected, and without anything anyone could call a fiasco. The missionaries praised her progress, and even Mark gave in and said she was doing a good job. Ruth took her shopping for clothes one day, and Eleanor Stephens had taken her on a tour of the city.

To top it off, wonder of wonders, the internet had even been up for several days in a row. Asha had messaged her parents, copying to James, with stories about the orphans and a few pictures of the city. She told them about the funny things that Milo said, and how she was glad to be there to help, with Ruth being ill.

Her parents' notes were full of interest and encouragement. James' notes held approval. Though he had originally wanted her to spend the summer working in his inner city ministry, so they could be together, he had come around.

"Your heart led you to India," he had written. "And that was where you were supposed to go. Keep following your heart."

Asha felt gratified. Not that she needed James' approval, of course. But it was nice to have it nonetheless.

As she left the Main Building for her daily devotions on the swingset, she noticed Mark in the courtyard talking with Ruth. She saw him wave and mouth, "Good morning." She waved back with a small smile then continued on her way.

"She has surprised you, hasn't she?"

Mark looked over at Ruth and nodded mutely.

There was a knowing twinkle in Ruth's eyes. "She fits well here. Like she belongs."

Again, Mark nodded. Asha had done very well with the orphans and the culture. He had to admit, he was impressed. In fact, he was growing daily more fascinated.

Initially, Mark had been very relieved at how well Asha was adapting, and how others were taking her under wing. He had not been restricted as he first feared.

As the days passed, however, without the excuse of being her "babysitter," he had no legitimate reason to spend time with her. He found himself wishing he did.

"She has not seen much of the real India," Ruth reminded him. "Perhaps the next time you go out, you could take her with you?"

Mark's mouth tipped. "Now, *Mashi* . . ."

"What?" She shrugged, then crossed her arms. "Well, you are not staying—what do you Americans say?—a spring chicken anymore. It is far past time you should be married. Can I help it that I want you to be happy?"

He chuckled in response, his gaze across the compound where Asha sat. "Thanks for the thought. However," he emphasized the word, "probability has it that I'm just feeling pleasantly toward her because we haven't talked enough over the past week to get in an argument."

Ruth pursed her lips. "Perhaps. However," she, too, emphasized the word, "seems it would be worth an hour or two of your time to find out."

"All right, all right." Mark conceded defeat, laughing. "You win. But first, I'm going to go see if I can fix the car. If I can't, I'll be riding rickshaws for a few days."

"Hmmm." Ruth started walking away, calling out behind her, "Asha loves to ride rickshaws, you know."

"See you later!" Asha waved as the children headed back inside for lunch. She stood and stretched her back, glancing over to the building that would one day be Mark's house. It sat silent and forlorn, like a lost child. Mark rarely worked on it.

Asha wondered if he did not like the place. Admittedly, it was very small. It would not do for a family if he were to marry and have children.

Now why had she thought of that?

After wandering the compound, trying to look like she was not searching for anyone in particular, she finally found Mark underneath the vehicle that had brought her from the airport to the compound. It was the only one available now that John Stephens had taken the Land Rover out of the city for the month.

And it was broken. Or at least it looked that way. Mark was tinkering beneath the hood, tools on the ground all around him. A Bangladeshi man was kneeling next to the car, holding out tools when requested. Asha could tell he was a good friend from the way he and Mark bantered back and forth. Another Bangladeshi man worked on the back tires.

When Mark emerged, covered in grease and oil, to see Asha standing there, the smile that lit up his face warmed her to her toes.

"Good morning, Sunshine." She was wearing a bright yellow salwar kameez. His face told her he liked it.

"What's the verdict?" Asha gave a chin nod toward the dilapidated car.

Mark wiped his hands on a well-used rag, spreading the oil over his hands more than cleaning them. "Well, I think she'll live, but she needs more help than I can give her right now. It looks like the starter might be shot. We'll have to have a replacement one sent in."

Asha did not know a starter from a transmission, but she nodded as if she understood what he was talking about.

Mark began putting away the tools, and the two men moved on to other jobs. "It's odd. I would have checked a couple other things while I was at it, but it seems several of the tools are missing." He shrugged. "Someone must be using them."

Mark stuffed the dirty rag back into the tool box for use another day. "In the meantime, I've got people to visit, and no car to visit them in. But I don't mind. It's slower, but I'd rather take a rickshaw any day."

He turned toward her suddenly. "Why don't you come along with me?"

Had she been a puppy, she would have wagged her tail in delight. Any chance to get outside and experience the real India was exhilarating. She told herself her excitement had nothing to do with the fact that Mark would be with her.

"I'd love to! But do you think I can? What about the kids?"

"When I saw Ruth this morning, she told me she was feeling well today, so it shouldn't be a problem."

"I'll go check with her, just in case."

"Okay." Mark looked down at his grease-streaked shirt. "And I'll go change and grab a snack. Meet you in, say, half an hour?"

"Half an hour it is, then."

Twenty-five minutes later, both ready. Asha had brought her camera along, and Mark smiled at her enthusiasm as she bounced on her heels, eager to leave.

Several rickshaws were parked across the street. Mark waved to a specific one, and the man came running, pulling the rickshaw behind his lean, thin body.

As much as Asha loved riding the rickshaws, being pulled by a man on foot was unsettling. She felt guilty, sitting comfortably and enjoying the ride, while a person pulled her around for such a paltry amount of money.

As they got started, Asha mentioned her feelings to Mark, hoping she was not stirring up a controversial subject right out of the gate, literally.

Instead of responding defensively, Mark seemed to truly ponder her statement. "I often feel the same way."

Asha was shocked. He noticed and grinned. "Didn't think I had any feelings, did you?"

She had the grace to blush. Mark instructed the rickshaw driver to pull over, then he paid him after he and Asha hopped down.

"For awhile I didn't want to ever use rickshaws because of how guilty I felt at how hard they had to work while I just sat there, enjoying the ride."

Asha could not believe how close his comments mirrored her own feelings. This was a side of him she never expected.

"But then I realized that, if no one ever used the rickshaws because of the deplorable conditions the rickshaw workers live and work in, then their lives would be even worse than they are now. Yes, they have an extremely hard job, but it is a job. And working, however hard, is better than starving."

Mark led Asha down a worn path past several vendors.

"The past few years, when I've come home for the summer, I've tried to use rickshaws more instead of less. The regulars in our area have gotten to know me a bit. They know I will pay them fairly, and even give them a little extra. They know I will treat them with respect."

Mark kept pausing to respond to greetings called out from vendors and several people walking along the path. Wherever they were going, it was obvious he was well-known here. And well liked.

"I wish I could do more, but I won't let not being able to do everything stop me from doing something. Even if it is only a small something."

Mark sent an Indian-style wave toward a rickshaw driver who rested against the wheel of his rickshaw, taking a break from the midday sun. The man waved back.

"That's Milo's father."

Asha whipped her head around to look at the man again. He looked so old.

"My dad met him out in this area last fall. The man told us about Milo, and how he did not have enough money to feed them both. That's when Milo came to the orphanage."

Because Mark was walking quickly, Asha had to concentrate on keeping her footing and could not study Milo's father anymore. So Milo's story had been true.

"It's interesting," Mark commented as they carefully crossed a rickety bridge over a low-lying pool of sludge. It was so narrow, she had to walk behind him. "I've read about groups that call it inhumane that men are pulling rickshaws by hand. They want to condemn the practice, revoke their licenses, and change all the hand-pulled rickshaws to bicycle rickshaws. It's a great idea, but who is going to buy all those bicycle rickshaws they're talking about? And what's going to happen to the men in the meantime? The very people who are shouting about it being inhumane might actually end up inflicting more suffering on the people they supposedly are trying to help."

Mark stopped and Asha ran into him from behind. He did not seem to notice but turned to her with a seriousness that seemed out of place in the bright, sunny day.

"Living in a place like this means having plenty of questions, big questions, some without good answers. In fact, the longer I live here, the more I find questions so big and so difficult that only God can know the answers. I have to trust Him with them. Like the Bible says, it's wise not to lean on your own understanding."

They ducked under a clothesline covered with wet, dripping saris. Once on the other side, Asha gasped. Before her was a panoramic view better than any picture she had seen in a magazine.

Mark swept a hand out. "This is beautiful, exotic India."

The land dipped down a good forty feet or more into a valley submerged. Across the river, up along the facing edge, a line of trees stood like soldiers at attention. The river was wide to the left, and Asha could see several canoe-shaped boats, small bamboo canopies arching over them to provide shade. Far in the distance, a ferry of sorts, perhaps ten feet square, carried passengers across the water. Asha wondered how so many men, women and children could fit on such a small space without some of them falling off.

"Welcome to the Hooghly River," Mark said. "Someday I'll take you to the famous fancy bridge a ways down, in the more modern section of the city, but for now, if you ask me, this is one of the best spots in India."

The sun was bright, shining down upon the scene as if in blessing. The trees stretched their roots down toward the water, some of them exposed due to erosion. The water eased by lazily, and Asha could hear children laughing. Edged along the river, as if gathered there for a meeting, stood clusters of bamboo houses on stilts over the water. Asha pointed. "The houses make me think of big, fat animals standing on four skinny little legs in the water."

The image made Mark smile. "Within the city, where water is scarce, living along the river is very practical. And for kids it's the best backyard ever. I always loved coming here growing up. My parents were good friends with one of the families." He pointed at one of the dilapidated bamboo shacks. "Down there. I couldn't wait till after the meal, when their boys and I got to run out the back door and jump right into the river. Doesn't get any better than that for a kid."

Asha pulled out her camera and zoomed in to take pictures. A group of boys splashed happily around mothers dipping clothes into the water to wash them. Turning slightly to the left, Asha focused on a woman in a yellow and green sari balancing a full waterpot on her hip. She snapped another picture when the woman lifted the pot and set it onto her right shoulder. Next, Asha zoomed in across the river at a woman bathing a naked child, a sibling nearby brushing his teeth, another child . . ."

Eyes wide, Asha lowered the camera. "Tell me I did not just see that."

Mark chuckled. "Like I said, the river is very practical. With no other source of water, the river is used to wash clothes, bathe, go swimming, get cooking water, and yes, it's a bathroom too."

Asha's whole face screwed up in disgust. "And your parents let you go swimming in there?" she squeaked out.

"This is life here." Mark shrugged. "You can't live here without accepting some of the way things are."

Asha's face did not change.

"Besides, have you ever gone swimming in the ocean?" he asked.

"Yes, of course." *Where is he going with this?*

"Did you ever accidentally get some of the water in your mouth?"

Now it was Asha's turn to shrug. "Sure. Why?"

Mark smiled. "Well, if you think about it, there are millions of fish and other marine life in the ocean, and it's not like they have floating port-a-potties to visit when they need to go . . ."

Asha's face did change then, but only to get more disgusted. "Okay, you have totally grossed me out."

He laughed. "It's easy to see things clearly when you come from the outside, but harder to see into what is familiar and normal in your own world. For example, Americans are disgusted when they find out that most people in Asia don't use toilet paper—they use dippers of water and their left hand."

Asha nearly gagged. Mark looked over at her. "You didn't know that? Sorry. That's why you aren't supposed to eat with your left hand or give things to people using your left hand. It's considered unclean."

"I'll say," Asha offered, flustered. "How-how do they get clean?"

"Ah," Mark said. "Interesting question, but perhaps not the right one. There are always two sides to every coin. Asians think it is disgusting that Americans use toilet paper without water. They wonder how we get clean without using water. And if you think of it, logically, toilet paper has only been around for about a hundred years or so, so most of the people who have lived on earth throughout history have managed without it."

Tilting her head to the side, Asha tried to consider the other perspective without gagging again. She could not. "Okay, I hear what you're saying, and I think I almost get it, but I think we'd better leave this happy little subject for awhile or I'm going to be sick."

Mark laughed out loud. Having heard nothing more than a chuckle from him since they met, Asha found it a welcome distraction. She liked his laugh. And she found herself liking his perspective on a lot of things, too. Maybe not on the whole bathroom thing, but on a lot of other things.

What a surprise.

She followed Mark down the tiny, precarious path. As they walked, Asha wondered what other surprises this place, and this man, might have in store for her.

CHAPTER THIRTEEN

When the path forked in several directions, Mark led Asha to the right toward several bamboo houses on stilts. A young man emerged from one and waved. Behind him, a woman followed into the sunlight, a welcoming smile on her face, two small boys right behind her. The boys rushed up to meet Mark, chattering excitedly to "Mr. Steben tree!"

"Mr. Steben tree?" Asha was curious.

Picking up the smaller boy and flinging him up onto his shoulders, Mark grabbed the other boy's hand and they continued toward the house. "The Indian language doesn't have the 'ph' sound, so the 'Steben' part is Stephen." When my grandfather first came to this area, these guys' great-grandfather was his first translator. They became lifelong friends, and my dad and his kids grew up together. They called my dad 'Steben two,' kind of like we'd say 'John Stephens the second.' So when I came along . . ."

"Mr. Steben tree?"

"Exactly. They don't have the 'th' sound either. The kids don't know what the words stand for; they just know that's my name—or a good attempt at my name anyway." Mark greeted the man and woman with the warmth of old friends. "This is the Mr. Hamal family—Mr. Hamal tree if you'd like."

Mark introduced Asha comfortably, then spoke to Asha in English. "You won't find a better family anywhere. Generous and good, and completely content with the blessings God has given them. And, despite what visiting Americans might think," he added, a gleam in his eye, "they are really happy with the free swimming pool right outside their door."

Asha wanted to swat him lightly on the arm, but just in time remembered that touching between genders was frowned upon in that culture.

Stepping inside the tiny bamboo home, it took some moments for Asha's eyes to adjust to the lack of light. Small cracks of sunshine filtered through the slits between the bamboo poles. That and the daylight coming through the open door were the only sources of light in the room. Asha noticed a tiny kerosene lamp on the table, but it was not lit, likely to save money by using the natural light during the daytime.

She looked around. Her home back in America suddenly seemed ridiculously luxurious in comparison. Even Mark's small house on the compound would be large enough for several families by this standard.

"Your feelings are showing," Mark whispered. Asha cleared her face immediately and plastered on a smile. She hoped Mark knew that the feelings on her face had not been disgust over the present environment, but rather an overwhelming sense of guilt that she had always had so much, and until this moment had never realized just how much it was.

Asha was impressed at how easily Mark switched from Bengali to English, talking to his friends and then to her as if this were the everyday way to have a conversation. She realized with a start that for him, it likely was. She could tell he spoke slowly when speaking Bengali, and appreciated his effort to include her in the conversation. When Hamal's wife asked if they wanted a drink, and Asha answered back in Bengali, it felt good to see Mark's surprise. Apparently Ruth had been right and it was only her accent that had been holding her back.

Every once in awhile she would look over to him blankly, and he would translate the discussion for her, but for the most part, she could keep up with the main ideas.

They settled into cross-legged positions on the floor. One of the children brought a bowl of puffed rice, and though she wanted to drop her handful when several ants crawled from the rice over her hand, she kept her smile in place and was rewarded by open admiration in Mark's eyes. He had been watching her responses. She was glad he could not read her mind and know she had almost asked earlier where the chairs were. She had not asked, not because of cultural sensitivity, but because she could not remember the word for chair.

Huge bowls of steaming white rice were placed before each of them, covered with a seasoned red sauce. Asha looked down at hers and remarked, "That bowl isn't just for me, is it?"

"You bet," Mark answered. "Hospitality is extremely important in Asia. They are showing that they are glad to have you in their home." Asha watched Mark use the fingers of his right hand to mold a ball out of the sticky rice and sauce, then use his thumb to push it into his mouth.

She tried to follow his example. It was harder than it looked. She laughed at her lack of coordination and the young boys laughed with her, their fingers expertly pushing the curried rice around and bringing it to their mouths.

When the host and hostess left the room for a moment, Mark drew Asha's attention to a one-liter bottle of Coke-a-Cola leaning against the wall nearby. "See that? Every time I bring a visitor here, they bring out one of those to serve."

Asha could tell this fact held significance, but she had no idea why. "And . . ?"

"That one bottle costs two days wages for them."

"Oh." Asha found her eyes filling with tears. How could people be so generous when they had so little?

"I've tried and tried to convince them not to buy them, but they only smile and tell me, 'Americans like Coke.' Their hospitality always humbles me. I wish I could be more like them."

Asha started to speak, but their hosts returned. By the end of the meal, Asha was almost able to get a bite from the bowl on the floor into her mouth without dropping some.

She was trying not to cry. Originally the tears were from how unworthy she was going to feel when they offered that bottle of Coke. As the meal went on, however, the tears were her eyes' response to the food. Spicy was not a strong enough word.

"I feel like a fire-breathing dragon," Asha whispered in English to Mark. "And I forgot to bring any bottled water. What should I do? I can't eat any more of this without something to drink."

Mark grinned. "I'd call you a wimp, but you've actually done great today."

His words warmed her heart, but did nothing to help her mouth. "So are you going to help, or what?"

Chuckling, Mark softly said something in Bengali. Asha caught that he was talking about her, about how this was her first time trying real Indian curry and rice, and something else she did not pick up, but she figured it must be some teasing comment. The boys laughed, the parents smiled, and Mr. Hamal tree's wife quickly reached for the bottle of Coke.

She poured some into a cup and Asha tried not to grab it immediately. Asha thanked her, then, trying to appear as if she were not desperate for some liquid, she slowly raised the cup and took a long sip. The Coke was warm. It burned all the way down her throat, but Asha was still grateful for it.

After that, Mark suggested that she try a paratha, a flat, pancake-shaped piece of bread that looked to Asha much like a tortilla. It took her quite awhile to rip a bite-sized piece off using only her right hand, but once she did, and got it into her mouth, she sighed with relief. The bread neutralized the spices still lingering on her tongue. This was much better than the Coke option.

"You are wonderful," Asha said in English. "I could hug you right now."

Mark's left eyebrow shot up and Asha made a hasty verbal retreat. "No—I mean—not literally! I just mean—well—whatever. Thanks for the bread suggestion."

They spent the rest of the meal in silence. Asha ignored Mark's grin, horrified at herself.

Trying to think of something neutral to say, once there was a break in Mark's conversation with his friends, Asha asked, "Should I drink my whole glass of Coke? Will it be rude if I don't?"

"Good question." Mark said in English. "Usually it's polite to accept what is offered, and enjoying it is a compliment. However, in the case of the Coke, I like to leave behind as much as I can. They never buy it for themselves, and they'll enjoy whatever is left."

Asha smiled at the two young boys. "I'm glad to hear it."

After goodbyes and thank yous, with a promise from the family that they would return the visit to Mark's house once it was finished, Mark and Asha walked up the hill back toward the road.

"Mark, thank you." Her voice conveyed her sincerity.

Mark smiled down at her. "I hadn't meant the afternoon to be a test, but if I had, you passed with flying colors. If God does call you to a future in missions, I think you'll do well."

They had scarcely gone a mile in the bicycle rickshaw Mark had summoned when he asked the driver to stop at a rickety bamboo stall on the side of the road. He hopped out of the rickshaw. "I'll be right back."

Asha did not mind the interruption. This outing could last forever as far as she was concerned. She had fallen in love with India completely.

And what about Mark?

Asha watched him, trying to mentally discard the question, until Mark climbed back in the rickshaw, grinning. "Your reward for doing so well today."

He handed her a glass bottle of Sunkist, complete with straw. Asha felt the wet coolness that told her the bottle had been sitting in ice. She smiled her thanks, and focused on the drink in her hand, suddenly shy.

She had never felt this way with James. Asha wondered what that meant, until the rickshaw jerked into motion again, throwing her off balance.

Mark reached to salvage her drink before it ended up all down the front of her. Their hands touched.

She could not look at him. Asha swallowed, and stared at their two hands holding the glass together. His hand was large and strong and sure, exactly as a man's hand should be.

"You got it?" came the question.

Asha looked up, startled. "Got what?"

Mark smiled. "Your drink. You're not going to spill it?"

"Oh." Asha let out a half-giggle. She was not used to her thoughts being this jumbled. What had he asked her?

The rickshaw driver turned around and asked Mark a question. Thus distracted, Mark removed his hand, and by the time he was finished talking with the driver, Asha had composed herself.

"Where are we going next?" she asked.

"Just one more stop." Asha had learned enough of the area to know they were almost to the compound when Mark had the rickshaw pull over again. He left for a minute or two, then returned with a bag.

"Pani puri," he told her before she had a chance to ask. "They're like little crunchy donuts with filling. Sort of." Mark grinned. "I'm in charge of bringing snacks to the next team meeting. Maybe these will help liven things up a bit."

Asha smiled. "They sound delicious, but I doubt anything can liven up those meetings."

Dusk was falling as they arrived back on the compound. Asha checked her watch. Five-thirty.

Mark walked Asha to the Main Building. "Well, thanks for coming with me today."

"I had a wonderful time." Asha beamed up at him, then looked down at her sandals. "Thank you, really, for letting me come."

They stood at the bottom of the porch steps in awkward silence until finally Asha said goodnight and walked toward the door.

Once inside, she breathed deeply. The day had been perfect. Well, perfect except for her mouth being on fire and finding out why the left hand was unclean, that is. She smiled as she opened the door to her room and slipped inside, thinking of Mark and how much more at ease he seemed among the Indian people than he was there on the compound.

A noise just outside the window startled her. Asha frowned. It was probably that annoying rooster that had become her personal alarm clock, just waiting until she fell asleep so he could wake her up. Well, she'd scare him for once instead.

Asha tiptoed across the room. She leaned toward the screen, looking for the rooster, when a face popped up from under the window.

Asha jumped back with a squeak that was meant to be a scream.

"Shhh! Asha *Didi*. No scream!"

It was Milo.

"Good heavens, Milo! You scared me half to death!"

Milo did not have his usual grin in place. In fact, she had never seen his face so serious.

"Milo, what's wrong?" she asked. "What are you doing here? You know you're not supposed to be outside the building once it gets dark, and—"

"Asha *Didi*," he interrupted her. "You are the only one who can help me. You must help me."

CHAPTER FOURTEEN

Sensing the need for secrecy, Asha began whispering. "Milo, what is going on? Why do you need my help?"

Milo's eyes darted back and forth as he talked. "Asha *Didi*, I know they say I cannot go outside gate any more. I know they say I cannot stay at orphanage if I go out. But I am missing my friends. My life. I just want to see them a little. And get some good food."

Asha's voice was stern. "If you're asking me if I will help you sneak out, Milo, I won't. You know—"

"No, no, Asha *Didi*. Already I go out. I go out while *Mashi* is sleeping. I go back to my place. I eat ice cream. I talk with my friends."

Asha was confused. If he had already snuck out and come back without anyone catching him, why was he confessing to her?

She asked Milo this. His eyes were panicked. "*Didi*, I leave my shoe there."

Asha leaned her head onto the top window pane. "You've got to be kidding."

"You know where I live. You have to go get my shoe!"

"Milo, I can't do that. I—"

"Asha *Didi*, with no shoe, the missionaries find out I go back, and they send me away for good. They told me this time my last chance."

Asha was torn. "But Milo, that would be deceiving them. I can't lie to—"

"It's no lying. Only not telling. You have not told something to keep from trouble before, yes?"

Asha thought of how she had not told her parents about the internet being down and no one knowing she was coming. Ouch. He had hit a nerve.

"Please." His eyes were pleading, breaking down her defenses. "Please only this one time. I never do it again."

Asha shook her head. This was a bad idea. She knew it. But maybe if she helped him this once, he would settle down and not need to keep wandering off.

She sighed. "Okay, when I go to the market tomorrow, I will go to your street and get your shoe. But only this one time! You understand?"

Milo was grinning. "I understand, *Didi*. No problem. Only this one time. Tomorrow I tell them shoe is missing and I look for it—until you come and give me shoe. Good plan."

Good plan. Good plan. The words rang in Asha's ears the next day as she stepped out of the gate and told Milo's street name to the first rickshaw driver who approached. He gave a little head jiggle, which she assumed meant he understood, and started off down the road.

I can't believe I'm doing this. So far trying to help this boy had only gotten her in trouble. Why had she let him convince her to go along with this ridiculous idea?

She argued with herself for awhile until, looking up, she realized she was on an unfamiliar road. This was not the way she remembered. Using Bengali, she asked the driver if he was going to the right street. She mentioned the street name again. He shrugged and kept going.

An ominous feeling swept over Asha. She could see he did not understand her. Was there another street name that sounded similar to Milo's? Where was this man taking her?

She was nearly in a panic when the man finally pulled over, obviously at his intended destination.

Only it was not where Asha had wanted to go. She tried asking him where they were, what the name of the street was, but got no response other than the same head nod that had started this misadventure. The word "fiasco" came to mind. She groaned as she paid the driver. He took the money and quickly left.

That was odd. I wonder why he rushed off like that?

Asha looked around, searching for any familiar landmark or street sign. Finding none, she began to walk. She would need to find another rickshaw, one that had a driver who spoke Bengali, so she could get to Milo's street, or at least get back to the compound and start over.

There were no rickshaws in sight, another oddity. What was this place?

She was on a thin, narrow street surrounded on all sides by dingy, dirty buildings, some several stories high. Men walked along the streets. She realized nervously that most of them were staring at her.

She was the only woman walking. All the other women she could see were leaning against the filthy buildings, as if in a line, waiting. Waiting for what?

A chill ran down her spine. Asha got the distinct feeling she should not be there. That this was not a good place. She looked around again, then up. On the second floor of the building to Asha's right, a girl stood at a window. When the girl saw her, she started, as if surprised. Asha smiled, which seemed to shock the girl even more.

When the girl disappeared, Asha wondered if she had offended her somehow. Her gaze dropped from the window to see a rickshaw coming down the road in her direction. It stopped about a block away and a man stepped from it, reaching into a pouch to pay the driver before entering one of the buildings.

Asha adjusted her *orna*. If she rushed, maybe she could get the driver's attention before he rode off again.

She started forward when a movement at the window caught her eye. The girl was back. Asha watched, puzzled, as the window lifted just a crack.

A small, pink piece of paper appeared through the crack. The girl pushed it until it left the window and fluttered and floated down to the street.

The girl looked at Asha intently. Spurred into action by the desperation in her eyes, Asha walked to where the paper lay and bent to pick it up. She heard a shout, a crash, then silence. By the time she stood upright again, paper in hand, the girl was gone.

Asha looked at the Bengali letters on the paper. She was good at understanding and speaking now, but still had no idea how to read the difficult language.

What did it say?

The lone rickshaw started moving away, and Asha knew she must catch it. Glancing one more time up at the dirt-covered window, still vacant, Asha rushed toward the rickshaw, chasing down her only chance to leave this frightening place.

Her heart pounded all the way back to the compound. Dazed, still uncertain of what she had experienced, she absently told Milo that she had gotten lost and did not find his shoe. She did not hear his complaints, walking woodenly until she was inside the orphanage. She waited in silence until Ruth came inside.

"Asha!" Ruth greeted her warmly. "How was your trip to the market today?" At Asha's face, Ruth sat and touched Asha's hand. "What it is?"

Asha did not know any other way to find out the words. She handed Ruth the note. Ruth read it. Her face blanched and her eyes widened.

"Where did you get this?" Ruth's voice was hoarse.

Asha gestured toward the note before answering. "What does it say?" She could see Ruth did not want to tell her. "Please, Ruth. What does it say?"

Ruth swallowed. She looked again at the note as if it were something truly dangerous. "It says, 'I was stolen. Will you help me?'"

Stolen? What could it mean?

"I don't understand," she told Ruth. "What does it mean?"

Ruth now had tears in her eyes. Asha was shocked at the depth of Ruth's distress, over a small note that had yet to make any sense to Asha.

"Where did you get this?" Ruth asked again. "Who gave it to you?"

Asha could see no way around it. She told Ruth about Milo sneaking out and her attempt to find his street so she could retrieve his shoe. She told about the rickshaw driver taking her to the wrong place then driving off again, leaving her on this strange road with a line of women.

As she talked, she saw Ruth's chest begin to heave as her breathing got heavier. Her hand raised to her heart. Asha became genuinely concerned and asked if she needed to go lie down.

"No. Tell me the rest."

When Asha told her about the girl in the window, Ruth began crying. Asha was now more concerned than ever. What was going on?

When Mark walked by, whistling, Asha felt an incredible relief. She called out his name, and her tone was so urgent, he rushed inside. Seeing Ruth, he knelt at her side, asking Asha, "What happened? What's wrong?"

"I don't know." Asha was nearly in tears herself. "It's my fault, but I don't know what I did. I accidentally went to this place. It was creepy and I could tell I needed to leave, but I don't really know why. And there was a girl on the second floor. She looked so desperate and sad, as if she were trapped or something. She dropped me a note, and I asked Ruth to read it, and she did, but it still doesn't make any sense to me."

Mark put a hand on her arm to stop her rambling. He spoke gently to Ruth, who nodded and then stumbled down the hall to her room. As she left, Mark read the note. His jaw clenched and his face hardened.

Asha watched Ruth go, her eyes pained. "Mark, I'm so sorry. I didn't mean to do whatever I did."

Mark touched her arm again. "I know. It's okay. I sent Ruth to go rest. Let's go into the living room where we can talk."

Once there, Mark turned to face Asha. "I know you didn't intend to, but you ended up in a very bad area. You should never go there again."

"But Mark, this note says this girl needs my help. I have to go back."

"No, Asha." Mark's voice was firm, leaving no room for argument. "You must never go back there. I need you to trust me on this. I will take care of this problem. You can forget about it now."

Forget about it? Forget about the desperation in that girl's eyes? The pain in Ruth's response?

"Mark, please tell me what this is all about." Asha would beg if she had to. She needed to know.

Mark shook his head. "The Bible says it is shameful to even talk of the evil things done in secret."

She grabbed his arm. "What things? Mark, I have no idea what you're even talking about! What was that place? Why is it so bad?"

She stilled when Mark's hand reached up to touch her face. His voice was soft and sad. "Would to God you could always remain as beautifully innocent and naïve as you are right now."

For a moment, her questions subsided, and her emotions rested in the tenderness of his eyes. Then the memory of the girl's desperate face floated before her vision, propelling her to plead with him, much as Milo had done with her the night before. "Mark, please?"

His hand dropped from her face and he sighed. "Okay, think about it, Asha. A road with no regular traffic on it. Dirty, unkempt buildings. Women standing in a line, but none walking anywhere. Men coming, and then going. Very few children in sight."

Asha heard all his words, but none of them were coming together to mean anything. At her blank look, Mark sat down on the living room couch, leaned his elbows on his thighs and rubbed his face with both hands.

"Prostitution," she heard him say from behind his hands. He took his hands down and looked her in the eye. "You accidentally wandered into one of Kolkata's red-light districts."

CHAPTER FIFTEEN

He could not be right. Asha could not believe it. That young girl behind the window—a prostitute?

"So . . ." Her brain was not functioning. The world was spinning. When Mark told her to sit down, she did so gratefully. "So maybe this girl was someone's daughter?"

Mark's answer was grim. "Asha, a lot of the girls in places like that are under eighteen."

Asha felt sick. She could not grasp all that Mark's words meant. "But the note said 'stolen.' I still don't—I don't understand."

She was grasping his arm, as if trying to hold on to something solid while the world spun in circles around her. Mark took both her hands and waited until she looked him in the eye. Then he told her the truth.

"Asha, the India you've seen so far is an exciting, exotic place. But it has a dark side. The sex trade here is very bad, and very prevalent. And many of the girls working the red-light districts are not doing so out of choice. They are girls that have been stolen from their neighborhoods, or were sold by a relative who either did not want them, or was desperate for money. There are thousands of girls trapped in those places, Asha. It is a terrible, terrible thing."

By now Asha was shaking. She had heard the phrase "human trafficking" before, but had always resisted learning anything about it, knowing she could do nothing to help. But here she was, with a note in her hand asking for help from a girl who had been stolen and forced to become a prostitute.

Suddenly the passive-sounding title "human trafficking" had a face, was a real person. It was no longer some vague thing happening someplace far away.

She did not even know she was sobbing until Mark pulled her into his arms. She buried her face into his shoulder, wishing she could run away and hide, find some place good and bright and full of truth.

But the innocent naivety Mark had seen in her was gone.

And she could never get it back.

Darkness fell earlier than usual. Asha ate supper mechanically, silently, then retired to her room.

Once the compound was shrouded in darkness, the power being out yet again, and everyone had gone into their homes for the night, Asha slipped out of bed and crept into the kitchen. She crossed the room and felt around the counter in the darkness for the phone plug. She hoped the internet would still be on.

Asha pulled a small wicker chair from the Main Room into the kitchen and set it up next to the counter. Her eyes adjusted to the darkness.

Taking one last look around to make sure she was alone in her vigil, Asha sat down at the counter, pulled her laptop quietly from her bag, and set it down on the hard surface. As she opened it, the light from the screen made her wince. It felt glaring, covering her lap, her arms, and her face in an eerie blue glow.

Asha took one more furtive look around. She could see nothing this time, the computer light adjusting her eyes to brightness, making the darkness seem darker than ever.

She bit her lip, wondering why she felt so sneaky. It wasn't like she was doing anything wrong. She wasn't stealing confidential information. She just wanted to know the truth.

And the internet was the best place to find it.

Her lips set in a firm line, Asha plugged the phone line into her computer, clicked a few buttons, and pulled up her internet search engine. She knew her computer battery would only last so long, and who knew when the power would be coming back on again? She did not have much time.

"Okay," she whispered shakily to the computer screen. "Time to find out the truth."

She typed in "Human trafficking Kolkata," and waited for what seemed like forever for the terminally slow internet connection to display results.

Taking a deep breath, feeling she was standing at the edge of a cliff about to jump, but not quite sure her parachute was strong enough to hold her, Asha clicked on the first website. There was no turning back now.

After an hour, Asha knew she could never go back. Never again could she pretend that the world was good.

She wished she had done her research in the daylight, surrounded by people, or birds, or anything that would remind her of goodness and hope. There, sitting in the dark, the knowledge of evil crept in upon her like the darkness of the night, surrounding her, mocking her, wanting her to give in to despair.

Suddenly the darkness won. It enveloped her and conquered every space with its hopeless, menacing power.

Asha shook herself, realizing her computer battery had died and the light from the screen had gone out. It was two in the morning, dark all around her, and she was not thinking straight. That was all.

Asha closed the now useless laptop and hurried back to bed, feeling foolish for rushing as if someone were chasing her.

She sprawled across the bed and tried to still her breathing, calm the irrational fears that haunted her thoughts.

Sleep was impossible. Asha stared up into the darkness, but kept seeing visions of women being sold, chained to beds, shrinking in terror as men came into the room, crying out for help . . .

It was no use. After trying to forget what she had read and seen, all that information she herself had chosen to find, Asha knew she would never be able to file it away in her mind and sleep as if she had never learned it.

She understood now why Mark had wanted her to move on. Now that she knew, there was no way she could not do something about it. There was no way she was staying uninvolved.

Would she ever be able to sleep again? Would she ever be able to rest, knowing that at this exact moment women were being horribly abused, bartered over like products, treated like animals?

Asha threw her flimsy sheet cover aside and once again got up. Back to the writing desk, this time with a flashlight and a pad of paper. Maybe if she wrote down the terrible facts she had found, she would be able to leave them on paper and they would stop haunting her.

Wiping her nose on her sleeve, she started by writing the statistics. The numbers that would not leave her mind. Horrible numbers she wanted to forget:

> *Up to twenty-seven million people have been trafficked, eighty percent of them female, up to fifty percent children.*

A sob let out. Asha kept writing.

> *Forty percent of women involved in prostitution began under age eighteen.*

> *Twenty thousand to sixty thousand—maybe more—work the red-light districts in Kolkata alone.*

Asha's pen dropped. Sixty thousand. It was impossible to imagine such a number. And to know that so many of them were not there by choice, but women and girls who had been stolen and sold, forced into a life without hope. And that was just in Kolkata. There were women and children being trafficked all over the world. Asha had even seen statistics on trafficking in America.

It was very late. Weary beyond description, Asha could not remember any more numbers, only the abominable fact that thousands of the girls trafficked and brought into Kolkata were from her own country. From Bangladesh.

The stolen girl behind the window could be her sister, her cousin. Asha stilled, looking into the darkness. Had she grown up in her home country, it could have been her.

Asha buried her head in her hands, and wept.

CHAPTER SIXTEEN

Staring motionless at her reflection in the mirror, Asha saw clearly the dark circles that testified of her sleepless night.

Dressing without care, not even bothering to brush her hair, Asha left the building, squinting in the morning's sunshine. It seemed out of place—too bright for the world she had just encountered. After what she had learned, Asha felt the world should remain dark. The sun should turn away in shame and refuse to shine.

Forceful hammering shattered the silence on the compound. Asha followed the sound to Mark's house. He was there, nailing planks into what would become a door frame.

She stood for some time watching him, numb, the hammering reverberating in her ears, increasing the headache begun the night before.

When he saw her, Mark's hammer stopped in midair. He stood, his eyes full of compassion.

Dust danced in the sunlight coming through the open door. They stood facing one another, the silence louder than the hammering had been.

Asha's voice was hoarse when she spoke. "I *cannot* ignore them. I cannot turn my back and pretend this never happened. I *must* help this girl."

When he took a step toward her, she backed up again. "I *must*."

"Asha, sit down."

At his command, she looked around the bare room. Finding no chair, she lowered herself to the dust-strewn floor, not caring about the wood shavings sure to collect all over her clothing where she sat.

He crouched down in front of her. "It is good and right that you care, Asha."

His words did little to penetrate her grief. "I understand that it's a bad area, Mark. I wouldn't put myself in unnecessary risk. Maybe I could send written messages, or go just once to find her, and then after that meet her in a safe place. Or I could—"

"You can't get involved, Asha. You have to listen to me."

Asha could feel her anger building. Had he not heard a word she said? How could he look her in the eye and calmly say she should turn her back on a woman with no other hope?

Maybe he just didn't know how bad things really were.

"Did you know that a lot of them end up getting AIDS or other horrible diseases?" she added. "Did you know that if they get pregnant and have children, those kids either grow up in the brothel or are sold themselves?" Her voice broke. "Who could sell a child?"

Last night there had been no tears left to cry. Today, already, more came. "And if a woman has an ugly scar from a C-section, she is considered even less worthy and can be abused even worse than the others?"

Mark started to answer, but Asha could see that he was never going to let her go. She could not bear to hear his refusal again.

"I—I have to go." Without looking at him, she stood and quickly left the room, stumbling over tools and scraps of wood.

Slamming the door once inside the Main Building, Asha tried to choke back her sobs. She had to do something. Anything. She had to talk to someone who would listen.

Asha looked up at the light fixture. A quick flip of the switch showed that the power had come back on. She rushed to her room, snatched up her computer, then ran to the kitchen.

She could not e-mail her parents about this. No, they would be too worried about her to understand.

James. She would write to James.

Asha's fingers flew with urgency over the keyboard. She told him everything, from the misguided rickshaw ride to the pink note to Mark's command that she stay away.

For the rest of the day, Asha stayed shut away in her room. She could not face the children. Their open laughter and innocent play only heightened her despair at those who had no freedom to play, no reason to laugh.

Later that evening, Asha tried to check her e-mail but the connection was down. Finally, near ten that night, the internet came up and her Inbox showed she had gotten a message back.

James was livid, she could tell. Of course she needed to help this girl, he wrote. Nothing else should be even considered. He said he wanted to come out there and let this Mark guy know he was not God, and could not hold her back from doing what was right.

For the first five minutes, his words were a balm. Then, as she read his message again, they became fuel for the anger that had been simmering in her all day. All the anger she had felt against those who stole and sold women, all the anger at how helpless she felt—she focused it on Mark.

Mark was the problem. He was the one who did not care about people in genuine, terrifying need.

Asha wrapped herself in her own righteousness and stormed outside toward Mark's house again. He was still there, a portable, battery-powered lantern lighting his work.

"So how do you decide, *boss*?" She said the term with contempt.

He looked up, not surprised to see her. His eyes held only sadness.

"How do you decide who to help and who to leave behind in the clutches of evil? These women—do they not measure up

117

because they're 'tainted,' not innocent or proper enough to be worthy of your attention?"

Mark stood. His fists clenched and unclenched. "Asha, there are things you do not know," he said slowly, each word emphasized.

"I know you would turn your back on this woman and leave her a slave!" Asha cried out.

"There are things you do not know," he repeated, his eyes piercing her. "You have to trust me on this."

She would not submit. Her heart felt as hard and painfully heavy as a stone.

"Tell me, then." She was sobbing now. "Tell me something that gives me reason not to despise you." The darkness was screaming at her, laughing at her. "James says you don't want to get involved because you're afraid it might taint the mission's reputation. Is that it?"

Mark strode toward her, his face cast in shadows. "Who is James?"

"A knight in shining armor compared to you at the moment." Asha wiped her face with her *orna*, but the tears kept coming.

Mark took her by the arm and would not let her pull away. "Sometimes, a guy's armor being shiny only means he's never actually been in a battle. Your James talks big, but he has no idea what he's talking about."

Asha stilled for a moment. She clasped tight hands on his shirt as her eyes begged him. "Please, Mark. She could be my cousin. My sister. She needs me. Please let me go help her. I *must*."

When he shook his head no, Asha tried to pull away, but he still held her arm.

"You have no heart!"

She did not know if she whispered it or screamed it, but his reaction was strong. Grabbing her other arm, he pulled her to him until their noses almost touched. He spoke through clenched teeth. "You know nothing about my heart."

He released her, and walked away. Snatching up the lantern, he turned one last time, the light flinging across him wildly as the lantern swung in his hand.

"Don't go back there, Asha. Ever. I told you I'd take care of it, and I will. As far as you're concerned, this is over."

He walked away then, leaving Asha alone in the darkness.

She stood still, silently crying, while her resolve built.

Mark was wrong. It was not over at all.

Not for her.

CHAPTER SEVENTEEN

Brighter than any carnival, the colors of the market beckoned and called, along with a chorus of voices advertising everything from oranges to eels.

Usually Asha had to consciously keep from wrinkling her nose as they passed the dried fish hanging in neat rows above a bucketful of tiny squid set out on the vendor's table. Next to it, a man held out a bag half-filled with water. A ten-inch fish squirmed at the bottom of the bag.

The section beyond it offered a rainbow of every fruit and vegetable imaginable, some Asha had never seen in America. Usually she enjoyed the variety, asking questions and talking animatedly with Ruth, but today there were other, more important things on Asha's mind.

By the time Asha had joined Ruth that morning, she had studied the area map in the guest room's missionary album until she had nearly memorized it, looking for any hints or clues that would help her find the red-light district with the girl in the window.

She had found three roads that could be possibilities. They were the only roads within two miles that had names similar to Milo's street, and Asha was fairly certain the rickshaw driver had not taken her farther than that.

As she and Ruth rode in a yellow taxi to the market that day—Ruth never liked riding rickshaws if she could help it—Asha kept a keen eye out at the roads and landmarks they passed. They rode past one of the streets on Asha's list. Looking down the road as the taxi rushed by, Asha could easily see it was not the right one.

Now she was down to only two. Asha settled back into her seat, certain that in two days, when she left for her trip alone to the market, she would be able to visit the other two roads and return to the compound quickly enough to avoid suspicion.

Once at the market, a *samosa* seller greeted her and Ruth like old friends, asking the typical small-talk questions as he had each time they visited so Asha could practice her Bengali.

Asha answered with little thought the same questions she had heard for weeks now. The Muslim call to prayer sounded from a mosque several blocks away.

"Asha? Did you hear what he asked you?"

She focused her attention back on Ruth and the vendor. Ruth was biting back a smile. "What did he say?" Asha asked.

The man repeated his question. Asha understood the words "husband," "father," and "why," but the rest was all spoken too quickly for her to understand.

At her obvious lack of comprehension, Ruth filled in the blanks. "He wants to know why you have no husband yet. Does your father not care about you? Why hasn't he arranged a marriage for you yet?"

"Oh." Asha tried not to roll her eyes. She really should put that on the list of everyday small-talk questions, since it seemed someone asked her that at least once a day. When the man started telling Ruth that he had a nephew who was the right age, etcetera, Asha moved down the narrow aisle to pretend a great interest at the spice table. It was covered with at least ten mounds of powdered spices, each one its own bright color, shaped up into a red or yellow or burgundy pyramid.

When the time came to go back, Asha and Ruth each carried a basket-full of fruit, vegetables and spices into another taxi. As they rode, Asha tentatively broached the subject that had been on her mind all morning. *"Mashi,* I am sorry about making you so sad the other day. When I brought back that note . . . I did not know . . ."

She waited, wondering anxiously whether Ruth would give her any more information about why the situation had upset her so. She wanted to ask, but knew that being direct was the American way, and not appreciated by most Asians.

Ruth looked at her with full comprehension. Her voice was quiet but firm as she responded. "Some things are better left in silence," was all she said. She looked forward as the taxi maneuvered through the flow of traffic. "There are things you do not know."

That was what Mark said. Asha's eyebrows knit together. Why was everyone being so secretive?

As if her thoughts had brought Mark's name to Ruth's mind as well, Ruth spoke again. "Mr. John Stephens' son is a good man. He cares for the people of India very much. You should trust him."

Asha felt a deep ache. *I want to, but I can't,* she wanted to argue. *He won't let me do what I must.*

But she kept quiet, and they rode the rest of the way in silence. Asha searched her memory for more details about the road where she had seen the girl behind the window, anything that would help her find it again. The buildings had all seemed clumped together, corridors between them only wide enough for a flight of outdoor stairs, and perhaps one or two people if they turned sideways when passing.

More details came to mind, like snapshots of what she had seen. Wires draping in every direction. Clothes hanging to dry on clotheslines strewn above the flat rooftops. Small, narrow alleyways, dark passages that led into even more darkness.

Asha hoped she would never have to see inside the buildings along that street. If the outer areas frightened her, how much more terrifying must the inner chambers be?

Once back on the compound, Asha went straight for the swingset, seeking some peace to settle the turmoil of her thoughts. She tried to pray, but could not think of what to say.

Could she ask God's blessing on this, knowing she was going against what the other missionaries wanted? But then again, didn't God want her to obey Him over man? Her thoughts argued back and forth, like two people bartering at the market.

Finally Asha left the swingset, knowing no peace would be hers that day.

Several hours passed before Mark sought her out. By then the pain she felt whenever she thought of him had settled into a dull ache. When she entered the Main Building to find him waiting for her, she willed her heart to stop its quickened beat. She would not feel anything for him. She could not.

She sat in the chair next to him. They both looked forward, avoiding each other's eyes.

Asha thought with a sigh that, though physically close together at that moment, emotionally they were now worlds apart.

When he finally spoke, Mark talked about how he was sorry that this had to happen. He wished he did not have to keep her from doing something she thought was important. He assured her again that he would be taking care of the problem and she did not need to worry about it anymore. He hoped that they could set the conflict aside and each continue in the work God had sent them to India to do.

Asha nodded in mute agreement to his last statement. They would put aside the conflict and be polite strangers. And they would continue the work. He with his national pastors and translation. She with finding the woman behind the window.

The conversation was finished. Mark had said what he had come to say. Asha had nothing to say at all.

They sat in silence until a rooster crowed. Then Mark brushed a hand over his pant leg, stood, wished Asha a good day, and left.

Suddenly she felt very, very alone.

Trying to forget her feelings as she rose and walked to her room, Asha thought again of her plan to find the girl who needed her help. She wished she could just ask someone how to get back to the red-light district. She wished she could talk to someone who knew the area well.

Unfortunately, Mark would be the best resource, but Mark wanted her to forget about the problem. Ignore it. Act as if it wasn't there. As if hundreds and maybe thousands of women weren't being stolen, sold, raped.

How could he ask her to forget? Didn't the Bible say that if a Christian saw a need and turned his heart away, that God would judge that person for the good they refused to do?

Well, Asha was not turning away, no matter what any of the missionaries said. Mark was not her authority, and she was not going to let him run her life. She had agreed to continue her work for God. He had meant her work with orphans, but Asha knew now that she had an even greater task to do.

She had to save a stolen woman.

Asha paced from the kitchen to the Main Room, then back again. Tomorrow was the day. She had drawn herself a map from the compound to the two roads she would visit, making sure she knew clearly how to get back from each place. She had the street names written down, had picked out a neutral-colored outfit to wear to avoid extra attention, and now there was nothing left to do but wait. How she hated waiting!

After what felt like the longest night and morning of her life, Asha dressed, stuffed her homemade map into her bag, and left the compound.

She hailed a bicycle rickshaw that day, knowing it would be faster than a hand-pulled one. She showed the driver the first street name. This time when she saw the head jiggle, she did not assume it meant he understood. Showing him the route on the map, just in case, she then climbed into the seat, twisting her hands in nervous anticipation.

Before they even arrived, Asha knew it was not the right place. Nothing had looked familiar the entire ride. When the driver turned to her, expecting her to climb down, she instead showed him the next street, and said the name. It was her only other option. If this was not the place, she had no idea what to do next to find it.

The surprised look on the driver's face, however, gave her hope. He knew the street she was talking about, and was hesitant to take her there. Asha offered a higher price for the ride than was normal, and he started off.

She held a hand to her racing heart. As they neared the street, she knew it was the right one. Here she was, in a place she had hoped to never see again, arriving on purpose against the direct instructions of the man responsible for her welfare.

Asha shook her head. No time to think of that now. This was too important.

She directed the rickshaw past several of the dank buildings, ignoring the curious stares, the leering eyes from several men loitering on the street, and passing the largest line of women. Asha noticed sadly that all the lipstick and bangles and brightly-colored saris could not hide the hollow emptiness in their eyes as they watched her pass.

Asha knew those eyes would haunt her the rest of her life.

When a child ran out from one building toward the next, Asha wanted to snatch him up and take him away, to find someplace safe and free from evil for him to grow up.

How many women lived in this horrible place? How many children were growing up here?

When they reached the right building, Asha had the driver stop under the window where just days ago a note had floated down and shattered Asha's world.

She knew she could not enter the building. She would have to wait in hopes that the girl would come to the window again.

Should she go across the street, where she would be more visible to those on the second story? But then, what if someone besides the girl noticed her there waiting? Would that get the girl in trouble?

Uncertain, Asha decided to remain safely inside the rickshaw—or as safely as one could be in an open vehicle—directly under the window. Asha looked up, willing the girl to come into view. She tried to pray, to ask God's help, but somehow words would not come.

Five minutes passed. Then ten. Asha's nervousness grew. It did not help that the rickshaw driver kept looking back at her, anxiety and confusion on his face. She assured him she would pay him extra for his time, but could tell that time and money were not the main reasons for his concern. In her internet research, she had read about police raids. She wondered if that possibility was what was making the driver afraid.

A movement caught her eye and Asha's gaze flew up to the window.

She was there.

Huge eyes in a young face widened impossibly when the girl saw Asha. Asha smiled and was about to wave when the girl shook her head, obviously terrified.

Asha waited, holding her breath, as the girl looked behind her into the room. Then, quickly, the girl placed her hand in front of her so it would not be visible to anyone inside the room. She motioned to the right, then with her other hand, made a gesture as if she were eating something. Her hand was rounded as if cupping something circular.

Asha looked down in the direction she was pointing. At the end of the road, around the corner, she saw the edges of a market. Asha pointed toward it, her eyes questioning.

The girl gave the slightest of nods, then disappeared.

Having watched the scene play out, the driver was ready when Asha directed him toward the market. His quick response caused the rickshaw to jolt forward, catching Asha off guard and off balance. She righted herself by grabbing the sides of the rickshaw canopy, wishing there was a way to stabilize her emotions as well.

The driver turned the corner. A small market appeared in view, perhaps twenty small stalls or less. Beyond it, the road stretched and revealed several stores, iron bars across the glass windows to protect them from theft.

Asha led the driver to the end of the market, then as she climbed out and paid him, she asked him if he would wait. She offered more money than he usually made for a full day's work if he would stay.

When he accepted, albeit reluctantly, Asha breathed out a sigh of relief. He and his rickshaw were her only chance at a quick getaway if the need arose. She did not like the panic that rose in her throat at the thought of him driving away, of her being left helpless and alone. She had been helpless and alone in this city once before, the day she chased Milo. But this time, no one would have any idea where to find her.

The thought was very disconcerting.

Walking back through the market, slowly, Asha looked around until she found a table piled high with bright, cheerful-looking oranges.

She stood near the oranges and waited, trying to pretend she was not as out of place as she felt. Though the market was busy, with plenty of people bartering and chattering, Asha felt herself standing out like the foreigner she was. She was thankful she was not white, then none of this would have been possible.

As the minutes passed by, Asha felt her anxiety rise. Would the girl be able to come? Would she be endangering herself by meeting Asha at the market?

Suddenly, Asha saw a lithe figure coming around the corner. Slim and willowy, with hair down to her waist and huge eyes, the girl's lips and eyelids were heavily painted, and her sari blouse was too tight.

When she saw Asha, there was no smile. No greeting. The girl quickly averted her eyes.

Asha stared. She held her breath. This was it.

And suddenly, at that moment, Asha realized she had no idea what to do next.

Part Two

To give them beauty for ashes,

The oil of joy for mourning,

The garment of praise for the spirit of heaviness.

Isaiah 61:3

CHAPTER EIGHTEEN

Asha had thought through every detail to get her to this point, but had not considered what would happen if she actually succeeded.

Not able to think of anything else, Asha turned back to the oranges and picked up two, pretending to compare them. She put one down and chose another.

After a painfully long time, the girl stood a few feet away from Asha. She, too, picked up an orange, asked its price in Bengali, and set it down again.

Looking over the selection of oranges, not looking at Asha, she spoke. Her voice was soft and articulate. "My name is Rani. I was deceived into leaving my home in Bangladesh. For weeks I have been trapped in this foul and evil place, with filthy, evil men. I will do anything to escape and return to my home."

For a moment, Asha looked around, certain the exceptional English was coming from a different source. She allowed herself a glance at the girl. The girl did not look up at her, but, feeling the gaze, she spoke again. "You were not expecting to find an educated woman here? Come, Western Bengali woman. Follow, and I will tell you my story."

Mouth agape, Asha could only stare at the girl's back as she walked through the market, head held high, toward a sari shop on the left side of the road.

How did she know that Asha was Bengali? How did she know she was a Westerner? Asha had not spoken one word to her yet. Mystified, Asha tried to follow surreptitiously, stopping along the way to look at several vendors. At one, she bought a set of bangles, thinking she would give them to the girls at the orphanage when she got back. At the next stall, she chose a few cheap plastic toys for the boys.

Eventually, Asha came to the sari shop and wandered inside. Long pieces of material draped across from one wall to the next. Most of the saris were folded and draped over bars in perfect, neat rows across the wall. An old man squatted near the back of the store, chewing on beetle nut, its red stain covering his mouth and the few teeth he had left. He completely ignored his two customers.

Asha stood uncertainly just inside the doorway. She knew nothing about acting in a clandestine manner, and every idea she could think of seemed foolish even to her.

The girl from the window—her name was Rani, Asha remembered—beckoned her to sit in front of an old, moth-eaten mannequin wrapped in luxurious folds of gold material. Asha sat and Rani lowered herself to sit beside her.

"You need not worry," came the soft voice again. "Because I have given no cause for concern as of yet, I have been given the freedom to leave my room twice each week. I usually go to the market and then come to sit here. Few men come into this shop, and the manager does not know English. We can talk here."

Asha could only stare. She was dumbfounded. She had been frantically hoping the girl could speak Bengali so they could converse on some level, but to find her speaking perfect English seemed impossible. "How—how do you know I am a Bengali— and a Westerner?"

The girl's facial expression had not changed since the moment she arrived at the market. It was devoid of feeling, as if all personal thoughts and emotions had been barred, shut away. "Your face tells me you are Bengali, as I am. Your face shape, the shape of your nose, your eyes."

Asha lifted a hand to touch her nose. She had a Bengali-shaped nose?

"Your face tells me you are Bengali," Rani repeated. "But your feet tell me you are a Western foreigner."

"My feet?" Asha looked at the one foot sticking out of her cross-legged sitting position. It looked normal to her, clad in her new sandals with tiny beads across the top strap.

"They have no calluses." The reason was simple and concise.

Asha shook her head, overwhelmed. "How—how—"

"You want to know how someone like me ended up somewhere like here. It is a story less unique than I at first suspected."

Asha listened in silence as Rani, stiff and unmoving, began her story, her English perfect and clear, with the slightest British accent.

"I am of the Brahmin caste. The highest caste among Hindus. My father was a garment factory owner. My family was one of the few in our city that could live a life of ease and comfort. I had beautiful clothes. My own phone. I went to an English-medium school. I had personal tutors who had studied in Europe. Everything I wanted."

She paused. "Then my father died."

Her voice held no emotion. Nothing but facts, as if she were talking of someone else's life being destroyed. "The man who had partnered with my father took over the garment factory. He misused the funds that were meant for my mother and our family. Soon we were poor. Our rich friends rejected us. We had to leave our home. Sell our things. My mother had no skills. She was lowered to working in the garment factory herself. My sister and I also worked there."

Asha watched a cockroach slip into the store from the road as if it were a customer. It zigzagged across the floor, and Asha imagined it was considering the variety of saris on sale.

When it scurried around the old shop-manager's feet and into the back room, Asha turned her attention back to Rani, wishing she could scurry away like the bug and not have to hear what Rani was sure to say.

"I had heard of a job in the capital city," Rani continued. "A maid was needed. The pay offered was more than twice what my mother and sister earned, and I would be given one weekend each month to return and visit my family."

A small tremor gave a hint of feeling. Rani sat silently until her face hardened again into stone. "I wanted to help my family. This way not only would I make a great deal of money to send home, but I also would be fed and clothed, and less of a burden to my mother. I left for the city, leaving a note explaining the new job opportunity."

There she stopped. Asha felt her chest rising and falling, heard herself breathing heavily. She tried to keep her face as impassive as this young girl's, but could not. One tear slipped out.

Rani saw it. "I remember falling asleep on the bus. When I woke up in a small, dark room, I was very confused. My body felt heavy and I was so tired. In time I was aware they had drugged me. And, by the next night, I found out why."

She swallowed once. "Your imagination can tell you the rest. There was no job. Only this."

Her voice hoarse and pained, Asha whispered, "How old are you, Rani?"

Rani's eyes held hers, eyes with far too much knowledge of the world and its evils. She lifted her chin. Then for the first time, her eyes dropped to the ground. Her shoulders slumped. She became a child. "I am sixteen."

Asha bit her lip hard to keep from crying. She tasted blood. Her chin trembled. *Dear God, how can there be such evil in the world?*

Rani did not cry. Her face became cold and hard again. Her chin came back up. She looked as lifeless as the mannequin behind her. "I must go back now. They only give me twenty minutes of freedom at a time. Will you meet with me again?"

Asha had not even told Rani her name. It did not seem to matter. She nodded and grasped Rani's small wrist. "I will come back. And I will help you escape. I don't know how, but I will do whatever it takes to make you free again."

For the smallest moment, a flicker of hope flashed into Rani's eyes. Then it faded. "I will come here again in two days, at this same time. If you will help me, I will escape. I will escape, or I will die trying." She looked Asha in the eye. "To stay here is to be kept alive, while already dead."

Asha waited until Rani had faded from sight before she allowed the tears to fall.

From the back of the store, the man eating beetle-nut looked her way, flung an arm in her direction, and laughed. The laughter spurt red juice from his mouth to land like blood stains on his arm and shirt.

Asha fled.

CHAPTER NINETEEN

The guard opened the gate to the compound and greeted Asha as she stepped inside. Asha said hello back, holding her hands tightly together so he would not see them shaking.

She had trembled the whole way back, praying desperately that God would show her some way to rescue this young woman. She walked toward the Main Building, lost in her thoughts, remembering Rani's lifeless face, her toneless voice. When Mark called her name, she jumped. Whirling around, she held both hands to her racing heart, her small bag of bracelets and trinkets swinging from her arm. "What is it?" she asked, breathless.

"Sorry," Mark said, his feet kicking up dust as he jogged the last steps toward her. "Didn't mean to scare you like that. Can we talk a minute?"

Asha nodded, thankful he assumed her demeanor was due to being startled. Her hands clasped again, nervously, as they walked together across the compound.

Mark spoke first. "I know you're probably still not very happy with me, and I was going to give you some space, but something came up and I need to talk to you about it."

Asha felt the blood drain from her face. Did he know? Had he somehow heard that she had gone back?

136

She waited, trying to remain calm, to look unaffected. "Yes?" she said.

"It's about Ruth, and about Milo."

A half-laugh let out, and Asha realized it had come from her. She took several deep breaths in relief. "What about them?"

"Ruth is getting worse. I'm sure you've noticed." When Asha nodded, he continued. "I talked yesterday to Dr. Andersen—he's back from the traveling clinic—and he said that she's going downhill quickly. She won't be working in the orphanage much longer."

He turned to face her. Asha could hear the sadness in his voice. Her body tensed up in response.

"She's dying, Asha."

Asha blinked several times. She shook her head. "But she can't be more than forty years old! Can't they do something? Isn't there medicine? Why—"

Mark touched her hand, ever so slightly. "Her immune system is compromised; it has been for some time now. When she got TB, we all knew she would have a difficult time fighting it off."

Asha's head was still shaking in disbelief. "I don't understand."

Mark took in a deep breath and let it out in a sigh. He looked down into Asha's eyes. "It's not the TB that is killing her. Ruth has AIDS."

Eyes wide, Asha let out a shocked cry and stepped backwards. "What?" The word was barely audible.

"We suspected it for awhile, but just found out for sure a few days ago." At her look, he waved a hand reassuringly. "We've taken every precaution with the kids, and with you, even back before we were sure. Ruth knew all the rules to keep others out of danger, and she followed them implicitly. You needn't worry about you or the children being exposed."

Asha had not even had time to think of that yet. She was still reeling from the word AIDS and what it meant. Death. More sorrow. More pain.

Was there anything good in this country?

She closed her eyes so tightly, she saw tiny sparks of light behind her eyelids. This could not be happening.

"How—how did she—how did Ruth get—?" Asha could not say the word out loud. She dreaded the answer.

Mark's voice was low. "I'm afraid I can't tell you that right now. And please don't ask Ruth." He looked at her deeply then. "I promise, the day before you leave the country, I will tell you everything."

Everything. What did he mean? How many secrets were being kept on this compound?

There are things you do not know. Asha remembered his words, and Ruth's. She shuddered, suddenly wanting to go home, to forget all of this, to pretend she had never come to India.

They had walked several steps before Asha even realized they were moving again. She could tell Mark had more to say. "What else?" she asked, her eyes down at the ground beneath her feet—her un-callused feet. "You mentioned Milo, too." Her eyes shot up to Mark's face. "He doesn't have AIDS too, does he?" *Oh, please, God, not him, too!*

"No, no," Mark laid a hand on her arm. "He's not sick at all. He's okay."

Her eyes closed in relief. "What about him, then?"

His eyes looked down on her with compassion. "Milo has decided to leave the orphanage."

Tears rushed to Asha's eyes. How could this all be happening at once? She looked back across the compound to where the children were doing exercises. As if sensing her, Milo looked up.

When Asha covered her mouth to keep from crying, Milo grabbed his crutch and hurried toward them. "Please don't be angry, Asha *Didi*," he called out as soon as he was within hearing distance. He closed the gap between them and looked up at Asha with big eyes. "It is you I will be most sad to leave. But I no can live here. I want to be with my friends. I want to get the good food." He gestured around the compound. "Here it is too hard. Too many rules."

Asha's attempt at a smile resulted in only a wince. She understood that part, at least.

Milo took her hand in his. "I need to be free."

Looking down at him, Asha's heart nearly broke. Was that not exactly what she was trying to get for Rani? Freedom? How could she deny it to this little boy?

Her voice was soft. "I understand," she said.

Milo's face broke into a grin. "I knew you would." He looked proudly over at Mark. "The *Didi*, she knows how it is with me. She has big heart. Big Indian heart."

He beamed up at her. "If you no like living here anymore, you come to my street. You can live there. I get you some good food, yes?"

Asha laughed. It was a pained, choked laugh, but he accepted it. He reached his other hand over to take Mark's. "And Mark *Dada*, he is taking all boys and girls and Ruth—" He stopped, looking with questioning eyes up at Mark. "And Asha *Didi*, too?"

Asha watched Mark smile. She saw with surprise that he, too, was having a hard time speaking. Her heart constricted again.

Mark looked at her. "Yes, and Asha *Didi*, too, if she wants to come."

"Yeah! You will come, yes?"

She looked from Mark to Milo. "Come to what?"

Mark took over then. "We're going on a field trip of sorts. On a boat ride down the river, then to the zoo. None of the kids have ever been to the zoo."

"I will see a famous Bengal tiger, *Didi*. I will be brave, and growl right back at him!"

Asha smiled down at the young boy she had grown to love. "It sounds wonderful, Milo. I would love to go with you."

With a satisfied smile, he hobbled away. Asha turned back, her hand to her mouth, her eyes closed. "Please . . ." was all she asked, then walked quickly to the Main Building. She had to get inside. She had to find a place where she could stop smiling, stop pretending.

Mark followed her, then remained close as she sat and put her head in her hands. He started talking again, his voice strong and sure. It calmed her.

"I wish Milo would stay. I don't like thinking of him out on the streets on his own. But he's been living like that for a long time. The freedom of life on the street is more normal to him than the life he would have here at the orphanage. It constricts him. He doesn't like to have to answer to anyone else."

Mark smiled into the distance. "Like someone else I know," he said quietly.

Asha cringed. He continued talking.

"We can't make him stay. He has a free will, and ultimately the choice is his. So we will let him go, but before he goes we'll have this big trip to the zoo—kind of a goodbye party. It's something he would never get to do on his own. That way he will know we love him despite his decision, and that if he ever wants to come back and visit, he will still be treated like family."

Mark turned toward her with a genuine smile. She could see that, for that moment, he had forgotten about the awkwardness between them and was talking to her as a friend again. She basked in it.

"You know, he told me that he had learned about our Jesus-God. How Jesus became poor and homeless and dirty so He could show love to everyone, even the low people. Milo said that he would be like this Jesus and go back to live with the street boys. How could he be like Jesus if he stayed here? No, he had to go back and be dirty and poor, and then he would tell them about the Jesus-God so they could know that God loves the street boys, too."

Asha could not help but smile. "Sounds like a little missionary, doesn't he?"

Mark nodded. "I hope he has learned enough during his time here to really understand. I've tried to communicate that God is everywhere—here on the compound and out there on the street—and that God takes care of His children. I've given him a hand-held, solar-powered cassette player with a Bible-story tape, so he can listen to it and have the other boys listen if they want to, and I've told him he can come back and talk to me anytime he has questions."

Mark's mouth tipped into a half-smile. He looked like a big brother about to send his younger sibling onto the playground alone for the first time. Only this was no playground. "I hope he'll be okay."

Standing, shaking a stray bug from his shirt-sleeve, Mark walked over to look out the window. "I know it will be tiring for her, but I asked Ruth to come along. She has told me many times about how, when she was a girl, her family would take trips along the river near her home up in northern India. She said she always felt most at peace when she was near water. So that's why we're going by boat. I tried to think of what we could do that would be special for her along with something special for Milo, since it will probably be the last time for either of them to be together with everyone."

Asha nodded, impressed at how much he did for the people he cared about. Why couldn't he care about the stolen women, too? "That's—that's wonderful, Mark. It will be very special for both of them, I'm sure. You—you do a good job taking care of people."

Asha left it at that. She wished she could be one of the people he was taking care of. But she forfeited that the moment she decided to go behind his back and return to the red-light district. It was a sacrifice she had been willing to make to do something that mattered. But now, looking at his face lit by the sunlight coming through the window, how she wished they could have worked together to rescue Rani. What a great team they would have made.

Mark turned and Asha glanced away to hide the regret in her eyes. "The trip will be all day Saturday," he said. "We'll be leaving early in the morning, around six. We'll take a bus down to the river, then a boat, then taxis to the zoo." His grin was wry. "It will be a long day with all those kids."

For the first time that day, Asha felt like smiling. "It will be wonderful," she said. "I'll bring my camera."

"And I'll bring lots of bottled water." Mark smiled. "Just in case somebody forgets to bring her own."

She offered a shy smile back. They looked at one another for several seconds.

Asha hoped that she could keep up this pretense long enough for her to help Rani escape. And then . . . how she hoped he would forgive her.

For at that moment, as Mark looked at her with those deep blue eyes, she wanted more than anything to have his admiration again.

CHAPTER TWENTY

Asha paid the rickshaw driver and asked him to wait, offering the same high price she had given two days ago on her first visit with Rani. She was taking no chance of not having one when she needed to get back.

Earlier, as the rickshaw took her through Rani's street toward the marketplace, Asha's senses were sharpened. She noticed details. Colors. Bare light bulbs. Thick patches of smoke. Asha's eyes took in the whole scene, wanting to notice everything, looking for any hint as to how Rani might escape.

The buildings had been painted long ago, dirt and grime from years of neglect streaking long dark lines down the walls. Graffiti, old and faded like long-abandoned dreams, stretched to make a backdrop behind the line of women.

As she walked through the market that day, Asha bought some oranges and mangoes, thinking that if she purchased some fruit she would look less suspicious to the people in the market, and to the missionaries once she got back to the compound. Then she headed straight for the sari shop.

Trying to keep busy as she waited, and to keep her nerves in check, Asha walked around inside the shop, looking over the selection of saris for sale. She fingered a stunning green sari bordered with a distinctly Asian pattern sewn in yellow thread.

Maybe next visit she would buy one to take back to America. She needed to buy one for Amy, too.

Just then Rani walked in. Asha smiled. She had been worried.

Rani's face was not negative, but she did not smile. Her face, like a painting in its beauty and symmetry, would draw attention wherever she went. Bright red lipstick and thick eye shadow only served to detract from the natural elegance of her face and form. Long earrings dangled from her ears, and a gold ring circled around the left side of her nose.

Rani pulled out a tube of lipstick. Before Asha could react and back away, she deftly colored Asha's lips with it. "You need to wear jewelry," Rani said. "And stop wearing brown clothes. If you wish to keep from drawing attention to yourself, you must begin to look like all the other women here. In this place, trying to avoid attention will get you noticed."

Asha had not thought of that. "I'll remember next time," she said meekly, trying to will away the strong desire to wipe the lipstick from her face. She tried not to think of the germs it might carry, vowing inwardly to buy her own as soon as she left the sari shop that day.

They spent Rani's twenty minutes of freedom brainstorming about how Rani could escape, but failed to come up with even one idea that was feasible. There were reasons why most of the women trapped there did not escape. They had to find a plan that overcame all those reasons.

By the time Asha said goodbye to Rani, left the sari shop, and stopped at a stall to buy her own tube of lipstick, a look at her watch told her she would have to hurry if she was to get back in time. The missionaries were holding a special dinner for Ruth, to thank her for her ministry at the orphanage.

All through the dinner, and even as Ruth was being honored, Asha found her mind kept wandering back to Rani. What could she do to get her out of that horrible place?

She lifted her eyes to see Mark watching her. He had told her once that her feelings showed. She wondered if he could see into her thoughts right then. If he knew that she was keeping secrets.

Asha excused herself from the table and went outside, where several of the children had come out after the dinner to play in the cooler evening air.

"*Didi*, push me!" a child called out from one of the swings.

Asha sighed, then purposefully put on a smile. For this special weekend, she would try her best to leave behind the red-light district and all its horrors. She would do all she could to make this a happy time for Ruth and Milo.

"Coming," Asha called, and ran toward the swing.

Yes, she could do this. For Ruth. And for Milo.

Five o'clock came too soon that Saturday morning. Even the rooster did not get up in time to wake Asha. She considered finding the annoying animal and waking it up for a change, but decided that would be rather immature. Besides, she did not have much time to get ready.

By five-thirty, Asha stood outside Ruth's door, dressed in her least-favorite outfit in case it got dirty or damaged at the zoo or on the boat ride. Ruth opened the door with a ready smile, but it dissolved as she looked at her friend.

"What's wrong?" Asha asked as Ruth looked her over.

"You are wearing this today?" Ruth asked.

Asha glanced down. "I know it's boring and wrinkled, but we are going off with a bunch of kids for the day, after all, and—"

Ruth was shaking her head. She laughed. "Sometimes I forget that you are American." She pulled Asha inside her room. "In India, my child, for an outing such as this, you should wear your very best!"

Ruth opened her own wardrobe and pulled out a deep blue silk sari embellished with hundreds of tiny gold flowers. "Oh, it's beautiful," Asha gushed.

"And for today, it is yours." Ruth ordered her to "remove that ugly thing," gesturing at her brown outfit. "Put on this underskirt and blouse in the bathroom, then come back."

Asha felt like a Christmas present as Ruth wrapped her in the bold, shimmering material. Next Ruth covered her arms in bangles. As a final touch, Ruth opened a box on her dresser and pulled out something that looked to Asha like a locket on one string. It was not a necklace. Ruth approached and carefully attached the golden strand down along the part in the middle of her black hair. The oval-shaped gold piece at the end of the chain rested on her forehead.

Ruth turned her toward the mirror. Asha saw a stranger staring back at her. She looked . . . beautiful.

"I know someone whose heart will sing when he sees you," Ruth said proudly.

Asha pretended she did not hear, but as she stepped out into the sunshine and the tiny gold flowers on her sari glittered in the light, she wondered what Mark would think when he saw her new look.

A whistle blew and a dozen children rushed past her toward the gate, giggling and cheering. Mark was waiting there with ready smiles and hugs. He ruffled the boys' hair, wrestled a few of them playfully, and teased the girls while they covered their mouths and giggled shyly.

Asha smiled. He really was a good man.

When his eyes lifted from the children to see her approach, the world seemed to stop. Children squealed and jumped and skittered around him, but Mark just stood there.

She could not read his face. What was he thinking? Did he think she looked pretty? Or was he thinking she just looked silly, pretending to belong in this world?

Several children noticed his stare and turned to see what he was looking at. Soon a group had clustered around to accompany Asha. "You look so pretty!" said one enthusiastic child.

"Like an Indian princess!" another agreed.

Milo parted the crowd and, as if he had special claim, took Asha's hand in his and walked her to the bus.

Mark had gone ahead and was helping the children board. There was no way to get on the bus without walking past him. Asha breathed in deeply. Was she ready to spend an entire day with this man who kept causing her heart to speed up, despite all her efforts against it?

"Ready, Princess?" Mark held his hand out to her.

Asha could not stop her lips from parting into a smile. She took his hand.

Oh yes, she was ready.

CHAPTER TWENTY-ONE

Laughter and songs and teasing filled the bus as they traveled from the compound to the river. Once there, twelve exuberant children practically fell out of the vehicle in their eagerness to get to the water.

Asha was taking pictures when Mark approached. "I thought about taking the ferry today, but with the kids being so excited, I was afraid one or two of them would run off and we'd lose them in the crowd." He chuckled. "I can't blame them, though. Not one of them has ever done anything like this, so it's a really big deal."

Ruth had followed the children to the edge of the water, where she was trying to keep them from doing any more than wading and splashing each other.

At Mark and Asha's urging, Ruth conceded to sitting down but would not separate herself from the children. She brushed away their concerns. "I shall live until I die. Today is a happy day and I will not miss it." She smiled at them, but her words were solemn. "Do not stop me from living this day fully by trying to protect me."

Asha's eyes met Mark's. When they nodded acceptance, Ruth smiled benevolently. "Now, if you will please turn away from your focus on me, you will notice that several of our children have already become soaked."

Twenty minutes later, a collection of children in various stages of wetness clambered into two long wooden boats. Six girls wedged into one boat; six boys in the other. Behind them, into the girls' boat, Ruth and her helper, Indira, carefully seated themselves. Mark and Asha climbed into the boys' boat, Asha with the boys at Milo's request.

The boats rocked and swayed as the passengers settled themselves onto the plank board seats. Two oarsmen picked up paddles and began rowing, their strokes sure, their muscles tight.

The two boats journeyed side by side. As the cool air rushed around them, Asha lifted her face to welcome it, feeling it flow around her neck and lift the edges of her hair. She looked around, ignoring the scenes of poverty along the edges of the river, focusing instead on the foggy haze that covered the river in mystery and the trees that stretched their branches up to touch the grey-blue morning sky.

She looked over at Ruth and saw the same refreshed calm that she herself was feeling. The weariness had faded from Ruth's face, and in its place was a beautiful peace.

Asha sighed in contentment.

Milo, sitting next to her, pulled on her hand. "You will come visiting me on my street, yes?" When she nodded, he turned to Mark. "You will come also? You can come together, yes? You like to be together, this I see."

Asha suddenly turned her attention down to the water swirling beside the boat. Her hand reached down just to the water's edge, allowing the waves caused by the boat's motion to trickle across her fingers.

"I would like that," she heard Mark say.

Through her peripheral vision, Asha saw Milo look from Mark to Asha, then back to Mark. Milo held his hand up in the "okay" sign with an exaggerated wink to Mark. Mark laughed.

A commotion drew their attention to the four boys in the foremost part of the boat. "They are getting ahead of us!" one of the boys said. "Don't let a bunch of girls beat us there. Go faster! Go faster!"

The oarsman looked to Mark, waiting for instructions. Mark turned to Asha. "You up for a little race?"

She grinned. "I only wish there were more paddles." Leaning toward the other boat, she called out in Bengali, "We're going to get there first!"

Paddles swooshed through the air, then sliced down into the water with speed and precision. The children began to cheer and scream. Asha took pictures. Ruth laughed.

To the boys' great dismay, the girls' boat won. The children scrambled onto the banks, arguing and joking about who was fastest.

Asha held up her camera and focused on Mark with the boat men. As they talked, it was clear the men had enjoyed the race. She snapped a photo, which caught their attention. The men then posed and smiled, motioning for her to take another.

Asha complied with a laugh, then turned to join the group as they walked up the banks of the river.

She assumed they would need quite a few taxis to transport the sixteen of them to the zoo, so was surprised when Mark summoned only three.

"You're in India, remember?" Mark shot over at her, once again reading her thoughts on her face. "There's no such thing as personal space!"

Five boys quickly layered themselves into the back of one taxi. Four girls into the second. Mark approached Asha. "Ruth, Indira and I will each ride in the front of one of the taxis, since we three know the way. You get the back of whichever one you'd like. I'm guessing you'd prefer the third taxi there," he pointed, "with only three kids in it." He grinned. "So far."

One bumpy, crowded, twenty-minute ride later, Asha gratefully opened the taxi door and exited. "I think I'm going to hurl," she muttered, determined never to ride in the back of a taxi in India again if she could help it.

The children did not give Asha much time to dwell on her queasy stomach. They pulled and prodded her toward the zoo entrance.

Happily, Asha followed as they skipped from one display to the next. They marveled at the elephants, laughed at the monkeys, called to the giraffe, and Milo even growled at the Bengal tiger.

It had been a perfect day. After they left the zoo, Mark surprised them all by stopping at a park for a picnic lunch, complete with sandwiches made by Mrs. Eleanor Stephens for the occasion.

It soon became clear that, to the orphan children, American sandwiches were a far cry from the curry and rice they were used to, but they ate them out of politeness. When the soft drinks and chips were brought out, however, they tripped over themselves rushing to get one of each, thrilled with the very rare treat.

Settling back against the base of a tree, Asha enjoyed the scene before her. The children were happy. Ruth was happy. Mark had succeeded. They would all remember this day as a very special one.

Asha's eyes wandered to the outskirts of the park. She saw a large European-style building casting a formidable shadow across the road. It shaded its high, obstructive fence, the rare tree along the sidewalk, and a collection of people and animals digging through a pile of rotting garbage.

She knew she should not stare, but Asha could not get herself to turn away. Wild dogs, a host of noisy crows, and even one cow picked and pulled at the pile of refuse.

The animals barely noticed when a man and a child joined them on the mound. The man pulled out several pieces of plastic—used water bottles, plastic shopping bags, candy wrappers. The child collected every kind of paper to be found, stuffing all into a worn burlap sack.

Asha was watching so intently, she did not hear Mark approach until he sat down beside her. He followed her gaze. "The cow is sacred in India, you know. As awful as the truth is, of all the life on that street, most of the people in India would consider that cow the most valuable."

Asha's eyes traversed the area all around the park. She saw a cluster of orange-clad monks walking toward a small Buddhist temple. In front of the temple, several beggars waited for spare coins, squatting on the concrete sidewalk under the shade of tattered umbrellas.

Not far away, a Hindu idol began to take shape under the hands of a carver, its many arms stretching out angrily. The finished idol next to it, newly painted, seemed to stare back at Asha. It was Kali, the goddess of death.

Asha shuddered, returning her gaze to the trash pile. She watched for several moments until she whispered to Mark, "How do you keep from—from giving in to the despair all around you?" She did not look up at him, but down at her own hands, fingering one of the golden bangles on her wrist.

"Asha," Mark said her name softly. He motioned, drawing her attention to the orphan children. Several of the boys were playing a rousing game of cricket. The girls were in small clusters, giggling and sharing secrets. A few of the children flew kites they had made from discarded plastic bags and sticks.

"Look, Asha. Tell me what you see."

Asha looked. "I see . . . joy. Hope. Resilience."

Mark nodded. "That is the India I love. But there is also a lot of sadness in living here. There is too much poverty for me to even make a dent in it." He smiled. "Not that I have a lot of money as a missionary anyway. There are too many orphans and street children for me to take in. There are too many women on the streets to rescue."

His words pierced her heart.

"But," and here he waited until Asha's eyes rose to meet his again. "I finally had to accept that I cannot save everyone in India. God did not send me here to do a task impossibly big for me. God is the only One big enough for all the street children, all the orphans, all the oppressed women, all the evil in this world."

He looked toward the trash pile with its forgotten humanity scrounging through it. "The moments when I look at the world as my responsibility, all I find is despair. I can never hope to make a difference."

One of the youngest orphans came to sit in Mark's lap. He held her as she curled into a ball and began sucking on one finger, content. "God has not asked me to take in all the orphans. He has asked me to take in little Shafique here, and these others. He has given me a task to do, and when I obey, I make the difference He has chosen for me. The rest I have to leave up to Him."

The small child reached out a hand toward Asha. Asha took it, rubbing her thumb across the tiny fingers. Yes, Mark and Ruth and Indira were making a difference in this young life. And God only knew how He would use this child in the future.

But what about the rest? The rest of the orphans. Milo's street friends. What about all the women who had no chance of being rescued?

Mark's voice penetrated her thoughts. "I can't explain His reasons for what He does and does not do, but I know God is good. He is big enough. And I can trust Him."

Asha nodded. That was the essence of her problem, she realized. She was quick to say she trusted God when He was doing things according to her understanding. But here, where nothing seemed to make sense, suddenly God was not exactly as she expected Him to be, not doing what she expected Him to do.

God did not fit into her box. The knowledge almost frightened her. Maybe Asha did not know God as well as she thought.

When the whistle blew and Ruth gestured for the children to gather, Asha came as well. Mark followed carrying Shafique, who had fallen asleep against his shoulder.

Asha sat cross-legged on the ground facing Ruth, and the children clustered into a semi-circle all around her. Mark squeezed in nearby with little Shafique.

The children looked up at Ruth expectantly, waiting for a story.

Then Ruth surprised them all. The story she began telling was her own.

CHAPTER TWENTY-TWO

Ruth's words transported them all to the tea plantations in the northern parts of India. They heard how she grew up, about her brothers and sisters, even the jokes her older brothers used to play on her.

Suddenly she stopped. A dozen pair of eyes looked up in expectation.

"I am telling you about my life for a reason," Ruth said. She was speaking in Bengali, and Asha listened with all her attention, trying not to miss a word. "My dearest children, I love you all very much. Each one of you is special. Unique. And God loves each of you even more than I do. He will watch over you even after I am gone."

"Where are you going, Mother?" one of the younger children asked, using the loving term all the orphans used when addressing Ruth. "Will you be taking a trip?"

"My young ones, I am dying."

All was silent. The children did not react with as much emotion as Asha expected. Then she remembered that here the subject of death was not avoided. For these children, death was a very real part of life, each of them except Milo having lost at least one parent to death already.

"Next week, I will go away to a hospital. I will die there."

Asha noticed several of the children inching closer to Ruth. One rested her head against Ruth's leg. Ruth ran a hand lovingly through the child's hair.

"I want to tell you about my life, so you do not make the same bad choices I made. When I was a child, I did not like the difficult rules in my home. My family and our religious community had many requirements. I did not like to wear the clothes of my religion. I did not like to always follow the traditions and holy days along with my family."

"When I got older, my father began to arrange a marriage for me. I did not want to marry. I wanted to live free. I wanted to do what I wanted to do."

She looked each child in the eye. No one stirred.

"So I ran away."

A collective gasp arose. The children peppered Ruth with questions. "Where did you go?" "Did your family look for you?" "Did you carry all your clothes with you?" "How did you find food?"

Ruth silenced them with a raised hand. "What I did was foolish. I had a little bit of money, which I used to travel to the city. I expected to get a job. I planned to be very rich, and do whatever I wanted. But my money soon ran out."

"What did you do?" a child named Rafi asked. Several more children scooted closer.

At this question, Ruth's eyes went down. "I did a very bad thing. I did many bad things," she said. Her eyes lifted to look straight at Asha. "In a very bad place."

Asha gasped. Rani's face flashed before her mind. A pink note. Ruth's reaction.

Ruth continued. "I was in the bad place for a long time. I wanted to live a better life. I wanted to be clean again. But I thought that I had done so many bad things that I could never do enough good to pay for it. I was certain God hated me."

Little Shafique had woken up. She sat up, horrified. "Oh, no, Mother! God does not hate *anyone!*"

Her passionate certainty brought a smile to Ruth's lips. "You are right, beautiful one. But I did not know this. My religion taught me that God would only love me if I did more good things than bad."

Ruth's sigh tore into Asha's heart. "But I wanted to be clean again, more than anything. At night, I would beg God, if He was there, to send some hope to me. And He did. He sent someone to tell me that God loved me. Me, as I was. That God had sent Jesus to forgive all my sins. That I could be clean again." She smiled. "I believed in Jesus, and God forgave all my sins. For the first time in a long, long time, I had hope. And peace. God had rescued me."

She looked again at Asha, love in her eyes. Then her eyes drifted to Mark. The love remained. "And then God rescued me from the terrible place where I was. He gave me a new life, here with you. And I have been so happy."

The children shifted closer as Ruth continued. "I am sick because of some of the bad things I did. God forgave me, but He did not take away all the consequences of what I did. Instead, He has been with me, and loved me, and He will stay with me until I die. Then after that, He will take me to Heaven to be with Him forever."

She reached her arms out as if to hug all the children at once. "I tell you this because you already know that life can be very difficult and very sad. You have to make choices about your own life. Believe in Jesus and follow Him, and you will always have joy and peace. This is better than anything else."

Her gaze found each child. "Do not be sad for me when I die. I will be with Jesus. And I will live in a place where everything is good, and clean. I pray that you will someday be there with me, too."

She then did reach out to hug them all. The children rushed into her arms. "I love you," Ruth whispered.

A subdued group left the park that day. As dusk settled in around the city, lights flickered on from every direction. The bus barreled toward the compound, swaying as it passed smaller vehicles, honking brazenly to clear its path.

Asha watched the city go by, swaying with the bus' movement as she looked out the window. Such a place of mystery and beauty. And paradoxes. Here she had seen more evil than she imagined existed in the world. She had also seen much good.

Entering the compound, the children clung to Ruth and asked her to sing to them before bed. Ruth agreed, and they walked toward the orphanage together, Indira following with the leftover food for bedtime snacks.

Mark and Asha were left alone. They stood quietly as darkness fell around them.

Now more than ever, Asha wished to tell Mark everything. She wanted him to know her heart. She wanted to ask more about Ruth, how she came to be rescued. Who rescued her? Who told her about Jesus?

She looked up at him. *Who are you, Mark? Every time I see a glimpse of your heart, it is good and honorable. What are these secrets you keep? This hidden side of you, is it who you really are? Will I ever see it?*

They walked in silence toward the Main Building. Once there, Mark opened the door for Asha. He looked down on her with a soft smile. "I'm glad you came today."

Her gaze, questioning and unsure, seemed to unsettle him. Shifting his weight from one foot to another, he looked off across the compound, glancing at his unfinished house. Then his eyes swept back to Asha.

She tried to smile. "Today was. . . it was perfect." She looked into his eyes. They were full of feeling, but Asha could not tell what the feeling was.

"Good night, Mark," Asha whispered. "And...thank you."

She slipped into the building. Turning at the entrance to her own room, she watched through the darkness as Mark sighed, then closed the door slowly, shutting it with a firm click.

Not bothering to turn on the bedroom light, instead flicking on the small nightlight near her bed, Asha removed the magnificent sari, folding then draping it over her desk chair.

Tomorrow was church. Monday, Ruth would be leaving.

The borrowed colored bangles clinked against each other as Asha slid them from her arms. As important as it was, she wished she could just skip Monday and all the sadness it would contain, fast-forwarding to Tuesday when she would meet again with Rani. Tuesday held more hope.

Surely one of them would have thought of a plausible escape plan by then.

Asha fell into bed with a sigh. She heard her own voice whispering into the darkness before sleep claimed her, "Don't worry, Rani. Tuesday we'll figure it out."

CHAPTER TWENTY-THREE

*O*nce near the sari shop, Asha pulled her new tube of lipstick from her bag and applied it liberally to her full lips. Having returned Ruth's borrowed bangles, she instead pulled out the set she had bought for the orphan girls, putting half of them on one arm, and half on the other.

Lastly, she raised the tube of lipstick to put one round, red circle on her forehead. She knew this was a Hindu mark, but hoped the Lord would not mind, as it helped her disguise.

Inside the store, the full-length mirror revealed to Asha a stark contrast to the woman who had entered a week ago.

Shedding her neutral, plain salwar kameez, Asha this time had chosen a bright red and yellow one with painted block designs all over it. Red, red lips and the red dot on her forehead drew attention to her face. It was like staring at a stranger.

Is this how they all feel at first? Like they paste on a different person, and they themselves have ceased to exist?

Rani arrived, but before Asha could greet her, Rani silenced her. "There are others coming. They will stay and they will talk. You must not speak. They will hear that you are a foreigner from your accent. You must not show that you know me. If they stay the full twenty minutes, I will have to go back with them. If that happens, meet me in two days, on Thursday, at this same time."

She was about to say more when two young girls—decorated like peacocks, Asha thought—meandered into the store, whispering secretively. Rani sat near the wall full of saris for sale, keeping a good distance between herself and Asha.

Asha tried to hide her disappointment by turning away, looking at the sari on the mannequin. When the salesman approached and asked if she wanted a sari, Asha nodded yes, hoping the man would not ask any questions she would need to answer with words.

She fingered several of the saris on display. The manager, still chewing beetle-nut, brought several more choices from the back and even modeled one for her. He asked Asha if she wanted a sari blouse made. Again, Asha nodded. The man directed her toward a small room in the back, telling her she must be measured for her blouse by the tailor.

Asha went inside and waited while the man shuffled through a door across from where she stood. Another room was revealed, facing the opposite road. Apparently the sari shop and tailor's shop were connected by this tiny room. A smart idea, Asha noted.

Hearing voices then, Asha slid back toward the door she had first entered, sliding it open just a crack to see several more women arrive and sit near Rani. She could hear them discussing things Asha had never been allowed to speak of, some things she had never even heard of.

For the first few minutes, Asha strained to listen, trying to understand the Bengali. After a few minutes of frank talk about what happened inside the rooms of the red-light district, Asha closed the door, swallowing down nausea. She did not want to hear any more.

When the shop manager returned, a younger man in tow, Asha hesitantly obeyed when he instructed her to hold out her arms for measurement. She gulped nervously as his hands brought a tape measure around her upper waist, then her arms, then across her shoulders.

When he reached around her to measure her bust size, Asha's face broke out in a sweat. Was this normal? Appropriate?

Did all women go through this when they bought a sari? Asha gulped, her nausea rising.

The tailor finished his work, marking numbers on a small brown paper. Finally, he left and Asha lowered her arms and held them across her chest.

The man had not taken advantage of the situation in any way, but still she felt a sense of invasion. Her thoughts went to the women in the room nearby. How must they feel, every day and every night, when—

Asha wiped her damp face with her *orna*, trying to refocus her thoughts. She did not want to think about it anymore.

Until Rani spoke. Her voice caught not only Asha's attention, but the other girls' as well.

"Have you ever thought of escaping?"

Asha could sense the immediate tension, as if someone had just walked in and offered them a piece of cake, but they feared it was poisoned.

Silence filled the room for one minute. Then two. Rani was the one to finally break it. In Bengali, she asked again, "If you had the chance, would you try to escape?"

With the beetle-nut man chattering behind her, Asha cracked the door again and peeked into the shop room to see all the girls looking down. Not one was looking Rani in the eye, or even looking at her face.

"I tried once," one woman whispered, as if afraid of being overheard. She kept her head down. "They caught me and beat me. I thought they would kill me. After that, I have never had the courage to try again."

Another woman, older, spoke next. "I worked for years to make enough money to buy back my freedom. Finally, I got enough money, and I went home."

She sat without speaking for so long, another girl asked, "What happened?"

The woman's voice became wooden, dead—like Rani's, Asha thought. "They did not want me. Everyone knew what had happened to me. It would damage my family's status in the community if they took me back. So they disowned me."

Eyes of hopeless pain lifted. "I had no place to go. No money left." Then she shrugged as if it did not matter. As if she did not matter. "So I came back. There is nothing else for me."

After a long and painful silence, a few girls tried to start up a separate conversation, their voices too high, too cheerful.

When the counterfeit attempts fell flat, one by one the girls rose and left the shop.

Asha negotiated a price for the pale green sari she had chosen, along with a black and gold one for Amy, taking care to speak quietly with the shopkeeper in case any of the women were still nearby. She asked how long the matching blouse would take to make. A week.

When she stepped back into the shop, Rani was the only one left. She stood to face Asha, her eyes for the first time filled with emotion. Asha saw fear. Pain. Hopelessness.

Rani spoke in English. "What good is it to be rescued *from* something terrible, if you are not rescued *to* anything good? Freedom is not the same as hope. If I do escape, is there anything good left for me?"

Before Asha could respond Rani turned and walked away. Asha ran to the entryway and saw her slowly round the corner, returning to a life more binding than any prison cell, to chains worse than any made of metal.

Oh, God, Asha's heart cried out within her. She could think of no fancy words. No impressive prayers. *Oh, God,* her spirit groaned. *Help.*

CHAPTER TWENTY-FOUR

℘t was a dismal day. Nearly as dismal as Asha felt.

She was tired, and deeply disappointed about the failure of yesterday's meeting with Rani. To go through all that trouble and not even get five minutes to speak together.

The gloomy grey of the afternoon sky weighed upon her emotions. Worst of all, her stomach had kept her up half the night complaining about the *samosa* she had eaten at the market the day before.

She had just finished the daily lesson and the children were playing under the watchful eye of Indira when Mark approached. She mustered up half a smile for him.

Not adversely affected by the weather, the orphan children laughed and swarmed around Mark like bees to honey. Not that Asha blamed them. Who wouldn't respond to the ready smile and quick affection he always had for them?

Mark neared the swing Asha had lowered herself into, a wide smile on his face. "You look cheerful today in that bright yellow outfit," he said, tentatively trying out the swing next to her. The swingset was ancient, the swings made out of old, cutout tires on chains. After looking dubiously up at the top beam, he stood up again.

"Yellow suits you," he continued. "Most American visitors look rather out of place in the Indian dress, but you look just right in it."

Again, Asha offered a half-hearted smile.

She could feel his gaze on her, studying her. Should she tell him she was feeling sad? Give him some reason why, say she was missing Ruth and Milo? It was true.

"Do you have time for a little trip?"

She eyed him. "What kind of a trip? To where?"

Mark shook his head. "Not telling. Do you have time?"

"Well, the kids will be napping soon, and to be honest, I was dreading the free time. Normally, I'd have my Bengali lesson with Ruth then, but now that she's gone away . . ."

She let her words trail off and thought about Mark's offer. If there was anything that Asha could not resist, it was a mystery. Her glum feelings began losing their hold and she felt the corners of her mouth turn upward. "Okay, Mr. I-live-here-so-I-can-be-all-superior, I do have some time," she said. "Try to impress me."

Mark responded with that grin she was coming to love. "Maybe I will. Come with me. There's something special I want to show you."

Asha left her black mood on the swingset and rushed to catch up with Mark. He opened the gate and motioned to a three-wheeled taxi called an auto.

The tiny vehicle looked to Asha like a brightly painted golf cart. She liked the autos. They had open-air sides, greatly appreciated after her unpleasant ride in the closed taxi the day of the zoo trip.

They climbed into the small vehicle and rode in what would have been a companionable silence had Asha not felt so curious. She pestered him with her eyes and her facial expressions to tell her what the big secret was. He would only smile back, that calm, devoid of passion smile that infuriated her, then look at the road again, or give an instruction to the driver.

After four or five minutes, which felt like a hundred to Asha, they veered to the side of the road and stopped.

Asha stepped out as Mark paid the driver, then followed as Mark guided them down a path.

When she saw it, Asha gasped in appreciation. Though originally she thought they were entering a grove of trees, a closer look revealed that the branches were all connected. Leaves overshadowed the entire area, with a hundred small shafts of light filtering through to shine lines of gold down all around them. Very thin trees, hundreds of them, somehow all connected, created a shrouded wonderland of color and light.

She had never seen anything like it.

"It's a banyan tree," Mark informed her, putting his hand out as if he were introducing it. "The roots grow from the top down, so all these long parts that look like skinny trees are actually roots growing down from the main tree's branches."

They walked farther inside the wooded area.

Asha smiled over at Mark. "This was worth all your annoying secrecy," she said.

Mark grinned. "The world's largest banyan tree is not far away, across the river. I think it spans over a mile altogether, with over a thousand roots. I'll have to take you there someday. But this smaller one here is my favorite."

Asha looked up at him in wonder. "I am totally impressed," she said.

His smile down at her was all tenderness. She could have melted right there at his feet.

They walked through the forest that was only one tree, light through the leaves covering them in a green haze. "It's like a fairyland," Asha whispered almost reverently.

"The banyan tree across the river gets lots of visitors. A fence was put up around it, and a road, but it keeps growing, and has overtaken the road in some places." Mark looked up. "I like this tree so much better. Always felt like it was sort of my own. I don't remember ever seeing anyone walk around in here except me."

He looked down at her. "And now you."

With the darkening sky, their fairyland became shrouded in grey, almost as if the day had skipped the sunset and gone straight into night. A welcome breeze swirled leaves in circles around them.

They meandered through the tree's hundreds of roots without talking. Asha did not mind. She could feel the silence between them was the good kind, the kind enjoyed by close friends.

Almost as if they had made a silent pact, neither mentioned that one subject, the topic that caused so much friction between them.

Mark sat on the ground at the base of one of the banyan roots. When he patted the area next to him, Asha took the invitation and joined him. She chose to ignore the fact that the ground was hard, and that the wind had picked up and the sky was darker.

As they talked, the wild edge to the weather seemed natural, a parallel to the tempest in her own heart. It warned her to beware. She should not fall for a man who lived on the other side of the world, who couldn't seem to agree about anything that mattered to her, who avoided people in desolate need.

But none of those things seemed to matter when he looked down at her and smiled like that.

Suddenly Mark looked around them, then rose to his feet.

"There's a storm coming in," he said, brushing leaves from his pants, "and it's not going to be a picnic sprinkle. I should have noticed the sky and gotten us home long ago."

He reached down and pulled her to her feet. "I'm sorry, Asha. I wasn't paying attention."

His eyes smiled down at her. "Guess I got distracted."

She grinned back, then followed as he led them quickly out from under the banyan tree. Once out in the open again, Asha felt like she was walking in the outskirts of a hurricane. She caught her scarf just in time as a gust of wind ripped it from her shoulders.

"Besides," Mark shouted over the noise of the wind as they climbed onto the seat of a bicycle rickshaw, "my dad came back from his trip this morning, you know. He went to visit some people this afternoon, but is supposed to be home around five, and if we don't make it back before he does, you can be sure he'll be waiting to let us have it."

The rickshaw driver began to pedal his way down the road. Asha turned to Mark in shock as the wind whipped her shoulder-length hair across her face and into her mouth. She pulled it away. "You mean we'll get in trouble for coming out here today?"

Mark's face showed chagrin. "No, not trouble, just teasing. Something along the lines of 'I was beginning to wonder if you two had run off and gotten married,' or something like that."

Asha's face flamed. "He would never really say something like that, would he?"

Mark's answering smile was unnerving. "He already has." He grinned. "More than once."

Just then, as if monsoon season decided to announce itself right over their rickshaw, the rain began in a torrent. People immediately began scrambling from the streets, looking for any kind of shelter.

Asha squealed, but could barely hear herself over the sound of thousands of huge drops of rain pelting them, the rickshaw, and the asphalt road. Or was it the sound of the rain hitting the hundreds of plastic bags clogged up in the open sewers? Asha could not tell.

Before she had time to wish for an umbrella, the rickshaw driver stopped and rushed back to pull the rickshaw's canopy over their heads. Next, from one side of the overhang to the other, he pulled a flimsy plastic tarp to protect them from the rain. Asha cringed; it felt like the inside of a shower curtain.

They watched as the driver pulled a random plastic bag from the street, wrapped it over his hair, then jumped back on the uncovered bicycle part of the rickshaw and began pedaling again.

Suddenly the two passengers found themselves cocooned within a small and cozy setting. The heavy rain and the noise made everything around them disappear.

Asha pulled her legs back from the tarp and relaxed against the torn, back cushion of the rickshaw seat. She would have been content to remain there the rest of the day in her rumpled, soggy salwar kameez, enjoying the ride and the company, imagining future possibilities.

Reality, unfortunately, had other ideas.

"Well, if it isn't my son and the little lady herself," a booming voice greeted them.

Asha turned to see that they had arrived at the compound and Mark's father, umbrella in hand, had opened the gate and was waiting to welcome them back. He grinned with delight, like a child with a new toy.

She knew it was coming. Mark even reminded her it was coming as he paid the rickshaw driver. But still she felt mortified when she heard it.

"You two were gone so long, I was about to think you'd run off and eloped or something," Mr. Stephens said with a laugh.

Mark looked back at her, rolling his eyes.

Asha caught herself smiling. She rushed through the rain into the compound and under the first sheltering driveway awning she could reach.

"Teasing is a sign of affection with my dad, you know."

Asha turned to see that a completely doused Mark had snuck up behind her. Despite the coolness the rain had brought, she felt the heat radiating from him.

She took a safe step away from him, certain her clothes would be dry in seconds from her own steam if she remained so close.

Mark was smiling. "It means he likes you."

With a sigh, Asha accepted this strange, incomprehensible fact. "He must like me a lot, then," she murmured.

"I think he does," Mark agreed. After a moment's thought, his face opened up as if he was having a revelation. "Maybe that's why I like teasing you so much, too."

Did he just say that out loud?

Asha watched, full of interest, as his face reddened.

With a short cough Mark excused himself, thanked her for coming with him, and took off running through the pouring monsoon rain toward his grandparents' house.

Asha stood still, as if she were a banyan tree root herself, watching him go with a sweet, small smile touching her lips.

All around her it was still a dismal, dreary day, but somehow Asha felt as if the sun had just come out.

CHAPTER TWENTY-FIVE

Early the next morning Asha typed a quick e-mail to her parents, copying it to James and Amy as she had since her arrival. She wrote about the orphans, about the zoo trip, and about the amazing banyan tree, noticing she had mentioned Mark a few times more than was necessary.

As she sat staring at the screen, wondering if there was anything else she should check while the internet was actually working, an instant message popped up. James was online.

"Have you rescued the girl yet?"

That was all it said. No "Hello" or "How's the weather?" or "How are the orphan kids doing?"

"Not yet," she posted. "It's complicated."

His response was quick. "You aren't letting that control freak Mark stop you, are you?"

Asha bit her lip and typed back, "No, it's not like that. He's not as bad as I thought." It was a small message, but hopefully it would give her some time to think of what she really wanted to say.

James' next short comment jolted Asha's world.

"You're falling for him, aren't you?"

She stared at the words on the screen. She thought of Mark— at the orphanage, under the banyan tree, sitting close to her in a rickshaw. She thought of his eyes and his voice and his smile.

Asha sucked in a breath.

With resolve, and only a bit of impulsiveness, Asha typed just one word and sent it.

"Yes."

James had always made it clear he was not interested in only friendship with her, so Asha was not surprised when his next message was a goodbye.

Asha knew she would no longer be hearing from him. Not even to ask about the trafficked girl.

His final note was kind enough, wishing her the best. But one line stood out to Asha. She thought of it as she sent her goodbye in reply, then left the building and went to find Mark.

"India has changed you," he wrote.

Asha smiled. Yes, it had.

She found Mark sitting on the porch outside his grandparents' home, a huge stack of papers on his lap. On the table next to his chair, a half-filled glass had been set securely over a batch of leaflets—to keep them from blowing away, Asha assumed, in the unlikely event of a breeze.

Asha stood with uncertainty at the foot of the porch steps until he noticed her. Mark's smile was welcoming enough. In fact, he looked very happy to see her.

What kept her weighted to the ground at the edge of the porch, though, was the newly realized fact that she had not thought of any legitimate reason for searching him out that morning. She had just wanted to be with him.

And that, she certainly could not say.

Mark indicated a nearby chair and invited her to sit. "Want some tea?" he asked. "Grandma was originally from the South, so it might be sweet enough for your taste."

"Real sweet iced tea?" Well, wonders never ceased. "Now that's something I didn't expect to find in India. I'd love some."

He started to set aside his mound of papers, but she motioned him to stop. "No, don't get up. I can get it. Just point me in the right direction."

He grinned. "That would be nice. I'm afraid if I set this pile down now, I'd be lost by the time I picked it up again. I love translating, but editing is just not my thing."

A few minutes later, having found the tea and returned to sit beside Mark, Asha's sigh was pure joy. "This is so good." She held up the glass and swirled the ice cubes, enjoying the clinking sounds they made as they bumped one another. The sight of them all crammed in the glass reminded her of the orphan children stuffing themselves into the back of those three taxis they took to the zoo. She smiled at the memory.

"Am I interrupting your work?" she asked. "I can come back later." If she came back later, she would have time to think of some excuse for showing up at his doorstep, instead of just wandering toward him like a lost kitten in want of attention.

"Actually, give me just one minute and I'll be done with this page." Mark gestured toward his lap. "Then a break would be nice."

With one final skimming glance, he penned a small notation at the bottom of the paper, then set the whole pile down with a thud, putting his foot on top of the pile to keep the pages from floating away. He turned to her with an expectant smile. "So what's up?"

Asha's mind went blank. She studied her glass of tea again, and got an idea. "I want to ask your advice about something," she said, relieved that her voice did not betray that her idea was completely impromptu.

"Oh?" His eyebrows rose. "About what?"

She licked her lips and took another sip of the tea. It had reminded her of her mother back in North Carolina, which brought her mind to her biological parents in Bangladesh. "About my parents. My real parents."

Mark turned in his chair so that he faced her fully, taking care to keep his foot securely on the papers. "I'm all yours," he said, then reddened. "I mean, you have my full attention." She smiled and he tried again. "I mean, I'm listening."

"Well, my parents adopted me when I was just a baby. They won't tell me anything about the circumstances, and every time I ask it seems to hurt them. I don't want them to think I don't love them. I love them very much. But I have this terrible need to find out what really happened. If my Bangladeshi parents are still alive. To find them and ask them . . . why they gave me away to strangers."

Mark sat quietly. His eyes had grown serious. He looked down at the floor and she knew he was thinking. She waited until his eyes returned to hers. "Why is it so important for you to know?"

Asha licked her lips again. She felt her fingers twisting, and purposefully clasped them still in her lap. "I saw a picture of you and your parents in the guest-room album." She could not keep the longing from her voice. "Your mother's face—there was such love there. I want to know . . ."

Asha was surprised when tears stung her eyes. She had never talked with anyone but her parents about her birth family, and not even to them about how she really felt. Why was she telling Mark now? "I want to know what was wrong with me that made them give me away."

Mark stayed quiet for so long, Asha finally looked up to see if she could decipher the feelings on his face. With precise movements, he reached down to pick up the pile of papers under his foot. He stood and carried them inside the house.

Most of the time Asha did not mind his silent thinking, but right then it was torturous. She reached a hand up to wipe a loose hair from her face and tried not to fidget as she waited.

When he finally sat down and turned toward her, she found herself falling into the deep concern she saw on his face. He cared about her. It was there, in his eyes. She breathed in deeply.

He spoke. "I think I understand now why you cared so much about that girl in the red-light district."

Asha was startled. Of all the things she had imagined him saying, that was the farthest from her mind. It jolted her upright in her chair. She could not look him in the eye anymore, certain that if she did, he would see right through her and know everything about her secret meetings with Rani. She grasped her glass of tea tightly and said with contrived nonchalance, "What do you mean?"

"That girl was trapped, and you wanted to save her. I think you felt so strongly about it—well, partly because you seem to feel strongly about a lot of things—but I think the real reason was because you feel trapped yourself."

Asha's head was reeling. What was he talking about? Rani's situation had nothing to do with hers. "I wanted to ask your advice about how I could start looking into finding my biological parents without upsetting my adoptive parents," she said, trying to steer the conversation back to a safer place.

"Asha." He took her hand in his, and she stared at it. "Your worth as a person does not come from whether or not your parents valued you. It also doesn't depend on whether or not you do some great worthwhile thing. Your worth is in the fact that God loves you, and that Jesus gave up His own life for yours. You don't have to try to earn that, or prove you are worthy of it." He took her other hand, now holding both in his. "Just accept it. Be loved."

The conversation was becoming dangerous. She had to leave, soon.

Pasting a smile on her face, she withdrew her hands and said, "I didn't mean to start such a melancholy subject. You'll start running away the moment you see me coming if I always begin conversations this deep." She laughed, but it sounded fake, even to her.

She picked up her glass, the ice cubes clinking cheerily as she took one more drink. "Thanks for the tea. I'll just go put this glass in the sink."

She felt his eyes on her as she retreated. Once inside, she held the cool glass up against her forehead. Why had he said all that? What even made him think that she wanted to rescue someone else to make up for the fact that she could not rescue herself? That she was afraid to really find out the truth, and yet desperate for it anyway? Afraid that she would find out, once and for all, that she was not wanted? Was not worth anything?

Her stomach churned. Asha placed the glass in the kitchen sink, then decided to give herself a few minutes respite from Mark's piercing eyes by washing the glass before leaving the kitchen.

You're hiding, her conscience told her. *You're afraid he's right, and you don't want to face it.*

She scrubbed the glass furiously, trying to block the voice in her head with the sound of the sponge squeaking back and forth over the surface of the glass.

The sudden hands on her shoulders shocked Asha so much, she dropped the glass. It clanged several times as it teetered in the sink and finally settled on its side at the bottom, thankfully unbroken.

Mark turned her to face him, but she resisted. "My hands are dripping," she said weakly, turning her back again to him and slowly drying her hands with the kitchen towel.

He moved to stand next to her at the counter, looking over at her face with a persistence that unraveled her. For one moment, she imagined leaning into his chest and crying out half a lifetime of fears and longings.

"What is it you're so afraid of?" he asked, his voice low.

She avoided his eyes, and his question. "Um, well actually, I think I'd better get going on my trip to the market." She again rinsed the glass and set it up on the counter to dry. "Maybe we can talk about this later."

Asha backed away from the sink with a "Have to practice my Bengali, you know!" She smiled and left the house without once looking him in the eye, telling herself not to ask his advice ever again on a personal matter.

Somehow he seemed to have the ability to see into her very soul. No one had ever gotten close enough to do that. No one had ever pushed through how she appeared to be, determined to see who she really was.

No one ever had, because she had never let anyone.

Within minutes, Asha had left for the market, not giving any thought to possible dangers on the streets as she rode toward the sari shop.

Her mind was too full of the danger she had just left behind.

CHAPTER TWENTY-SIX

Mark's words swirled and tumbled in Asha's mind, as if someone had thrown her brain into a washing machine and hit the spin cycle button. Could his intuition be true? Was she desperate to rescue Rani because it would result somehow in a rescue of a part of herself as well? Give her validity? Worth?

No, Asha shook her head resolutely. She wanted to rescue Rani because it was the right thing to do. Because God loved Rani and wanted her free.

And today she would be carrying that very message. Not just freedom *from* something, but freedom *to* something.

With effort, Asha blocked the entire scene with Mark from her mind, and by the time she stepped into the sari shop to see Rani waiting there, her mind was focused and clear. Knowing they had little time, Asha sent up a swift, silent prayer, then sat beside her friend.

"Rani," she barged into the subject, skipping any small talk that might waste precious time. "I'm so glad none of the others came today. There's something really important I need to talk to you about."

Rani had said nothing since Asha's arrival. Asha noticed that her eyes seemed as deadened as they had the first time they met. She wanted to ask how Rani was doing, if she was being treated well, but the complete ridiculousness of the question itself stopped her. Of course she was not being treated well. Of course she was doing badly.

Even more motivated, Asha rushed on. "First, I need to apologize to you."

A flicker of a question flashed in Rani's eyes.

Asha took that as permission to continue. "I wanted to help you escape so much. All I could think about was you needing to be free from this terrible place and these terrible circumstances. But your words last time I came have pierced my heart. What you need most is something that freedom from this place cannot give you. And I did not think to tell you. I'm so sorry."

Asha took a deep breath, about to embark on a journey into brand new territory for her. "Rani, do you know that God loves you? That He cares about what happens to you?"

This brought an instant reaction. Rani's face shot up. "God?" she said cynically. "Which god?"

She gestured up at the idol guarding the entrance to the shop. Its elephant head and human body stood still as death. Incense wafted up in front of it. "This god maybe? Or one of the hundreds of others? The ones that were supposed to watch over my house, the ones who should have kept my father from dying, the ones we prayed to so they would keep our family wealthy and safe?"

She sat, a cloud of despair nearly tangible around her. Asha had never seen anyone look so completely alone. She sat down and touched her friend's hand. "Rani, have you ever heard of Jesus?"

When Rani remained still, not answering, Asha told her an old, old story, one that has been told a thousand times before. Of a God who created all things, who loved His creation, who sent Jesus to bridge the gap and restore the relationship that was broken by sin. Rani sat unmoving, showing no obvious interest, but not interrupting. Asha wondered if she was even listening.

When she had run out of words, Asha stopped. Rani's face was passive, but then filled with pain. "This God, He sounds so wonderful. So good. He does not play with people's lives like our gods. He does not change His mind. And if it is true that He loves—this is a greater God than I have ever heard of."

Asha's heart beat with joy at Rani's words, but confusion at her actions. Rani stood and turned her back. Her voice was hard. "Had I heard of this God in my life before now, nothing would stop me from believing in Him." She turned to Asha, and the hardness in her face caused Asha to physically back up.

"But if your God is pure and holy, He will not accept one like me. He will not want me in His great family. I am not clean or pure or holy anymore. I have nothing to offer."

Her face was hard but her eyes were full of such an ache that Asha heard herself responding with urgency, "No, Rani! For one, what has happened to you was not your fault. And for another, even if you had chosen this life, God would still love you. He would still be waiting for you to come to Him, to believe in Him."

Quickly, her fingers clumsy in their haste, Asha untied a smaller bag inside the larger bag she carried everywhere. She pulled out a Bible, written in Bengali, that she had bought just the week before when she and Eleanor Stephens had gone shopping together. She had been excited about taking it back to America and learning to read it, but now held it out to Rani.

"This is God's book. It is all about how much He loves you. It is about how He wants people to live. And it is about Jesus."

Rani looked at the offering, skepticism still plainly written across her features. "Does it have any prostitutes in it?" she asked with scorn.

Asha's eyes lit up. "Actually, yes, it does."

Her answer had its effect. Rani sat back down and looked at Asha warily.

It had always been one of Asha's favorite stories. She opened the Bible to the book of Joshua and checked her watch. They only had ten minutes left. It was not long enough.

She handed the Bible to Rani. "I'd tell you the story, but it is so much better if you read it yourself. Read chapters two and six. They are about a woman named Rahab, a prostitute."

Rani was a fast reader. Her eyes poured across the pages, widening as she read. When finished, she looked at Asha, and for the first time since they had met, a tiny glimmer of hope shone through. "Your God rescued this woman. This Rahab. Do you believe He would rescue me?"

Asha's eyes filled with moisture. "I do. And I think it is not just about rescuing you from something. More important even than rescuing you from this terrible place, God wants to rescue you from the despair and the fear. He wants to rescue you to something beautiful and whole."

"To what?" Rani's voice was breathless, her eyes wide.

Asha grasped her friend's hand. "To peace. To hope. To love."

Rani rose. She stood looking down at Asha. "I will think about this God of yours. This Jesus. If He is what you say, to belong to Him would be better than anything. You will tell me more next time you come?"

"I will." Asha could not help herself. She stood and hugged Rani. At first Rani recoiled, as if any touch frightened her. Then she stood stiffly until Asha stepped back. Her body remained tense but her face filled out into a smile.

Asha had never seen her smile. She was transformed.

"If this God of yours is true, I think perhaps He sent you to me." Rani's words brought tears to Asha's eyes.

Rani turned to go. At the doorway to the shop, she stopped and looked back. "You know," she said to Asha, "I have heard one other person talk of your Jesus. A few weeks ago a man came to my room. He had paid, but he did not touch me. He told me he was a follower of Jesus. A follower of the God who loves women. He asked if I wanted to leave my life here and have a better life."

When Asha just sat there, stupefied, Rani continued, "I thought that the men in my building might have heard about my meeting with you, and were trying to trap me. So I said no. I did not believe him. What man could want to help a woman like me? But now I wonder, maybe your God sent him to me also."

Rani looked at the Hindu idol at the front of the shop. Unseeing eyes did not respond. "The gods I tried to appease all my life never did anything for me. They certainly did not love. I will learn more of the God who saves the prostitutes. Will you come on Tuesday, next week?"

When Asha nodded, Rani gave a hint of a smile, then was gone.

All the way home, Asha's mind puzzled over the story Rani had shared about the man coming to her room and offering her an escape. What could it mean? Was the man trying to trap her, as Rani had thought? Or had he truly wanted to help?

Asha wished she knew who he was. She would love to find the man and ask for his advice. If he was sincere, he had likely helped other women and would have some good ideas on how Rani could escape.

But other than this unsolvable mystery, her time with Rani had been better than she hoped. Asha thanked God for giving her the words to say, and especially for having her bring her Bible so Rani could read the story of Rahab.

"And God," she whispered as her rickshaw meandered through the streets on the way back, "thank You for being good. I always took for granted that You are good and never change, and that You love me. But I'm learning what a beautiful gift it is."

A soft smile fluttered like butterfly wings at the edges of Asha's lips as she entered the compound. It died swiftly when she looked across the way and saw Mark, sitting again on his grandparents' porch, the pile of papers back in his lap. He was hunched over them, eyebrows pinched so tight in concentration he looked like he was grimacing.

Asha knew she was grimacing, and it was not from concentration. She forced herself to walk toward the Stephens' house instead of rushing to her own room. She was standing in front of the porch, her hands on two individual beams, before he noticed her.

"You're back," he stated the obvious. His eyes were looking at her, but they seemed closed off somehow. She had feared him looking into her with his probing eyes, but now found that to have him look through her without seeing her was far worse.

She swallowed. "I'm sorry for running away like that earlier. You were trying to help, and I think there may be truth to what you said. I will think about it. Okay?"

He set his papers aside, and stood. Four steps brought him to the porch railing, where he rested his weight onto his hands and looked down to where she stood on the ground below.

"I shouldn't have pressured you to talk about something you were uncomfortable sharing. I can be kind of . . . intrusive at times."

Oh, you have no idea how you have intruded upon my life, Asha's heart said.

"Truce?" he smiled down at her.

She smiled up in return. "Truce."

He laughed then, ruefully. "You know, maybe one of these days we'll make it through a conversation without one of us needing to apologize."

Asha smiled, and by the time she had reached her room, she was humming. She and Mark were back to being friends. Rani wanted to know more about Jesus.

Things were really starting to look up.

CHAPTER TWENTY-SEVEN

Asha marked the days off her calendar, marveling at how quickly the time had flown by. Five and a half weeks she had been in India. Less than three left. The thought made her unaccountably sad.

Before coming, Asha had wondered if eight weeks would be too long. Now here she was, wishing she could stay longer.

Faces she had come to love flashed through her mind . . . Rani . . . Milo . . .

Mark. When she heard the familiar voice outside, her heart quickened.

"Hey, Sunshine." Mark stood at the screen door, calling out instead of knocking. Asha smiled. In so many ways, he was more Asian than she.

When she appeared, wearing her bright yellow salwar kameez, he smiled. "Perfect."

Asha looked away self-consciously, then up into those mesmerizing blue eyes again. "Good morning, yourself." She smiled. "What's up?"

He actually shuffled his feet, standing there at the door, hands in his pockets. He looked so adorably insecure, Asha wanted to hug him.

"Well . . ." He was stalling, she could tell. But about what?

"Today's my birthday, and—"

"It is?" Asha's hands flung wide. "Why didn't you say so? Happy Birthday! Are you going to do something special?" Asha thought of home, how on her birthday her parents always took her to her favorite restaurant. "Want me to treat you to lunch somewhere? Where's your favorite place to eat?"

He half-smiled. "Actually, out here, if it's your birthday, you are the one who gets to do the buying. I don't even get out of it with my birthday falling on Saturday this year. I'll still be expected to go out and buy some snacks for break-time Monday."

Asha eyed him. "You're joking."

"Nope. This is a culture where you aren't supposed to draw attention to yourself as an individual. So I guess if you have to buy, you're less likely to make a big to-do over your own birthday. Or something like that." He shrugged.

Asha's peal of laughter was music around them. She put a hand to the screen door from the inside. "Well, then, why don't you buy me lunch instead?"

Embarrassed by her own boldness, Asha looked down at her feet, thinking absently that her favorite pair of sandals were now not only broken in, they were nearly falling apart. She would have to replace them soon. She heard Mark speaking, but did not look up.

"Wish I could, but we'll have to be here at noon for a team meeting."

That did bring Asha's head up. She groaned. "On Saturday? We just had one last week." She sighed. "Don't tell me we have to endure another whole hour of discussing where those missing tools could have gone."

Mark grinned, and reached his arms up to the top door frame. He leaned his weight onto his hands, his head forward near the screen. He looked around, then leaned in to whisper, "Well, rumor has it that there's a surprise party planned. They say we're having a meeting, but I know better."

He chuckled. "They've done this every year on my birthday for the past ten years at least. I don't know why they still expect me to be surprised about it."

She laughed with him, then was surprised to see his face grow serious again. He was still leaning close to the screen. She stepped nearer on the other side, close enough to notice a small birthmark at the edge of his chin.

"But until the 'meeting' at noon, I have the day to myself. I'd planned to work some on the house, but . . ." He looked at the small structure and frowned.

After a heaving breath, he faced Asha to say in a rush, "I'm going out to the banyan tree and I want you to come with me."

Asha's face filled with concern. What was bothering him? She put a hand up again, flat against the screen door, fingers spread. "Of course," she said softly, watching as one of his arms dropped from the door panel and he placed his hand on the screen to touch palms with hers.

"Thank you."

She stared at their hands. "You're welcome," she whispered.

All the way out to the banyan tree, they rode in silence. Mark seemed lost in his thoughts, and Asha spent the time wondering what those thoughts were. Finally, once they were sitting under the tree in what she thought of as their spot, the place they had sat the first time he brought her, she said, "Want to talk about it?"

He looked down at her with his analytical, assessing look. She smiled to reassure him that she really did want to know.

"Today's my birthday . . . and my Dad's back from his trip, you know . . ."

Asha nodded, waiting for him to continue.

"This will probably sound childish, but it feels like he still sees me as just his kid, not as a man. Even my grandparents, though they've tried, still think of me as a grandkid more than a fellow missionary. And that house. It's so—so—"

"Tiny?" Asha offered. She did not think he was the type to complain about a lack of space, but maybe he felt it symbolized how small they saw his role there on the compound.

Mark shook his head no. "I don't care about the size." Then he smiled. "Though it is pretty dinky, isn't it?" He waved off a mosquito. "I wouldn't mind living my whole life in a house that size, if only it wasn't . . ."

Asha leaned toward him unconsciously. "Wasn't what?"

He sighed. "Wasn't *there.*"

"There? What do you mean?"

Mark gestured as if pointing out the house to her. "There. On the compound. I've told my family for years that once I finished seminary, I wanted to move off the compound. To live within the culture. Be part of it. Have Indian neighbors instead of just American ones. Live someplace where my Indian friends and national pastors could come to visit without feeling out of place. I want to live like they live. I feel like it would be more appropriate for the things I believe God has called me to do."

When Asha sat in silence, processing, he put in quickly, "Not that I'm judging any of the others, don't think that. I know especially for the clinic workers that having the compound is really important and necessary. They'd have people at their door day and night if they had no boundaries. And for the ones who travel around in ministry, it's great to have a set-apart place so they can be revived when they're home, so they're ready to go out again."

"It's just that for me, personally, I feel the Lord wants me out there, being with them and living like them as much as I can. And that house there on the compound, it just—it just shows that all those years, nobody took me seriously. I guess they thought I'd grow out of it or something."

Asha wanted to comfort him, tell him that she believed in him. "You really love India, don't you?" she whispered.

Mark leaned forward and rested his elbows on his knees, his hands clasped together. "I do. I love this country. I love these people. I want to be faithful in doing what God has gifted me to do."

"So why not just move out?"

Mark looked down at his hands. "For one, I know it would be going against my dad's authority, and that would be Biblically wrong. For another, it seems the missionary team feels like my desire to live away from the compound is some kind of an insult, and I don't want to keep bringing it up until they understand that it's not a rejection of any kind."

Mark frowned. "But my biggest reason for waiting is my grandparents. I don't know what to do about them."

"Do you feel like you have to stay to take care of them?"

Her question seemed to shake him out of his solemn mood, at least partly.

"No, nothing like that." The frown became a wry grin. "It's that they've lived here so long, some of the Indian philosophies have kind of seeped into their thinking, honoring the ancestors being one of them. I'm not supposed to dishonor them by setting off on my own. I'm supposed to stay and continue the work they began."

"And truly, I do honor the work they began," Mark continued, looking off into the distance as if seeing into the past. "They are my heroes. They came not long after India had gained Independence, faced years of pent-up hatred against anyone white caused by generations under British rule. Grandfather says they often wanted to leave, but they knew God wanted them here, so they stuck it out. They were pioneers, and I admire and respect them. In my way, I am continuing the work." Mark sighed. "This one thing, me wanting to live on my own outside the compound, is the first thing we've ever really disagreed on. I don't know what to do."

He looked at her as if Asha could be holding the answer.

She had no idea what to say. So she shrugged slightly, and smiled, then offered a piece of advice that must have come from the Lord, for it certainly surprised her. "You have time, you know. If God is the One who gave you the desire, then it is His responsibility to make a way for you. You don't need to feel the burden of making it happen yourself."

Mark just looked at her, apparently as surprised as she that such an idea would come from the girl who had been pushing her own heart goals since the day she arrived. He cocked an eyebrow and a teasing smile hinted of a comment to come.

But then Asha watched him clamp his mouth shut. When he opened it, his voice was sincere.

"Thank you, Asha."

Asha ducked her head, self-conscious.

Mark reluctantly looked at his watch. "We'd better get back."

He helped her stand. As he turned to leave, Asha touched his hand. "Mark?"

Mark turned back to face her. He did not move his hand, and she did not move hers. Their hands did not clasp together; they just barely touched. Asha felt hers tingling. She licked her lips.

"Yes?" Mark looked down into her upturned face and wondered what it was about her that captivated him so.

She removed her hand from his touch, and he noticed her twisting her fingers.

He took the hand back, this time holding it in his own, rubbing a thumb across her hand to calm her nerves. It did not seem to work. She bit her full bottom lip, looked down at his hand on hers, then back at his face. He waited for her to speak.

"I think that wanting to live off the compound is a desire the Lord has given you," she said. "But you're right that it would not be a good start to ministry to have your family and your missionary team unhappy with you."

Mark grimaced in agreement. That was true enough.

"So what if you continued praying about it, while working to finish the house?"

"But I don't want to live in that house. What would be the point of—"

With excitement, she interrupted, "No, you finish the house, all the while praying that God will change all the hearts that need to be changed so you can move out with their blessing. See, if you work on getting the house ready, then everyone, your family especially, will see that you are honoring them and their wishes. But the whole time you will be praying that God will provide for you not to need that house at all. And maybe by the time you're finished the Lord will have made a way for you to move out."

She grasped his hand with enthusiasm. "So that way no one would feel dishonored, you won't have to feel like you have to convince them anymore because you can leave it up to God, and to top it off, there will be a house all ready for whatever missionary comes next!"

Mark just stared down at her. He looked at her face. At her hand tight around his. She had certainly shaken up his world. All sunshine or storms, she was the most fascinating—and frustrating—person he had ever known.

He wanted her to stay. He wanted her to stay in India, with him, and knew with pain that she could not.

Asha's enthusiasm faltered. "I'm—I'm not telling you what to do, of course," she said.

"No." He shook his head. "No, that's—that's not—"

He could not quite find words for what he was feeling. This was nothing new, except that for the first time he really wanted to. He wanted to be able to tell her, to translate what his heart was saying.

His free hand reached up to cup her face. "It's like . . . like I am a prism and you are light, and when I am near you—there are colors everywhere."

His voice was soft and she gasped at his words.

Her eyes called to him, invited him to come closer.

He almost did. But Mark could not pretend the facts away. The fact that she was leaving in less than three weeks. The fact that, even if she did come back someday, it would not be for at least another year. And the newly realized fact that his heart was fragile, and he was suddenly afraid of what would happen to him if she took it away with her.

Clearing his throat, Mark dropped his hand, took a step back, and turned away. From her. From the unreasonable desire to fold her into his arms and ask her to stay.

Asha blinked away tears. What had just happened? She felt the unsaid rejection like a knife.

She followed Mark numbly, her eyes down, watching her feet. When he suddenly stopped and turned to face her again, she ran into him, hard. His hands reached out to steady her. Hers grasped his shirt to keep from falling.

This time he cupped her face with both hands and looked at her with an intensity that took her breath away.

"Asha," he breathed out, her name beautiful when he said it, "I thank God for sending you here. What you said about the house, and waiting for God to work is a great idea. I could not think of what to do, and you have helped me. Thank you."

She tried to follow his train of thought. His words did not match up with what his eyes and the muscles clenching in his arms were saying. "I wish—" he began, but cut himself off.

"What do you wish for, Mark?" she whispered. Her voice sounded gentle like a breeze, so unlike the storm in her heart. She knew what she wished for. Right at that moment, she could think of nothing she wished for more than him kissing—

The sudden sound of a traveling fruit seller's cart passing near the shelter of the banyan tree startled them both into jerking apart, turning toward the sound.

An awkward silence followed.

Finally Mark cleared his throat, then garnered up a teasing tone and a smile that did not quite reach his eyes. He gestured for her to follow him. "Well, let's get going then. You don't want to miss me pretending to be surprised at my surprise party, do you?"

Asha mentally appreciated his effort at lightening the mood, but her emotions wanted to press the rewind button and go back to just moments ago, when he was looking at her like she was rare and precious, someone he wanted in his life. She did not want to go back to being the visiting short-termer who would be leaving in a few weeks. She wanted to forget that fact. Forget all the facts except for the fact that she was falling in love with this man.

She tripped over an exposed, jutting root. At her small cry, Mark turned. "You okay?"

No, I'm not okay, she wanted to say. *I won't be okay until you tell me how you really feel about me.*

Instead, she pasted on a smile. "Sure." She passed him and headed resolutely toward the nearest rickshaw, turning back to say with false cheerfulness, "Hey, you should buy me a Coke on the way back, it being your birthday and all."

CHAPTER TWENTY-EIGHT

When Asha walked into the sari shop the following Tuesday, Rani was there waiting. She started speaking before Asha even sat down. "First, tell me how I am to pray to this God of yours. Do I prostrate myself? Should I burn incense to speak with Him?"

Not minding her directness, Asha answered, "No, you can just talk to Him. He is always here. You can talk to Him anytime."

Rani pondered the information, then nodded her head. "I want to hear more about this Jesus. But today there is no time. We must make a plan."

Asha sent a quick look around the shop, suddenly wary. "No time? Do you have to leave?"

"You must listen for I may need to leave quickly if anyone sees that you are here." Rani stood and motioned toward the ever-present shopkeeper. When the old man approached, carrying Asha's new sari blouse and motioning for her to try it on, Rani followed Asha into the back room where there was privacy. As Asha dressed, Rani spoke with urgency.

"Someone told the men in my building that I was talking about escape. Remember when I asked the others if they had ever tried?" Asha nodded and Rani continued. "The men have threatened me, and are very suspicious right now. I fear they may begin to have me followed. There may be someone watching this shop even now." Rani took one furtive look out, then closed the door to the back room, making it darker, but also more private.

The shopkeeper entered, muttering complaints about the lack of light, circling Asha and putting in a pin here and there to make the arms of her sari blouse tighter. Asha paid no attention. Her focus was completely on Rani's words.

"We must make a plan soon." Rani spoke in English so the shopkeeper would not understand.

Asha nodded. "It would be good for us to have another place to meet, if there is an emergency of some kind or if you find out the shop is being watched."

"Good idea. Do you know the market two blocks down from here, the one with the large booth with pig meat for sale?"

Nose wrinkled at the memory of the horrid smell, Asha nodded the affirmative. When looking for alternate routes, she had passed that particular market, and found the aroma of pork left out in the sun more than she could bear.

"I think that would be a good place," Rani said as Asha tried to remove the newly tightened sari blouse. "The men will not go there if they can help it, and behind the pig stall is a small road that is not lit at night. There are several alleyways, very dark, where we could meet if we had to."

Asha could not get the blouse off. She removed the pins, to the objections from the shopkeeper about the blouse needing to fit her arms better. Asha told the man in Bengali that she had to take the sari home that day, so there would not be time to alter it.

The man was unhappy, but when Asha handed him the full payment, his red-stained, toothless smile returned.

As her purchase was being bagged, another thought came to Asha's mind. "But if there is an emergency, how will you contact me?"

Clearly, Rani had not thought of that problem yet. They stood silently, until Asha brightened. "Wait, I know!"

Asha mentioned Milo's street. "Do you know where that is?" she asked Rani.

"No," Rani said. "But I could find it if I needed to. Why?"

"There is a little boy there. His name is Milo and he has only one foot. He uses a crutch. He begs at the big intersection there, usually in front of the ice cream shop."

Just thinking of Milo made Asha smile. She would have to go visit him soon. "If you are in trouble, send word to Milo. He will come find me."

Relieved to have some sort of backup plan, Asha sat back down inside the main shop area and invited Rani to join her. Since no one else had arrived, and it seemed no one was watching the shop, Asha spent the rest of their time telling stories from the Bible.

Rani drank them in with joy, like a traveler in the desert would a cool drink of water. She especially loved the stories about Jesus. How He showed compassion on the sick and the needy. How He preached deliverance for the captives. And how He looked in love at a condemned woman and told her accusers to only cast a stone if they themselves had never sinned.

Reluctantly, Asha picked up her sari purchase, thanked the salesman, and turned to leave the shop. The time had gone all too quickly once again. "I look forward to telling you more about Jesus on Thursday," she said to Rani.

Rani smiled. As it had the week before, the smile took Asha by surprise. She hoped with all her heart that soon Rani's smiles would not be the rare gems they were now.

Riding home that day, Asha's prayers were for Rani's safety, and for some kind of miracle plan that would enable her to escape.

"I have less than three weeks left, Lord," she murmured with fervency. "Something has to happen soon. Please let something important happen on Thursday."

Thursday came. Asha and Rani met.

And something important did happen, but not what she had expected.

By Thursday evening, Asha was floating on air. Even if she had to leave tomorrow, even if she had never met Mark, her trip would have been worth it.

Rani had accepted Christ. Asha felt like she could fly. Now her sister in Christ, Rani was full of questions. She wanted to know everything. She asked if she would be able to have her very own Bible once she escaped.

Asha had offered her one that day but Rani refused, saying she had no place safe to hide it. The book would not only cause suspicion if found, but would likely be destroyed. Rani could not bear to take that risk.

So instead, Asha determined to spend all her free time that weekend writing verses—she was thankful Rani knew English since she still could not write in Bengali—onto tiny sheets of paper that Rani would be able to hide. She would find verses to comfort Rani when she was afraid, verses to give her courage as she waited to escape, verses to remind her God was always with her.

Asha wanted Rani to know that God's love for her was boundless, a greater and more beautiful love than she had ever known. A pure love.

Tears of joy slipped unnoticed down Asha's cheeks as she wrote. She had to keep stopping to get on her knees beside her bed and thank God for saving her friend. She asked for wisdom on how and what to teach her in the short time they had left.

When a still, small voice reminded Asha that, however wonderful Rani's new faith was, all of Asha's actions were being done without approval, Asha tried to ignore it. She returned to her desk to continue writing, but the voice would not be ignored. One word would not be shut out. Her soul kept whispering it.

Deceit. She was living in deceit.

Asha cringed at the ugly word. Surely God understood. Surely He did not mind; after all, Rani was a believer now, and how would she have heard about Jesus had Asha never returned to find her?

Once Rani escapes, I'll tell Mark everything, she prayed silently. *I'll make it right before I leave India. I promise.* Ignoring the continued discomfort, she asked God's blessings on her plans for helping Rani escape. Time was running short. She and Rani had made a tentative plan. The next time they met, they were to finalize it, make sure of all the details, and decide on the exact date.

Asha could barely contain herself as the weekend passed. She tried to stay as busy as possible to keep her impatience at bay, as well as the tugging at her conscience.

Finally, Tuesday morning arrived and Asha arose full of restless energy. Forgoing a rickshaw ride, she decided to walk. It was far, but not too far, and she was too excited to just sit all the way to the market.

She did not even think to pay attention to her route, or her surroundings. All was familiar. She had come to this same market to meet Rani twice a week for several weeks now.

It did not occur to her to be careful. Not until she stopped to admire a stand of fresh bananas and saw a shadow nearby making a hasty retreat, as if someone did not want to be seen.

Asha looked around, suddenly alert. Biting her lip, she left the fruit stand and continued down the road, more slowly this time, taking care to look toward the side and check with her peripheral vision to see if the shadow came back.

It did. It sped up when she sped up, and slowed down when she slowed. She turned around and the shadow fled.

Someone was definitely following her.

A line of sweat started down her back.

Whoever it was, he was not making much pretense about it.

Then again, perhaps the follower knew she was the vulnerable one. He had no need for stealth.

But why? If someone wanted to mug her, there would be no need to stay out of sight. The person could have just snatched her purse while she stood unaware at the fruit stand and run off with it.

The only reason she could think of why someone would want to follow her from a safe distance was Rani. Someone knew Rani was sneaking out to meet with her.

Adrenaline pumped through Asha's body, but she did not know what to do with it. She thought of running straight back to the compound, but Rani might wait for her too long, putting herself in danger.

But what of the danger of Asha showing up with a stalker on her trail?

Asha skirted around a corner and almost tripped over a goat. She rushed down an alley to the left and then snuck into a dark spot between two market stalls.

Had she lost him?

She sank down, curled her knees up to her chest, wrapped her arms around them, and buried her head. Her thoughts drifted to Mark. Regret burned along her skin. Resolutely, she determined that if she made it through this day, this meeting, she would return back to the compound and tell Mark everything.

"God, help me," she whispered, and stepped hesitantly back into the sunshine. Now familiar with the area, she took a different path than usual, one that would bring her to the sari shop from a different direction. She hurried, knowing Rani would be waiting.

When Rani came into view, standing across the entryway to the sari shop near a booth selling spices, Asha's relief was tangible. Unfortunately, it was also only temporary. Within seconds, she realized that the shadow was back. She was still being followed.

And she had led the person right to their meeting place. Right to Rani.

Swallowing a sob, Asha looked to her left and right.

Just as she decided to run into a maze of shanties, drawing the predator away from her friend, Rani saw her. Her welcoming smile fell at the look on Asha's face. Very quickly, Rani's features turned fearful, almost childlike in their terror.

What would happen to her friend now? To herself?

Asha had never known such pain.

The only thing she could think of was to whirl upon her follower, surprising him by confronting him outright. Maybe if

Rani saw whoever it was, she would realize she was in danger and run before the attacker could reach her.

For a split second, Asha wondered what the person might do to her personally, but she pushed the thought away. It was her fault that Rani was in danger now. She would take the consequences.

Asha turned. She rushed toward the shadow that had suddenly shrunk down behind a long men's shirt hanging on display. Nearing the vendor, allowing anger to overcome fear, Asha flung the shirt aside and gasped.

Her surprise was so violent, she fell to the ground.

"Milo!"

The boy huddled back against a table decorated with necklaces, bracelets and rings. For a moment he looked more than contrite. He looked genuinely fearful.

Asha's eyes were wild. Her body flooded with relief, anger, confusion, then more anger.

"Milo!" she snapped. "Do you have any idea how much you scared me? You—you—why are you following me?"

The boy regained some courage, and stood up. "*Didi*, you should no be here. This is lie. This is not the market you say you go to. This one near bad place. Even I know not to go near to this bad place."

Asha glanced around, hoping no one within hearing distance could understand Milo's English. "Milo, please!" she shushed him.

He stood to his feet, shaking his head solemnly. "Asha *Didi*, this no good. This not like me sneaking out to get the good food. This bad sneaking out. I come to the orphan house today to see you. But you are leaving. I follow you because you look so happy, like you are going to meet a man you are feeling love for. But now I find you here, in bad place."

He did not stay to hear an explanation. He turned, but then turned back, speaking to her as if she were a wayward child. "You tell Mr. Mark where you go. You tell him today. Right now."

Asha thought of her inner promise to do just that, made when she feared the worse. The idea suddenly felt much less palatable than keeping her secret just a little longer. She rubbed her arms. "Milo, I can't. Not yet. He doesn't underst—"

The boy interrupted her. "I am coming to him later today. If you no tell him, I tell him."

Asha swallowed with difficulty. The truth would be even harder to swallow. Milo was right. This had gone too far.

"Okay, I will tell him." She tasted her defeat. It was bitter.

Milo nodded his head once, then disappeared back into the shadows.

Now the dread of being chased and captured morphed into the dread of having to admit everything to Mark. Originally she had not wanted to tell him because he was being unreasonable and too cautious. Then she did not want to tell him because he would keep her from meeting Rani anymore.

The past few weeks however, she had not told him because she had not wanted to shatter the bond between them, the beautiful friendship that was weaving into something more.

Now everything would be destroyed.

When Rani approached from behind, her footsteps soft and tentative, Asha turned to assure her there was nothing to fear. She'd been followed, but it was only her young street friend.

Asha felt Rani's confusion when she told her they would have to cancel their meeting, have to wait to work on the rescue plan until next time. "I'm very sorry, Rani, but I have to get back to the compound. There's someone—there's something I have to do. I'm sorry."

Before she left, Asha told Rani not to worry, that everything was okay.

Only it was not okay. And they both knew it.

CHAPTER TWENTY-NINE

She had to tell him. She promised Milo she would.

It had seemed a good idea earlier when she was being followed, when she'd been scared senseless and was wishing fervently for a deliverer, even an angry one.

But here, on the porch of his grandparents' house, hearing him talking on the phone inside, the idea bordered on the insane.

Asha twisted the thumb and forefinger of her right hand around the pinky finger of her left. Looking down, she wondered how many years it had been since she had allowed herself that nervous habit. She had willed herself out of it before heading off to college, determined to look and act competent even if she did not feel it.

Well here she was, and no amount of acting or looking competent was going to overcome the feeling of dread that wafted around her like bad perfume. At this point, she might as well look as apprehensive as she felt.

Maybe he was a softy for a helpless female and it would help.

When the screen door swung open and a whistling, happy Mark nearly ran over her, she had been thinking that he would not believe her helpless front even if it was sincere. Like the boy crying wolf one too many times, she had cried independent too many times to convince anyone at this point that she needed help.

But when he practically tripped over himself apologizing for not seeing her, she almost allowed herself to burst into tears and beg for some kind of reassurance that he would not hate her once she told him the truth.

Her face must have shown her inner agony, for he began to look truly concerned. Taking her hand, he led her inside into the main room created with warmth and openness for entertaining guests. He sat her down, then sat next to her, looking down at her with all the feeling she could have hoped for, but only because he was afraid he'd stepped on her.

"Are you all right?" Mark looked her over for bumps or bruises. "Did I step on your foot?"

Asha nodded her head no as she absently looked around the room.

Mark noticed the twisting fingers. "Did I hit your hand with the screen door?"

"No." Asha's voice was half a moan. She looked down at her hands. "It's a nervous habit. I used to do it as a kid all the time. Drove my mother crazy."

She offered him the hint of a smile. "Growing up a Bengali in a small, all-American town in North Carolina, there was plenty of reason to feel out of place."

"Different is not so bad," he said.

"Not if you're accepted."

Mark wondered how many kids had alienated Asha before she got her nervous habit, but he wondered more why it had come back just now. What had happened?

"I guess I should say I know how you feel." He could see his comment took her by surprise. "I grew up in India, you know. The only white kid for miles. At the time, the only other missionaries either had no kids yet, or their kids were grown. I was it."

Asha tilted her head to one side. "I never really thought of that. We both stood out in our opposite worlds, didn't we?"

Mark continued. "It didn't bother me much when I was a kid, except that I didn't like all the extra attention I got whenever we went out of the compound. But as I got older, no matter what I did or didn't do, I never really fit. I ended up staying inside and studying a lot. Partly because I was a rather brainy kid, but partly to avoid making everybody else uncomfortable, trying to figure out how to treat me."

Asha was leaning toward him now with avid interest. He had hit upon something that mattered to her. Not quite certain what it was, he continued talking, hoping whatever he was saying would help.

"When I went back to America for college, for the first time, I looked like everybody else. But I found that I felt more out of place there than I ever had before. There wasn't anyone to talk to about the things I remembered and missed, or the people I cared most about."

Mark willed a smile. No sense thinking about things that could not be changed. "So I went back to studying. One benefit to not being very popular was having the time to get really good grades."

The joke fell flat as Asha searched his eyes again. She was looking for something, but Mark had no idea what it was. He tried to decide if he should encourage her to talk about whatever was on her mind, or if he should try to get her mind off whatever it was.

Mark sighed. Trying to guess what was going on in a woman's mind was downright impossible. He gave up trying to think of something else to say and simply said the thought already on his mind. "I bet everybody back home thought you looked exotic and beautiful." Mark put some humor in his tone so she would not notice too much that he used the word beautiful. Not that he wasn't thinking it.

"Exotic, yes," was Asha's response. "A good word in fashion, but not exactly on the list of cool things to be in Weaverville, North Carolina."

Her voice had gotten so soft, he had to lean in to hear her. Doing so, he caught the scent of her hair, something fresh and clean and fruity. He loved it. Made him want to pick up a big handful of her hair and bury his face in it. Except since her hair was only shoulder-length, to do so he would have to lean into the back of her neck, and . . .

Forcing himself back to the moment at hand, Mark heard her whisper, "I have never told anyone but you how I always wondered why my family gave me away. Why they didn't want me." A breath. A sigh. "I guess it has followed me around my whole life, but I was too afraid to talk about it. I always wondered who I was and if there was anywhere in the world where I really belonged."

Mark's heart constricted. How could this woman come across so confident when she felt so insecure?

He tilted her chin up until her eyes met his. Big, deep brown eyes filled with sadness. "Asha, do you think the orphan kids here at the mission are less important because they are orphans? Do you think of Milo as a lesser person because he was born without a foot? Or little Shafique? She has family, but they didn't want her because she was a girl. Is she less of a person, less precious in God's sight?"

Anger flashed in Asha's eyes. "You know I don't think that about any of them."

"Then why think of yourself that way?" he quietly replied.

Asha's face stilled and some kind of awareness filled her eyes. A tear escaped. Another followed.

Mark wiped away the first, then the second. Asha was looking at him as if she were trying to look into his soul. Mark was not sure he was ready for her to see what was there.

But still he heard himself saying, "Asha, don't you know how beautiful you are?"

Her eyes widened. His wandered over her face. What was this hold she had over him?

The screen door slammed. Milo stormed in, banging his crutch as he hurried into the room, not bothering with even a hint of the usual formalities.

Mark was about to reprimand him for not knocking or asking permission to enter when Milo steadied a look on Asha and asked, "Did you tell him?"

Mark looked from one to the other. "Tell me what?"

It was then that Asha turned those entrancing eyes away from him. She looked at the floor, as if she were ashamed.

"Asha?" Mark's question was hesitant. He thought of the fact that she had been standing outside the door earlier. He had assumed she was coming to visit his grandmother, but she was always gone this day of the week. Asha knew that.

She had come to see him, Mark realized with a jolt.

The momentary pleasure that came with the realization faded as Mark looked from Milo's stern face to Asha, who had stood from the couch and walked to the open window, her back now to them both.

What had she planned to tell him? Was it something bad? Was that why she had been so nervous, so preoccupied?

Finally, Asha turned around. Her eyes were pained. He wanted to say it didn't matter. Whatever it was, he didn't care. He wanted to say anything to get that look out of her eyes.

"I came to-to tell you-" Asha stumbled over her words. "To-to tell you-about-"

"Oh, no. You are too late, *Didi*." Milo was speaking now, in a tone sounding as if he were the adult and she the child. "You wait too long. Milo tell the story now."

Confused enough to feel frustrated, Mark willed himself to remain quiet and wait for someone, anyone, to give him whatever information he needed to clear up the emotional shrapnel suddenly flung all over the room and all the people in it.

What was going on?

CHAPTER THIRTY

$\mathcal{F}$ive minutes later, Mark had the answer to his question.

He had found out what was going on.

And he was angry. At Asha. At Milo. Mostly at himself.

The screen door slammed again, only this time it was not Milo who flung it so carelessly. Mark marched from the house, muscles taunt with frustration.

How could he have been so duped? He had let those big, innocent-looking eyes suck him in, all the while she was sneaking out over and over again, deliberately disobeying the rules and putting them all at risk.

Did she not understand that she was jeopardizing everything?

No, Mark remembered, she did not understand. She did not know.

But while that may excuse her desire to continue meeting with the trafficked girl, it still was no excuse for deception and outright refusal to obey even the simplest of rules.

Mark wanted to kick something. The girl was worse than Milo!

He would have to tell the team. They deserved to know about this new risk that Asha had presented by her impulsive, emotional behavior.

He had wanted to protect her. A part of him wanted still to refrain from telling the others. To keep her secret and figure out some way to fix this problem on his own.

But that would be neither right nor honorable. Resolutely, Mark walked to each house on the compound, informing families that there would be an emergency missionary meeting that evening right after supper. He felt certain the meeting would be less than pleasant.

He was right.

Asha paced outside on the porch, her hands wringing as she waited to be called in. She heard voices inside volleying back and forth. Mark's voice, too low for his words to be understood, Eleanor Stephens', then Renea Miller's, her words clear, her voice high-pitched with worry. "She has put the entire mission at risk!"

Several voices responded at once. Asha tried to hear, but no one spoke as loudly as Mrs. Miller had. Why was everyone so worried? Did Mrs. Miller think the men from the red-light district would come and harm them there on the compound? Asha could not fathom why there was such a haze of fear surrounding the entire subject.

When Mark opened the door and summoned her, Asha followed him inside with dread, stopping just inside the doorway as every eye turned to her.

They all looked as if she had committed some terrible crime. "I'm sorry for causing so much trouble," she offered cautiously.

Silence. Stares. Asha bit her lip.

She felt like a child in the principal's office. Hating the silence, Asha broke it by defending herself. "I know I shouldn't have gone behind your backs like that, but you're all acting as if I did something truly terrible. I was trying to help someone! Don't you care about the women who are trapped in that horrible place? Don't you care that—that—" She stopped when Mark turned around to face her, his patience obviously run out.

"Accuse us all you want of not caring, but emotion alone is not going to rescue those women," he retaliated. "If you don't know the culture and if you don't understand the system, sometimes what your emotions lead you to do will hurt more than help."

Dusk was falling outside. Like every evening since Asha had arrived, it was heralded by the sound of a thousand crows leaving the city for the night. She wished she could fly away with them.

"So better to do nothing then?"

Mark turned away, then back to face her again. He opened his mouth to speak when his grandfather's steady voice filled the room with its calm.

"My dear, may I ask you a question?" Lloyd Stephens looked kindly at Asha.

His unaffected demeanor did much to settle Asha's feelings. She looked over at him and nodded meekly.

"Have you witnessed to all the people in your neighborhood in America?" he asked, his voice slow and aged.

The question seemed so out of context, Asha stood for a moment without responding. "No, sir," she finally said.

"Have you held Bible clubs for the children in the inner cities near you?"

Again, her answer was no.

"Have you ever been involved in reaching the homeless in your state? Or worked in a pro-life clinic, or for that matter, helped rescue the women being trafficked in America?"

Once more, Asha had to answer no, by now twisting her fingers again.

Mr. Stephens' smile was gentle. "My dear, it is easy to see, in another place, all that should be done. If one of us came to your hometown, we would notice ministry opportunities that were not being done by you. Should we judge you for not doing all those things?"

Asha's shoulders lowered. She felt the tension of her anger flow down her body and away. In its place came conviction, and shame.

Lloyd Stephens saw the change. His voice was loving. "Then perhaps you should not judge us?"

Asha nodded mutely. She had judged them, all of them. "I'm sorry," she choked out.

"Each of us must do what God has given us to do. Nothing more. Nothing less."

This ignited a spark again within Asha. "Then why can't I be allowed to do what I feel God wants me to do?"

Mr. Stephens started to answer, but Mark spoke up first. "You don't have all the facts, or all the knowledge you need to do something like that. You don't even know the area well, and your language isn't fluent yet. And most of all—"

"But I care." Asha felt her temper rising again at Mark's words. "At least that's something!"

"What good is caring going to do when you and some woman are running for your lives, with men on your trail, and you have no idea where to go?" Mark's voice was taut with restrained feeling. "Think about it Asha, if it was easy for Milo to follow you, how easy do you think it would be for men who do this sort of thing for a living? How is caring going to help you actually rescue anybody?"

Asha brought her chin up. She had no answer for his question. But she had an answer for his attitude. "You have lived here so long, you've lost your vision. You have no passion!"

"And you are all passion, without any regard for common sense!"

They stared at each other, breathing hard.

Eleanor Stephens spoke into the heavy silence. "Mark. Asha. The problem at hand is not your rather strong feelings for one another..."

Mark felt his eyes, still locked with Asha's, widen. Her face paled. For several seconds, all was silent. He attempted to settle his breathing, and had nearly succeeded when his father burst out laughing.

"You two have enough chemistry between you to open a pharmacy!" He roared with laughter, completely forgetting the problem at hand.

Seemed everyone else forgot it as well, or so Mark thought as all eyes swiveled to him, then Asha, then back to him. A few people snickered. Most of them tried to pretend they hadn't heard, though John Stephens' laughter was still ringing throughout the room.

For Asha, it was clearly too much. Her composure unraveled. Mark felt genuine regret when she turned and ran from the room.

He turned to his father. "Dad—" But what was there to say?

Mr. Stephens looked genuinely contrite. "I didn't mean to hurt the little lady's feelings, Son. You can tell her that for me. But I do think you two might as well stop all this squabbling and get around to being friends, so you can get around to being more than friends before she up and leaves the country in a couple of weeks."

Mark cringed. Did his father not remember that the entire missionary team was still present?

Mr. Stephens dismissed him with a wave. "Get on with you. Let her know what we decided. She gets the same condition Milo did; she can stay if she stays within the rules. Absolutely no visits to the red-light district again. You know what is at stake here."

Mark cleared his throat. "Don't you think somebody else should go and talk to her at this point?"

"Scared?" Mr. Stephens chuckled, until he saw the look his mother was giving, which immediately silenced his mirth.

Though thus subdued, he still was not wavering on his choice of ambassador. "No, Son. You're in charge of short-termers. It's your job, no matter how you feel about the particular short-termer in question."

Mark nodded, dreading facing Asha after the meeting, confrontation, and especially his father's comment. To top it off, now he had to tell her to behave or she would have to leave.

Groaning inwardly, he then looked around the room and realized that just about anything would be better than staying here in the fog of awkward emotions emanating from the people all around him.

He left the room, taking in several deep breaths of fresh air before heading outside and looking around the compound.

She was gone. Mark stood outside the door of the Main Building, knocking, though he knew it was futile. All the interior lights were out, and Asha always left at least one small light on when she was inside—to keep the bugs around the light and off her legs while she slept, she had said.

Mark's heart thundered. Surely she had not gone back to meet Rani. Mark's head told him that was ridiculous, impossible. Even Asha would not go that far.

But a nagging worry from the direction of his heart kept arguing with his mind. Would she try to punish him by leaving the compound, knowing he would feel responsible?

Mark felt like the emotional minefield he was in had just doubled in size. But still he had to walk through it, though he was sure he was not going to make it without something blowing up in his face.

He walked toward the water-tower ladder. Had she ever used that to sneak out and meet the girl? He wished he could just chop the thing down, and maybe duct tape Asha to the base pole until she submitted to reason.

When a muffled sniffle came from the playground area, Mark felt some of the tension release from his neck and shoulders.

He tipped his head back, working the muscles of his shoulders to loosen them. Taking a few more deep breaths, preparing for battle, he turned and walked toward the playground, and the encounter he wished he could avoid.

She was sitting on the swing, gliding slowly back and forth, looking down at her feet and randomly wiping her *orna* across her nose with a sniff.

The moment Mark came into view, Asha bolted from the swing and backed away. "Please," she whispered. "Please, I can't talk to you tonight. I'm—I'm sorry. I'm sure you're here to tell me how disappointed you are in me, and how angry. And likely the rest of them have sent you to tell me—well, I don't know what, but probably something bad. And I just can't . . . ."

Mark watched her take in a shaky breath. He waited, and finally she said, "Please, can it wait until the morning? I'm sorry, but—please? I just—I just don't think I can take any more tonight."

Mark wrestled with himself. Could it wait until morning? Was she really that upset?

He would rather just get it over with. But she looked so miserable, Mark's heart tightened. "Okay," he heard himself say. "But promise you'll meet me first thing in the morning?"

She nodded, still backing up. "Thank you," she said quickly. "Thank you, Mark." Then she turned and ran to her room.

Mark waited until she was inside. He waited until the door shut behind her. A maddening tension taunted him. He punched one of the wooden stakes that held up the swingset.

Why couldn't she just follow the rules? Why couldn't she just trust him?

He waited, but no light came on behind the curtains of Asha's window. Mark expected her night would be far from restful.

He knew with certainty he would not be getting much sleep.

CHAPTER THIRTY-ONE

"Asha *Didi*! Asha *Didi*!"

Before Asha had even shut her bedroom door, Milo's voice put her on full alert. She closed the door, then reached for the light.

"No, no light!" His voice stopped her hand in midair. She crossed the room to look out the window, seeing nothing but darkness.

"Milo?" she whispered. "What is it? Why are you here?" She almost asked him if he had run off again, but then remembered that he had moved out of the orphanage last week and was now living back on his street. What could have brought him back, and at this hour?

Milo stood from where he had crouched below the window. Asha could see the outline of his face. He did not mince words.

"*Didi*, big problem. I go back to my street after I talk to Mr. Mark, and I see your friend, the lady from the bad place. She came to find me. I show her place to hide."

"A place to hide?" Asha's heart began pounding, beating a cadence of confusion and fear. "Milo, I don't understand. What has happened?"

"She tells me come find you. Give you message. The men, they get suspicious of her. They say they will sell her and send her across border. She runs away and finds me." There he stopped and Asha could see him almost smile through the darkness. "That good idea, *Didi*. Tell her to come find Milo. Milo help good."

She motioned urgently for him to continue.

"She say she escape tonight, or she lost for good. She say tell *Didi* to come to emergency meeting place. A place with pigs, she say." His mouth curved downward in concern. "This is not in the bad place, yes? You will not go to the bad place again. You will go and help her where the pigs are, yes?"

By now Asha was pacing. Her heart pounded; her mind raced. What could she do? Every missionary on the compound was already upset at her for sneaking out before. How could she do it again?

But how she could do anything else? She could not ignore Rani now, when she needed her most.

Should she tell Mark? Asha desperately wanted to find him, tell him what had just happened, and beg for his help. But she feared that, though he would care, he would still prevent her from going.

No, this one last time, she had to go on her own. She could only imagine the meeting the missionaries would have about her after this. But what else could she do? She could not abandon Rani. Not now.

For a moment, she considered having Milo keep Rani on his street and Asha could meet her there. But the idea of bringing Milo into the danger was unthinkable.

"Milo," she said with sudden resolution. "Please go back and tell my friend that I will meet her behind the pigs, like we planned. I will come as fast as I can."

She could see Milo nodding. Once she reassured him the pig stall was not inside the red-light district, he said, "I go fast, *Didi*!" Then he was gone.

Asha started to change clothes, her fingers fumbling and shaking. It took several minutes to dress, as she kept dropping things and having to feel around the floor blindly to find them. Finally, she was ready.

Swallowing convulsively, she turned the front door knob and slipped out into the night. Knowing she could not exit through the gate without someone seeing her, Asha resigned herself to the humiliating task of somehow climbing over the wall that surrounded the compound.

Looking around, Asha recalled how Mark's father once mentioned that Milo most often escaped by climbing the ladder to the water tower and sneaking over the wall from there.

She neared the water tower and studied the option. As it was only ten or fifteen feet off the ground, the method would not be as daunting a task as she had at first anticipated.

Trying to hold six yards of sari material to keep from getting it caught as she climbed, however, turned out to be a fair bit more daunting than she expected.

Asha wished grimly that she could have worn something more practical, but Amy's sari was the only black outfit she had. As it was vitally important she be able to disappear in the darkness behind the pig stall, there really was no other choice.

What would she do once she met up with Rani? Asha tried to concentrate equally on climbing the ladder without her sari getting caught, as well as trying to develop an immediate plan for Rani's escape. If the men were already searching for her, Rani had nowhere in the area to hide. The men would have connections at all the area hotels and likely the stores, too.

Mark had been right. Caring was not enough to rescue anyone.

Mark. Of course. Asha would bring Rani back to the compound. She would tell Mark everything, and once he saw Rani, of course he would help. The missionaries would be angry for awhile at her sneaking out again, but once they heard the situation, surely they would all understand.

Yes, that was what she would do. Mark would be able to help. She was sure of it.

Asha slipped over the wall, careful to avoid the shards of glass embedded across the top ledge. She fell ten feet to land in a heap on the ground outside the compound.

Once she had regained some measure of equilibrium, Asha crossed the road and hired a bicycle rickshaw, pulling the canopy up to shroud her as much as possible as she traveled.

As the market came into view, Asha covered her face with the hanging shawl of her sari, leaving only her eyes to see and be seen. To the right, the left, her eyes flicked back and forth.

Few people walked along the street. Two men argued heatedly in front of a market stall. Across the street Asha saw a man prostrating himself before a shrine adorned with goddesses, flowers and plates of food.

"Ignore the goddess and give the food to the women living near you in poverty and pain," Asha whispered as she climbed down from the rickshaw.

Unable to walk the narrow bridge toward the pig stall without looking into the sewage-filled waters below, Asha felt her face grimace at the sight, and even more so at the smell.

Stepping gingerly across the bridge, Asha kept her sari held against her face. How did people live in such squalor?

She turned a quick left after the bridge and let out a deep breath. She had made it. She was safely behind the disgusting, filthy pig stall. Now all she had to do was choose one of the dark alley spaces and wait for Rani there.

Suddenly all thoughts of smell and squalor left Asha's mind. An arm reached around her waist, and a hand curled into her vision to cover her mouth.

She felt her body being pulled back. Whoever had grabbed her was strong. Asha struggled, wanting desperately to cry out, but the arms pulled her back several more steps until she felt the darkness wrapping tightly around her, smothering her.

Once inside the small space, only wide enough for her own body and the man who held her, Asha felt terror envelop her as fully as the darkness.

She hesitated and forced her body to relax for a moment, pretending to give up until she felt the arms around her loosen their hold. Like a cat then, she wrestled and scratched and clawed. If she could only get her face free to scream!

"Asha. It's me, Mark. Be still, woman!"

215

He called her name several times before it registered in her consciousness. She was writhing and thrashing until his voice filtered through the fear and washed over her. She felt it, felt it cover her, flow over her, wash away her terror as the monsoon washes away the filth alongside the road.

A weakness flowed down her, starting with her head, down to her toes. She could no longer stand.

Mark's right hand, the hand that had covered her mouth to contain her scream, left her face and wrapped around her waist along with his left to hold her up as she fell. He pulled her back against him, whispering her name.

For what seemed like hours, she knew no thoughts but the inexpressible relief of finding herself saved instead of doomed, held in the arms of good instead of the evil she had feared.

Then past that, a new feeling crept across her. A realization that she was being more than just held up. She was being held. By Mark. By his arms.

His voice behind her ear made her shiver. It took full minutes before she understood any words, anything more than his voice.

Finally, more than emotions permeated her consciousness. She became aware of details, her head resting back against the curve of his neck, his head leaning forward until his cheek was a whisper away from her. Her back was against him, his arms were around her waist. She was breathing hard from fear and her struggle.

And her heart was racing. Racing more in the awareness of finding herself in Mark's arms than it had even when she feared the worst.

"Are you all right?"

She heard it again. He had said it several times already. She let out in one breath a small sound, an attempt at a yes, nodding when her voice failed her.

The moment he let her go, reality hit her full force. No longer a warm monsoon shower, the full awareness—Mark was here, Mark had followed her—was a heavy, storming rain that pelted and pricked her.

She whipped around to face him. Her turn swung her away and into the light.

A flash of feeling on his face was all she saw before he reached out and pulled her back into the sheltering small alcove of darkness.

For a moment she was held tight against him, their faces inches away, their breath mingling.

Asha looked up into his face. A small, thin ray of light from the street, very faint, allowed her to see Mark's eyes as they flashed confusion, then a sudden intensity that took away what little breath she had left.

For one heady moment his eyes dropped to her lips. His face inched forward toward hers.

Asha forgot about Rani. She forgot why she had snuck off the compound, why she had come to be in a dark alley, even where she was. Long gone was her disgust with the smell. Nothing existed but this moment in this alley. There was no world outside the few feet they shared.

Then the light flickered, Mark blinked, and the moment was gone. To replace it came anger. Asha could see it in his gaze. She felt it as his arms released her and his hands grasped her shoulders and gave her a small shake.

"What on earth were you thinking?" he whispered fiercely. "Do you have any idea what would happen to you if they caught you?"

His jaw was clenched, his teeth grinding. Hands tightened on her arms. "Are you listening to me, Asha? Do you have any idea what you're getting yourself into?"

Asha opened her mouth to speak, to explain. She wanted him to see into her heart and understand. But her flesh responded before her spirit, and she found herself spitting out, "I won't endanger the precious reputation of your mission, if that's what you're so worried about. I'll make sure—"

"Can you be so utterly foolish?" Mark interrupted her. If it was possible to yell while whispering, he was doing it. "I'm not here to rescue the mission's testimony. I'm not worried about you endangering my work. I'm here because I care about *you*, you ridiculous—frustrating—"

Mark stopped speaking. He was biting his lips closed.

His hands framed her face. "Asha," he whispered, "you have no idea the evil you are walking into. If they caught you—"

Asha felt herself bristle in defense. "I knew there were risks before I came," she whispered hotly. "I'm not afraid of—"

"Of what?" Mark's concerned tenderness was gone. "Let's stop playing the nice word game and talk about reality. This isn't about being imprisoned for your faith, or even martyred. Nothing so noble."

Asha's ready retort died as his words sunk in. "What do you mean?"

Her genuine confusion only intensified his frustration. "Are you really so naïve? Do you see yourself as somehow protected because you're American, or because you're a Christian, or—"

Asha's anger was rising to match his. "What are you talking about? I'm trying to do something good here, and all you can think about is staying safe? Avoiding risk?"

"Rape, Asha."

Her eyes flashed up to meet his.

"Let's talk in real terms. Skip the 'spiritual' words and walk with me into the sewers of India. If they catch you trying to steal what they consider their property, they're not going to swat your hand and send you on your way. They're going to hurt you. Badly. They will take you and treat you the same way they treat them. You will become a product, and after man after man abuses you, you will start to see yourself as only a product."

Mark let out a frustrated breath. "And Asha, they would make sure you could never get free."

Asha had visualized what Rani's life must be like a hundred times. But she had never really placed herself there. Mark's words put her in Rani's building, tied her to Rani's bed. When she imagined men walking into her room, Asha closed her eyes and shook her head, trying to shake free of even the thought.

Why had she never considered what would actually happen to her, personally, if she were caught and trafficked? A verse from Proverbs came to mind with bold-letter clarity: *He who trusts in his own heart is a fool.*

She was a fool. There was no other word for it.

"Mark, I'm—"

"Asha?"

The questioning whisper from around the corner stopped them both cold.

It was Rani's voice.

Asha gasped and looked up into Mark's face. His eyes were trying to speak to her. She could tell he desperately wanted her to keep quiet, to stay still.

Why?

Her eyes asked questions. So many questions. What did he know that he wasn't telling her? What was going on? Why did he seem to know everything about her plan despite her secrecy?

"Asha?"

The call came again, faint and hesitant.

Mark's arms wrapped around her and tightened protectively. His head nodded very slightly, but she saw it. No, he was saying. Don't go. Don't call back to her.

Was he that heartless? For the smallest moment, a suspicion raised its head. How did he know so much about the women of the night and the way the red-light system worked?

Asha's eyes shut tight. No, no, she knew Mark was good. His integrity was unquestioned by any who truly knew him.

When her eyes opened again, they held tears.

Did she truly know him? Did she know him at all? Would they ever be able to trust each other?

When they heard Rani's voice the third time, everything in Asha compelled her to run out into the street and fight for her. Rani was struggling, she could hear it. And now she could also hear the voices of angry men.

Mark held her tight against him. She knew it was to keep her from running to Rani's side, but his hold felt almost as if he was comforting her in her pain. She could do nothing, and she knew that somehow he had known that before she did. His arms were tight bands keeping her safe while her friend was pulled away into danger.

The voices faded, then died away.

Mark's forehead was against hers as the silence once again reigned.

He held her as she cried. She had enough sense to cry quietly, muffling the sound by burying her face into his shirt.

When she knew it was safe to speak, Asha whispered brokenly, "Why, Mark? Why did you keep me from helping her?"

She looked up at him with wounded eyes. "Why didn't *you* help her?"

Mark drew in a deep breath. She felt the frustration leave him.

He did feel compassion. It was clear on his face. Then why? Why did he let them take her back to the very gates of hell?

His breath was ragged. "Asha, there's so much you don't know. Please, trust me this night. Tomorrow I will answer all your questions."

Resigned to her failure, the terrible, rending pain of losing her friend to the evil of another night of slavery, Asha could only rest her head against his chest and nod. Yes, she would trust him. He deserved that.

The journey back to the compound was made in silence. Mark guided her through narrow passageways, seemingly hidden trails among the shacks and shanties. For a moment Asha wondered how he knew this disreputable area so well, but then fatigue held sway, and Asha concentrated only on keeping her footing and keeping up with her rescuer.

Cheerful house lights, in a familiar U shape, finally appeared to welcome them back to the security of the compound. Asha let out a small, broken sob of relief, and thanked God for bringing them safely home.

Home. Why had she thought of that word?

Mark walked with her up the steps to her building, then unlocked her door and held it open for her. For a moment, he looked down at her, opened his mouth to speak, but then shut it again.

"Mark," Asha started, "I—"

His hand soft upon her face stopped her. Again he opened his mouth, then closed it again.

"Goodnight, Asha," he said, then turned and walked into the night. She watched him cross the compound until his own door shut behind him.

What had he risked to find her that night? What did he know that she had yet to understand?

And the question that would not let go, even as the terrible weariness pushed all others from thought, would the answers of tomorrow tear down the wall between them, or only make it more impenetrable?

CHAPTER THIRTY-TWO

So many hopes. All destroyed.

A moan escaped as Rani rolled on the bed. If the men's hands had been rough when they dragged her into the room, they were brutal once the door was shut. She had screamed and fought as they beat her, hearing from her own throat sounds she had heard other nights from other rooms.

She could have withstood one man with the force of her desperation and the remnant of hope remaining that this night she would escape. Two men, however, meant two hands to hold her captive while two fists slammed into her body. A flat palm against her face silenced her screams. Chains suddenly fastened around her wrists stilled her wild thrashing.

When they hooked the chains around the bed posts, she pleaded, all pride gone. "Please. Please! I won't run. I promise. Don't chain me."

A grated laugh answered her. The chains jerked tight as one of the men yanked them back, forcing Rani to fall onto the bed. "Please," she whispered.

"Shut up." A booted foot kicked her midsection. Rani's body curled around the pain, her arms held taunt above her head near the bed posts.

She cried, knowing they would see they had won. The harsh laugh nearby faded to a growl. "Get her," he ordered.

"No!" Rani begged. "No, I'll behave. Don't get the madam, please!"

"You try to run, you pay the price." The sound of the door opening then shutting shot through the blood pounding in her ears. Pain throbbed and pulsed in the silence. When the door opened again, Rani did not open her eyes. She cringed and curled tighter, seeing in her mind the unkempt hair, painted features, blazing eyes. The madam's fury could be felt.

Rani winced at the sound of a hard slap, but when her body did not feel the impact, she opened her eyes to see one of the men holding a hand to his right cheek.

"Idiot!" the madam screeched. "You know not to damage the merchandise." She slapped the other side of his face. "Her eye is almost swollen shut, you fool!"

"She kept kicking at me!" the man whined.

"You were supposed to bring her back, not beat her senseless," the woman roared. "What good is she to me now?"

Rani watched in horror as the other man, the one who had not been slapped, crossed his arms and grinned at her. "We have a client who likes bruised ones. Sell her to him."

The madam grunted. "Get out of here."

When the two men were gone and the madam focused on her, Rani clenched her eyes tight. She heard the madam's shoes slap the concrete, louder as they came closer…closer….

"Jesus God," Rani whispered in English. "You care for the rejected and alone. Please…deliver me."

A voice crossed her senses, too cold and cruel to be God's answer. "I will conquer you. You are my property and will be until you die or one of them kills you. You are nothing. You will always be nothing."

Rani pulled her arms, futile effort against the chains, until the skin around her wrists shredded. Raw, bleeding, and bruised, she turned from the deepest pain, the madam's words, and wished for the dark freedom of unconsciousness.

CHAPTER THIRTY-THREE

The nightmare came again. She was running, running. But the men were faster. They grabbed her. This time Mark was not there to save her. For she was not Asha. In the dream, she was Rani. And the men who pulled her away were the men who owned her body, who had bought her to use her as their slave. Their hands were hard as concrete; their faces full of hate.

She thrashed, trapped and held down. A scream tore at her throat.

Asha woke, the terror as tight around her as the disheveled bed sheet she struggled against.

Her entire body was soaked in sweat. Her chest heaved. Focusing all her energy on trying to still the panic still screaming through her body, Asha looked around. She tried to process details, anything to replace the faces in her dream. The hands.

It was still dark out, and her clock flashed midnight. The power must have flickered off then on again. She had no idea what time it was, but her fatigue told her she had not slept long.

How could she sleep again, knowing the nightmare would be waiting for her?

Asha reached for the one thing she knew could help. Her Bible lay open on her bedside table. She pulled it into her lap, then turned on the small lamp nearby. She needed those same verses she had written for Rani just days earlier.

"God is our refuge and strength," she read aloud from Psalm forty-six, "a very present help in trouble."

Asha closed her eyes. The moment the words faded from view, Rani's face came to mind again. Rani's face filled with fear.

Oh, God. Help her. Turning to Isaiah, Asha found chapter forty-one, verse thirteen, and read it out loud, as if her life depended upon the words. She knew Rani's did. "For I, the Lord your God, will hold your right hand, saying to you, 'Fear not, I will help you.'"

"He will help her," Asha said into the darkness. "Rani is God's child. He will help her."

The words dispelled the fears swirling and attacking like demons all around her. Exhausted, Asha lay back again and asked God to send the morning quickly.

By the time the rooster announced the surrender of the night to the day, Asha's eyes were circled with the evidence of a long and terrible night. Every hour or so, the nightmare had returned, terrifying her even after she awoke.

For Asha knew that for Rani, it was no dream at all.

When Mark called out softly from the Main Room, Asha dropped both the hairbrush she was holding and any hesitations that might normally have held her back. She did not care how disappointed or angry he might be feeling toward her. She flung open her bedroom door and with one despairing cry, threw herself into his arms.

He held her, silent. Either he understood enough to know she did not need any hollow platitudes, or he had nothing to say.

They stood thus until Asha's heart question could no longer be suppressed. The question that had haunted her through the night even more than the dreams.

"What happened to her, Mark?" She looked up with imploring eyes, begging him to refute the nightmare by telling her Rani was all right. "What did they do to her last night after they caught her trying to escape?"

Mark's eyes were glazed with fatigue. He was unshaven, and his hair looked as if only a hand had run through it all morning.

Once the question was out, he could no longer look her in the eye. His head turned away, and his voice was gruff with emotion. "Don't ask me that. You know you do not want the answer."

Grief consumed Asha's entire being. She slumped into the nearest chair and wiped her hands over her face, willing herself not to cry. "It's my fault, isn't it?" she whispered brokenly. "I have the feeling what you're going to tell me this morning will prove that completely."

Mark sat next to her but did not touch her. "I'm going to tell you a story, and I want you to listen to the whole thing without interrupting, okay?"

When she nodded numbly, he began. "Three years ago, the Andersens and Stacy put up a temporary clinic in the inner city. They were planning to run the clinic for two weeks as a way to help the poorest of the poor, and also give them the Gospel. The first few days went great. They had some heartbreaking cases, especially among the beggars, but they were able to help nearly everyone who came, and several people believed in Christ and left the clinic with hope for the future."

He sighed. "Then a group of several women came at one time. They approached Stacy and told her that they were all prostitutes from Sonagachi, the biggest red-light district in Kolkata. All of them had STDs, and one of them was pregnant. Stacy helped as much as she could, but hearing the stories of how they ended up in prostitution really burdened her."

Mark ran a hand through his hair. Asha had the momentary desire to go get her brush and comb it out for him. Something about his disheveled appearance made him look vulnerable. It frightened her.

Asha focused on Mark's words again. She had missed some of the story, and knew that, for some reason, this story was important to Mark. She needed to hear all of it.

"When Stacy came back to the compound that night, she told us about the women. She talked about how sad she was

226

about the life they had to live. But then she was excited because later that day some of the—the—" He stopped and his face contorted. "I hate the word—the pimps, they came and asked Stacy and the Andersens to come into the red-light district and treat more of the women there."

"We all agreed this would be a great opportunity to make a difference there. So the next day, all three of them left the temporary clinic for a few hours to go see the red-light women."

Mark's jaw clenched. "They returned to find the clinic ransacked and all their equipment stolen. They had taken or destroyed everything."

Asha's hands clasped in her lap. He continued. "We had to close down the clinic and leave the area. All the potential help that might have been given was ruined."

He stood and began to pace. "We all realized that if we wanted to help the women in the red-light areas, we would have to find some undercover way to do it."

At that, Asha sat upright. She opened her mouth to ask the flurry of questions that flew to her mind, but remembered Mark had asked her not to interrupt until he was finished. She clamped her mouth shut with force, biting her lip to keep it closed.

Mark walked to the window. He looked out stoically for several moments. Then he turned to face her. Asha held her breath.

"For the past three years, we have been involved in an undercover ministry rescuing trafficked women from the red-light districts here in Kolkata."

Asha gasped audibly. She covered her mouth with her hand.

"And you," Mark continued, still looking at her with those piercing eyes, "by not trusting that I would take care of things, as I said I would, have put our entire ministry at risk by your overt attempts to help Rani."

A liquid fire poured throughout Asha. She could not bear his eyes any longer. His voice continued and she listened, her head down, her eyes closed.

"We started the ministry slow and small, knowing we had much to learn and it would be easy to do things that would be more harmful than helpful."

Asha cringed. The ache in her chest spread.

"So we asked our Indian brothers and sisters in Christ if anyone knew of any nationals with a burden to help rescue trafficked women. We found out about a couple in a village outside the city, and several others, who became part of our ministry. In fact, I sent someone to find Rani, based on your description of the area and her room. He did find her, and offered her the chance to escape. She sent him away."

Asha's face blanched. The man had indeed been willing to help Rani. And Rani refused because of Asha's involvement in her life. Had Asha trusted Mark, Rani might be free already. Guilt swept over her in waves upon waves. Why had she been so stubborn?

"Our ministry has been small and we only do a rescue every three months, to avoid suspicion and also so we have time to learn to do this well. Each time we do a rescue, we try to rescue several at once, because once even only one woman escapes, the whole district goes on alert and it is very difficult to be involved at all for some time."

Mark returned to the chair and sat again next to Asha. She wanted to bolt from her place and run as far away from him as possible. Shame filled her; she felt herself shrinking into her chair.

"I won't tell you the details about what we do or how we do it. The less you know the better. I will only say that nearly every person on this compound is involved in some way. So far we have rescued twenty-six women."

He looked at her then. "The first woman we rescued was Ruth."

A tear slipped out and ran down Asha's cheek. Mark stood and paced again. "Her original name was Alia. She was one of the women who came to see Stacy at the clinic. She was the one who was pregnant."

Mark's sigh was audible, close to a groan. "When the men finished destroying the clinic, they punished the women for coming to ask foreigners for help. They know that foreigners can get media attention and cause difficulties for the corruption that runs rampant in the prostitution business."

He leaned his forearms on the windowsill. "By the time we were able to help Ruth escape, they had beaten her so badly that she lost the baby. She was devastated. It took months of love and rest and God's mercy for her to even smile again." Asha could not see his face, but heard the pain in his voice. "When she finally recovered, she decided to stay with the mission, knowing her family would not take her back after what she had done. The orphan children seemed to heal a broken part of her heart. She remained here and has been a mother to those children ever since."

At this, his head bowed over his hands. "And now she's dying."

He turned to her with eyes that reproached her for her betrayal. "I hate what happens there. I hate what those men do. We will never be able to do as much as I would like, but we are doing what we can. Asha, you should have trusted me. You should not have assumed that because you could not see what we were doing, that we did not care."

Tears were flowing freely now. Asha barely noticed them.

Mark turned his back to her again. "We will be having a meeting tonight to decide what to do about Rani. We had planned an escape for several girls three weeks from now, but with the men already being suspicious, and now Rani's failed escape attempt, we will have to change all that. Unfortunately, often when a girl tries to escape, they sell her off to another part of the country, or even overseas, to break her will and keep her captive. We will have to act soon if Rani is to be rescued at all. And now the others are at risk as well."

He turned to look at her then. The entire time, Asha had not spoken one word. She looked mutely at him, at his face so grim, his eyes so admonishing. "I don't want you to come to the meeting," he told her. "The more people who know details about what we do, the more dangerous it becomes."

His gaze shot through her like a knife. "Will you trust us this time?" His question had no tone. No feeling. He wanted to know a fact. Yes or no.

She nodded. Yes.

His face did not change. He did not believe her. She hung her head. Of course he didn't. She had given him no reason to trust her. He asked again, "Will you let us rescue Rani? Will you promise not to interfere, and especially not to do anything behind our backs? You have no idea the entirety of what you would risk if you went out there again. Not just for yourself, and for Rani, but for our entire mission."

He looked at her. "Will you promise?"

Asha nodded mutely again. Yes.

The door was open and he was halfway out of the room when he turned one last time to say, "I will let you know what we decide to do about Rani. You can pray for her, and for a successful escape." His eyes bored into hers. "But from this point on, praying is all you can do."

He shut the door firmly behind him. Asha felt as if the door to all of her hopes shut with it.

CHAPTER THIRTY-FOUR

"No. Absolutely not," Asha heard Mark say.

"You know we have no other choice. She's the only one who can do it," another voice answered. Mrs. Miller's perhaps?

Asha had not intended to eavesdrop. She stood hesitating outside the door to the elder Stephens' home, where the missionaries were having their meeting. She was determined to apologize.

She had spent the afternoon doing some serious soul searching. Instead of asking her heart what was right, she looked deep into the Word of God. After hours of reading and praying and asking God's Spirit to instruct her, the truth became clear. All she had done to this point—her trip to India, her work with the orphans, her desperate desire to help Rani—everything had been more for herself than for God.

She had wanted significance, something to give herself worth. Some action that showed herself and others that she was valuable. Mark had been right. She did feel as trapped as Rani. Only she was in a trap of her own making. Bound by her own need to prove herself.

Deep down, Asha had felt God would love her more if she did some great thing in His name. On His behalf, as James had once put it.

231

Now, through His Word, God showed her gently that she was loved and valued, not for what she did for Christ, but for who she was in Christ. She realized that, just as much as Ruth was not held back from God's love by her sin, she was not held back from God's love by any good actions or lack of them. Trying to earn God's love diminished it, and cheapened the cross.

First, Asha asked God's forgiveness. Her heart, truly contrite, was cleansed and made clean again. But next, she knew she also had to ask forgiveness from the missionaries. The idea filled her with dread, but she knew she would not know full peace until she had made things right.

When Asha approached the Stephens' home later, much debased, a sliver of fear made her hesitate before knocking on the door. That was when she heard the conversation inside.

Whatever they were discussing, Mark was unhappy about it. His voice was strained. "This has already gone too far where she's concerned. She's already put herself in danger multiple times. This is going to be risky, more risky than any attempt we've made before. She can't be the one. No."

A voice Asha recognized as Mark's father's spoke up. "Are you sure she's not the one, Son?" His teasing tone met with silence. Asha imagined the looks he must be getting. "Sorry," she heard him mumble.

A sigh sounded from the inside. "Let's take a five-minute break, then we need to pray about this."

Before Asha had a chance to retreat, the door swung open and Mark suddenly faced her. His features showed surprise, then wariness. "Tell me this is not what it looks like," he said.

"It's not what it looks like," Asha responded quickly. "I didn't come here to listen in or eavesdrop. I came to-to apologize to everyone. I knew this was when you would all be together, so . . ."

Mark looked over her face. Apparently convinced of her sincerity, he nodded, then gestured her inside.

All mingling and conversation stopped the moment Asha appeared. As if on cue, each missionary returned to their place and sat, waiting.

Asha bit her lip. She felt her fingers twisting. But she was determined to stop trying to prove herself. Stop trying to present herself as competent and in control. "I'm sorry." She forced her voice to speak through the tears. "I disobeyed the mission authority and put you all at risk by my impulsive choices. And Rani, I...I..." She wanted to leave it at that, to hold off that final taste of humiliation, but knew she had to say it. "It's my fault and I'm sorry. Will...will you forgive me?" Her voice rose barely above a whisper. "Please?"

John Stephens rose from his chair and enveloped Asha in a fatherly hug. "You had good intentions. We all know that. And even if you hadn't, the Bible says we have to forgive anyway, so we're stuck having to forgive you no matter what you did!" He chuckled, and this time several others joined him. "But do try to hold off on any other secret adventures before you leave. You've only got one week left. Try to keep it a little less dramatic, okay?"

Asha almost smiled, surprised at the immense relief she felt to have no more secrets, nothing to hide.

Eleanor Stephens spoke. "My dear, tonight in our meeting, we have been discussing you."

Asha nodded. She was not surprised. She waited for the reprimands, a lecture, recriminations about her behavior. Instead, she was shocked when Mrs. Stephens told her they wanted her help with the upcoming rescue attempt.

"Me?" she said. After all she had done? "But I messed up everything! I thought I would be the last person on earth you would trust to help rescue anyone."

"I still don't like the idea," Mark cut in. It was obvious the break-time was over. Mark was sitting on the edge of his chair, his body tense, hands on his thighs.

Asha sat down heavily as the argument commenced again. Mark saying it was too risky. Others saying there was no other choice. Finally, she could stand it no longer.

"Would someone please tell me what ya'll are talking about?"

The southern accent brought them all back to focus on Asha.

"Perhaps we should back up a little and explain things to you," Eleanor Stephens said in her quiet way. "We have connections, dear, within the red-light district system. We found out that your friend, Rani, was beaten badly last night after she was recaptured."

At Asha's gasp of pain, Mrs. Stephens spoke again quickly. "This may prove to be a blessing."

"A blessing?" Asha was certain she could not have heard right. She felt tears overflow. "How could it be a blessing that they beat her?"

Mark watched his grandmother reach out a comforting, delicate hand to Asha. His mind rebelled against the whole idea. How could they even suggest that she get involved? She was so new to the area, so new to even the concept of human trafficking. She would not know how to adapt if something went wrong.

The reality that they really did have no other choice filled him with a nameless dread. He knew he would not be allowed even the slightest involvement, his white skin and well-known face making it impossible for him to be undercover in any way. He would not even be able to follow her and intervene if she needed him. It had been hard enough to follow her the night before without attracting undue attention.

Mark squeezed his eyes shut. An image of Asha being captured, hurt, filled his whole being with a fear like nothing he had ever known.

His mind returned to the present when his grandmother spoke again. "Well, I hope you will pardon my frankness, but . . . because she was beaten, she will not be able to . . . 'work' for a few days. That is a blessing." Her voice carried the distaste for the subject. "And also, because one of the men lost his temper and left bruises and marks on her face, which they usually try to avoid, they cannot sell her right away. Her price would be greatly lowered because of her appearance."

Her price. He saw Asha wince at the word.

"So because of this, we thankfully have a little more time to set things up for a rescue. There are two other girls ready, and we will attempt to rescue all three of them in one night."

Stacy Richardson held up her glass as if in a toast toward Asha. "And that's where you come in," she said.

Asha looked over at Mark's face. It was solemn, closed. She looked back at Eleanor Stephens. "You know I want to help," she said. "I desperately want to help Rani get free. But I promised Mark I would not get involved again. I've already caused enough trouble. I could not do anything without his permission to revoke that promise."

Everyone turned their attention to Mark, the one person in the room who did not want Asha to be involved. A low sound proceeded from his throat. He spoke, his face still focused on the floor, his tone still displeased. "You know I don't like it, but if that's the way it has to be, you can go."

John Stephens smiled in approval, then turned to Asha. "Usually in such cases we bring in a national woman from a different area. You don't need to know who, but this person is not known in our area, and so she can work without risking as much as someone well-connected with the mission. These men are ruthless and have no qualms about, shall we say, removing a person who continues to be a problem, or harming those they love in order to . . . um . . . motivate them to stay away."

A shudder ran down Asha's back. She glanced at Mark again. He looked tormented. Was he that angry that she would be allowed to be involved? Or was it something else altogether? Could he be worried about her?

"Anyway," Mr. Stephens continued. "There isn't time for us to get word to that person and have her travel here. By the time all that could take place, it would be too late for your friend. And we don't want to ask any of our Indian friends here in Kolkata.

Though many are involved in unseen ways, it would be too easy for someone to find out where they lived. Like I said, their lives and their families would be endangered."

Asha's hands were clenching again. No wonder Mark used such urgency in trying to get her to understand the risk. The situation was fraught with danger, so much more than she had thought.

John Stephens shrugged. "So that leaves you, little lady. You are the only one of us with the right color skin. None of us can go, obviously." A chuckle split the air and broke up some of the tension in the room. "We stand out like neon lights in the dark. Like a big flashy sunflower in the middle of a rose garden. Like the time I got a glass of milk and found a big brown cockroach in it!"

He laughed at himself and Asha smiled at him. He was the only person she had ever met who could enjoy a joke when talking about life and death issues.

"Anyway, we've got a plan, but it needs you. Do you want to do it?"

Before she could respond, Eleanor Stephens added, "There is risk involved, Asha. You need to know that before you decide. Normally, we would never allow any short-termer to even know about this, much less be involved personally. But," and here she, too, smiled, "you seemed to have gotten yourself involved without our help, and it does you credit." Her eyes shone with understanding.

Asha started to say yes, to say she was willing and ready to go. That night even. Then she stopped, remembering that what her heart said was not necessarily what God wanted. She wanted to appear spiritual by saying yes right at that moment, but a still, small voice reminded that true spirituality was doing what God directed. No more. No less.

"I'd like to pray about it, please," she said softly, a new calmness in her voice. For the first time in ten minutes, Mark looked up from the floor. His gaze on her was full of surprise.

Asha's smile was secure. "You know I want to say yes and rush right out there." She saw Mark's mouth tip in a half-smile.

He knew, indeed. "But if I've learned anything from the last week, it's that my own understanding is very faulty, and I should not trust my feelings."

Eleanor Stephens looked across at her with approval. Then she turned to speak quietly in her husband's ear. Lloyd Stephens, seeming frail and unwell that evening, nodded his head, then spoke with quiet authority. "We shall all pray this evening, asking for God's direction in this matter. In the morning, anyone who does not have set responsibilities, meet back here at—say, ten?"

Heads bobbed in agreement. The pioneer missionary then dismissed the gathering with prayer, and each returned to their homes.

Except Asha. With feeling, Asha crossed the room to embrace Mrs. Stephens, whispering a sincere, "Thank you."

"For what, dear?"

"For understanding."

Eleanor Stephens looked up at Asha with a gleam in her eye. "Oh, I understand, child. If I see past the fact that we look nothing alike, I would feel like I was watching myself at your age. You have made mistakes, but you are teachable, and as such, God will take your many gifts and use them for His glory."

She then smiled a knowing smile. "Just be careful you always remember that they are for His glory, and not your own."

Asha felt a comforting warmth fill her heart. Acceptance, like light, rose like the sunrise through her. It filled her with hope. Maybe God could use her after all.

She left the house that night, saying a quick, soft goodbye to Mark, who looked deeply at her but said nothing. She started for her room, but then detoured. She needed to talk to God. The best place to do that was on her swing with the night sounds all around her, under a thousand stars.

As she looked up in wonder at the heavens, her heart filled with peace. God was in control. He would take care of them all. If He wanted her involved, she would obey with all her heart. But for the very first time, she did not feel that Rani's safety and freedom were her personal responsibility.

And in that darkness, the breeze whispering peace all around her, Asha found for the first time in her life that she, herself, felt free.

CHAPTER THIRTY-FIVE

"*It's all settled then.*"

The meeting was over. The plan was set. Everyone had agreed that Mark should oversee the rescue attempt and Asha should be the one to carry out the rescue.

They had told her only what she needed to know to do her job, leaving the rest of the details unknown so she could honestly claim ignorance if questioned or caught.

Now that it was all set, Asha could hardly stand the intensity of her impatience. How was she going to bear waiting until tomorrow night?

She paced idly around the compound. She returned to her room to rest and ended up pacing around her room. She set out the outfit she had chosen for the rescue, changed her mind, and set out another. She wrote an e-mail to her parents, trying to sound casual, though she could not help envisioning the possibility of everything going wrong, and how this might be the last chance she had to contact them. She told them she loved them and thanked them for always being there for her.

Mark would probably tell me to stop being so melodramatic. She shook off the feeling of concern with a smile.

She spent her daily time with the orphans, who teased her for her absentmindedness. At one point, she even stopped talking mid-lesson and just stood there lost in her thoughts, imagining scenarios of the rescue and how she would react if something were to go wrong.

The next day, Asha spent a long time in preparation. Knowing that the spiritual preparation was even more important than physical preparation, Asha prayed, read Scripture, and sang. She prepared her heart.

And finally, finally, it was time to get ready. Asha dressed with care, pinning her *orna* in several places so she would not have to worry about it falling off. That would cause delay if she had to return to get it. Or it might betray the direction she was heading, or a place where she was hiding, if it dropped without her notice.

She painted her lips with a thick layer of red and her eyes with a heavy line of liquid eyeliner. She covered her arms in bangles and slipped several necklaces around her neck. Lastly, she added a few small touches that Stacy Richardson had taught her were indirect signals that she was a woman of the night.

Looking at herself in the mirror, Asha tried to calm her nerves by thinking with wry amusement that she never in her life imagined dressing to look like a prostitute on purpose.

Taking a deep breath, Asha prayed out loud. "Lord, this night is in Your hands. Help us. Give me wisdom to know what to do if something goes wrong. I am totally incapable of doing this without You. I give myself, and Rani, and the other girls into Your hands."

Again at peace, even as her veins pulsed with adrenaline, Asha walked from the safety of her room into the dangers of the night.

Mark was waiting for her outside. His eyes traveled over her. Asha felt certain he did not miss even one of the details that proclaimed her a woman of the streets.

Mark spoke, almost as if he were feeling nostalgic. "I could not believe my eyes when I saw you sneaking across the compound toward the water tower the other night. I had been waiting until a light came on in your room—I remembered how you said you always kept one light on, even when you were sleeping. When no light came on, I stayed outside to pray for awhile about how to get through to you. Then, quiet as night, there you were, rushing across the compound."

He almost smiled. "You were quite the sight, climbing that ladder to the water tower with one hand while your other hand tried to hold your whole sari skirt up to your knees." He looked down at her feet and said absently, "You have nice legs."

Asha burst out laughing. He smiled with chagrin. "I said that out loud, didn't I?"

Just as quickly as the smile came, he sobered again. "Promise me you'll be careful?" he said.

His eyes. So intent. His eyes were the only thing that gave her pause about this mission.

"Mark." She stepped closer. The smell of her perfume drifted up and around her. Mark stepped back.

Her face filled with regret. "Mark, I've told you before, but I really am so sorry about all I've done. I know that I should have let you take care of it, like you said. I should have trusted you, and the others. I will try to do a good job tonight, or at least show you that I can follow directions when I put my mind to it."

She had smiled as she said it, but when he did not smile in return, she stepped toward him again. "Please give me a chance, Mark. I know you don't want me to go. But I don't understand why. Do you think I will mess it all up?" Her eyes searched his. "Do you feel nothing for me but distrust?"

He reached a hand up to touch her face. His thumb caressed her cheek, causing Asha to shiver. "I have many feelings for you," he said, his voice husky, "none of them distrust."

Then he grinned slowly. "Or at least very few of them."

She could have lost herself in his eyes, his voice, but the guard approached to inform them the rickshaw was ready.

"It's Milo's father," Mark told her, retreating back into the facts at hand. "I have explained some of the situation, and paid him a very high price to take you to the rescue point and wait there until either you are ready to come home, or he is certain that you and the others are safe. Milo will be at a designated spot as well."

When she began to resist, not wanting to involve a child, Mark stopped her. "Milo knows that particular area better than anyone we know. He will watch from a safe distance across the street—he's a street kid, Asha, remember? No one will think a thing of him standing around. However, if he sees that you need help, he can lead you through any number of back routes if need be."

Asha's heart melted. He had gone through so much to try to keep her protected. "I wish you could come with me," she said softly.

Mark nodded. Cleared his throat. "I will be praying for you," he said. Then he stepped back, letting her go.

Asha turned to leave. She saw the guard slip outside the gate to talk with Milo's father. The eight-foot high gate swung wide. As she and Mark were standing between it and the compound wall, it closed them into a moment of seclusion from the rest of the world.

Asha started to walk to its edge, to circle around it so she could exit the compound, when suddenly Mark said her name, and pulled her back behind the gate.

For a moment, she felt as she had when he grabbed her in the dark alcove behind the pig stall. Her heart raced. Had something happened? Was there danger already?

Then she looked up into his face, and her breath deserted her. His eyes told her he was not thinking of danger, or even of the rescue mission at all. His eyes were full of her.

He kissed her then, softly, urgently.

His lips held hers for the briefest of moments, but Asha felt her heart reaching out to cling to his. She loved him, there was no hiding it. No denying it.

Too soon, his lips left hers, and he backed away. "Be careful," he said again.

She wanted to stay, to fall deep into the look in his eyes as he gazed down upon her.

But she knew she must go, and quickly. The guard pulled at the gate and motioned for her to come. She took one last look into Mark's eyes, then slipped into the night, leaving him behind with a small smear of lipstick on his mouth.

CHAPTER THIRTY-SIX

The hotel was impressive only for its garish décor and lack of cleanliness. Bare, exposed light bulbs hung on wires crossing the road at the entrance to the hotel. A man swept the street with a broom made from bundled straw tied at the top for a handle.

Several women stood in front of a row of hand-painted movie posters. Men walked the streets, pausing to look over the women just as they would pause at a fruit stand, looking over the produce to see if anything caught their interest.

Asha turned her gaze in disgust. Her stomach recoiled. When Milo's father stopped the rickshaw on the opposite side of the street, across from the hotel, she stepped down gingerly, trying to avoid the piles of trash littering the sidewalk, packed down into soggy mounds by recent rains.

She turned to tell Milo's father thank you, but the slightest shake of his head indicated they should not speak to one another. Not once looking directly at her, he flicked his chin toward a nearby corner. Her eyes followed. Milo stood in the shadows.

The sight of a friend was nearly Asha's undoing. She almost ran to Milo's side and asked him to take her away from this terrible place. To take her back to Mark. To purity and goodness.

Milo nodded slightly, but did not smile, or show any indication that he knew her. The lack of welcome reminded Asha of the importance of her mission. Three lives depended on her.

She squared her shoulders and lifted her head, ready to cross the street and begin her part of the rescue. Halfway across the street, observing all around her, she noticed that not one of the women were walking with shoulders back and head held high.

She had forgotten not to walk like an American. How was she going to pull this off if she could not even remember a simple thing like that?

Slowing, and taking smaller steps, Asha tried to merge into the chaos of sight and sound all around her. Reaching the hotel steps, she hesitated only a moment before walking through the open front doors. Tonight, her feelings did not matter. Her desire to run from this place and never look back had to be set aside.

Rani needed her. And God had told her to help Rani, so there was nothing more to be considered.

The hotel lobby had once boasted plush carpets and elaborate elegance in design. Now only a hint of the former glory remained. The carpets had burn holes and were covered in stains. The columns, Greco-Roman in style, were chinked and several were covered in graffiti. Low lights gave a disreputable air, reminding Asha of old movies set in gangster hideouts where corruption reigned.

Her eyes swept the lobby, trying to take in information without revealing that she did not belong there in the remotest sense of the word. At a far table, a man caressed the arm of a young girl. His touch was soft, but there was no goodness in it. The girl seemed to hunch within herself. Her head turned away and her shoulders pulled forward as she crossed her arms across her chest.

She started to rise from her chair, but an older woman with a harsh face and a great deal of makeup on gripped her arm so tightly the girl winced in pain. The woman's hand remained tight, though her face never even looked toward the girl. She continued talking with the man, smiling slyly when money was slipped across the table toward her.

Asha could no longer watch. She rushed to the open doorway and inhaled a lungful of the night air. It was not fresh, but compared to inside the lobby it felt like freedom itself.

A man climbed the hotel steps and approached Asha, his eyes raking over her body. When he reached out a hand to touch her hair, Asha stepped back in shock. She wanted to slap his leering face and tell him what she thought about men who came to places like this, until she remembered how she was dressed, that she looked like she was advertising herself.

For the first time in her life, Asha wished she was ugly. Ugly as dirt. Beauty here only made a woman prey. With grief, Asha thought of how Rani was beautiful, much more so than Asha. No wonder Rani had said she would escape or die trying. Who could live in this degrading world without being destroyed from the inside out?

Another man had joined the first on the steps. They talked and joked, glancing at her often, their eyes and words emboldened by each other's presence. Asha understood enough to know they were saying that she must be new and untried. She was still skittish.

Asha's breathing grew more and more shallow. She was starting to feel lightheaded. When one of the men asked her what price she charged, adding an obscene gesture, Asha could keep up the pretense no longer. She tore down the steps, the fading sounds of the men's laughter trailing behind her.

Once across the street again, hiding behind Milo's father's rickshaw, Asha grasped the wheel to keep upright and tried to regain control of herself.

Yet before she had a chance to rein in her wild torrent of emotions, Milo approached, his crutch clacking deliberately along the concrete. He passed beside her, touching her arm so slightly Asha almost missed the subtle signal. Lifting her head, she saw him walking away, his eyes focused across the street.

She looked.

It was Rani.

Tears sprang to Asha's eyes. How had Rani endured months of this horror? Rani walked like one dead, her face a mask of containment. Her clothing was bright and cheerful, possibly to distract from the heavy makeup that did not quite hide the bruises still on her face.

She looked so small, walking next to the tall white foreigner. Her eyes stayed down. Her entire body declared resignation and defeat.

Rani had given up.

Asha wanted to scream out to her, to plead and cry for her not to give in to despair. There was hope. She was not alone.

The man escorted Rani into the hotel, Asha watching after them, her mouth clamped shut by her hand to keep from calling out to her friend.

With furtive steps, Asha again crossed the street, re-entering the filthy hotel in time to see the man follow Rani into an elevator. The doors shut, closing them in.

Asha looked around the lobby again. No one had seemed to even notice the man and Rani. Her downcast eyes. His aura of ownership. Here, it was normal.

Again, Asha had to fight the nausea that rose up within her. What was wrong with the world, that places like this could not only exist, but thrive?

Asha waited until the elevator doors once again opened to the lobby, this time empty. She rushed inside the small box and pushed the button several times to shut the doors, praying no man would slip in before they closed.

With a grateful sigh, Asha watched the elevator doors join each other, enclosing her into a cocoon of momentary safety. The elevator lifted, and her eyes followed the numbers as they counted up toward the eighth floor.

As badly as it had looked, Asha knew that, for once, Rani need not fear the man who had paid for her company for the night. The missionaries would not tell her who he was or where he came from, but she knew that the white man who had accompanied Rani that night was a believer, one who had helped rescue girls before. He would not harm her friend. Rather, he was probably explaining the plan to her right at that moment.

The elevator doors opened to a hallway nearly dark, only a few flickering lanterns hanging to light the way. Asha squinted to read the numbers of the rooms. Three. Five. Seven . . .

She passed by every room until reaching number seventeen. There, she paused only long enough to give the slightest taps— one, two, three—on the door, before continuing on toward the stairway at the end of the hall.

Once there, she waited breathlessly. The stairwell was even darker than the hallway had been, but this time the darkness felt comforting. It would hide them.

The door creaked and Asha flattened herself against the wall behind it. She tried not to move, not to breathe, until she was certain it was Rani herself.

When the familiar face came into view, Asha's relief was overwhelming. She whispered, "Rani!" and saw her friend jolt in fear. But when she saw Asha, hope leapt once again into her eyes.

Asha hugged her as Rani whispered, "I prayed God would make a way. I had almost given up hope." Her voice broke.

"With God's help," Asha told her friend, "tonight, you will be free."

There was no more time to talk. The two women rushed down the stairs. After several flights, Asha fought dizziness. It was taking too long. They still had so far to go. How much longer would they have before Rani's owners found out she was gone?

Finally at the bottom flight, Asha pulled Rani back before they exited the hotel. "There are two others. Since they were not under as tight suspicion as you, they said they could probably escape on their own. They are supposed to meet us outside, behind the hotel."

Asha faced her friend with the grim news. "If they are not there, we are to wait ten minutes. It will heighten the risk, but we cannot leave until we are certain they are not coming."

Rani's face was pale, but she nodded in understanding. Asha fought the desire to run as quickly and as far as possible from the hotel, knowing distance and speed were their only means of attaining safety that night.

At the bottom of the stairway, she slowly and cautiously pushed open the exit door. It creaked and groaned, making Asha want to groan herself. They slipped outside, down the few stairs, then stood uncertainly, looking around.

They were behind the hotel. Though it had seemed impossible earlier, the back of the hotel was even worse than the front. Dank, rotting garbage filled the air with its pungent smell. It was piled in huge mounds in the area between the hotel building and the narrow, shoddy road. Several piles were over four feet high. All the trash and leftover food from the hotel must be dumped right there. Asha covered her nose with her *orna*.

"Where are they?" Rani's hushed voice brought Asha fully alert again. There were no people in their immediate area, or down the two alleyways visible. It was a stark difference to the bustle and traffic on the opposite side of the building.

"I guess nobody wants to walk back here around these big mountains of refuse," Asha joked. She quickly sobered at Rani's expression. Oh dear, she sounded like John Stephens, trying to lighten the mood when it was not the time. "Sorry."

Asha twisted her fingers, then forced them still, determined to at least appear calm. *Think about something good*, she told herself. Anything to keep the fear at bay. *Think about Mark. About how his eyes looked right before you left. About how his lips felt. About how you should tell him someday that it was your very first kiss, and how it could not have possibly come on a more memorable night.*

As the minutes slowly passed, Asha could sense Rani's fear growing. Her own was not far behind. Finally, she suggested they pray. Bowing their heads, but with a quick glance up every few seconds, Asha asked for divine help, and for the rescue of the other two girls. She really did not want to leave them behind, knowing that if they had tried to escape and somehow failed, they would be in even greater danger than before.

Suddenly Asha heard footsteps, too many to be just one person.

Whoever they were, the people were running, and they were headed directly toward where she and Rani stood.

CHAPTER THIRTY-SEVEN

*R*ani grabbed Asha's hand, holding tight. Both girls stepped back behind a pile of garbage, trying to avoid breathing in the smell, Asha's head just peaking out above the pile to see who was coming.

When she breathed out in relief, Rani questioned, "What?"

"It's them," Asha whispered. She stepped out from behind the trash pile, a victorious smile on her face, to welcome the other two girls.

But it was short lived. The girls were out of breath. "They are coming!" one said in Bengali, hunched over, holding her ribs. "They saw us escaping out the window. We had a small head start, but they are too fast. They will be here soon!"

Asha looked around. There were three directions they could go. One would lead them onto the busy road in front of the hotel. That was not an option, as people might be looking for Rani by now. The other two alleyways looked dark and would be good options for trying to lose their followers.

"We'll run down this road," Asha decided, randomly choosing one of the alleys.

"We can't," one of the girls said. For a brief second, Asha realized she did not know either of the girls' names. Then she heard the words.

"Can't?" Time was running out. They had to run soon.

251

The one girl had fallen to her knees, still hunched, holding her ribcage and trying to catch her breath. "It was too far already," the other girl said. "We cannot run anymore."

Asha felt her courage eroding. She tried to swallow the panic that filled her. *God, what are we to do?* She did not want to imagine what would result if all four of them were captured trying to escape together.

Seemingly out of nowhere, Milo appeared. "They are looking already. Big danger, *Didi*," he said.

The three other women had clustered together in fear when Milo appeared. Asha looked all around. *Think*, she told herself. *Stop feeling and think!*

"Okay," she said, trying to sound much more confident than she felt. "I have an idea, and we're all going to hate it, but I think we would all agree that to be captured would be far worse."

Three pairs of eyes looked at her, wide with fright.

"We're not going to run. We can't. So we're going to hide."

"Hide?" Rani's voice was wary. "Hide where? Back inside the hotel? You know they would find us."

"No." Asha wrinkled her nose, even as urgency propelled her to speak quickly. "We're going to hide right there." She pointed to the piles of garbage. "We can split up. You two can hide in that one." Asha pointed toward the largest mound, at least five feet high and as many feet wide. "Rani and I will hide in this one." She indicated the second largest pile, nearly as massive as the first.

She was not surprised at the looks of disbelief that came in response. There was no time to argue about the idea. "Would you rather be caught?" she asked, her voice harsher than she normally would have wanted. She had to instill in all of them the reality of the dangers they were facing.

It worked. And whatever hesitations might have lingered were quickly dispelled when Milo whispered urgently, "I see them coming!"

Four women threw themselves into the heaps of rotting, slimy, foul waste. It took all of Asha's will to not jump right back out as the smell assaulted her from every direction. It seeped into her pores. It overwhelmed every other sense.

Then sounds filtered through the decaying fish and rotting banana peels and soggy tissues. She could hear the sounds of men, several men, running. The footsteps came closer. Closer.

Asha held her breath. She prayed that none of the girls had accidentally left an *orna* or a shoe or anything in sight, betraying their presence. She prayed they had had the good sense to cover themselves in the trash after they had jumped in. Even one patch of hair, or one swatch of cloth would give them all away.

Voices. Angry shouts. The men were not happy, but Asha could not understand what they were saying. They must be speaking in Hindi. Were they angry because they could not find them? Or had they discovered one of the girls, and were shouting at them to reveal the others?

Asha prayed like she had never prayed before. She wanted so badly to cover her mouth and nose with her *orna*, or even her hand, to block out the smell. Even the danger outside the pile could not distract fully from the grime and slick surfaces that slipped and soaked into her. She felt like she was drowning in filth, a mighty metaphor to the lives these girls had lived since their capture.

God, deliver us!

Just then, Asha heard Milo's voice. *Milo, get away!* she wanted to yell. What was he doing?

She strained every nerve to decipher his words through the several feet of trash buffeting the sound of his voice.

He was begging. Begging for money. Of all things. Asha pictured his pathetic face, his body leaned over onto his crutch to make him look all the more needy. She almost smiled, but any movement only made the trash slip and slide on her skin. Her body retched, and she fought against the feeling with all her might, knowing she must not move or all would be lost.

The men were distracted by the young beggar boy. He was telling them he had not eaten for the longest time. They yelled and she heard a slap. She winced as if they had slapped her instead of her young friend.

"You are lying!" the men said in Bengali, using the language Milo had been using.

Asha could hear the mischief in Milo's voice as he responded that he had told the truth. He had not eaten in the longest time. It had been an hour or two, at least, and he wanted some ice cream.

The men laughed at him. She heard Milo laugh, too, then he said, "You are looking for some girls, yes? Maybe the ones running and looking scared?"

He had their attention. And Asha's too. What was he going to say?

"I think you should go down that road," he said. He must have pointed down one of the paths Asha had originally chosen to flee. "They would be too smart to go back on the main road. They would choose a dark road, like that one."

"Did you see them go that way?" one man barked.

Again, Asha held her breath. What would he say? Milo had learned at the orphanage that God hated lying. Would he lie anyway to protect them? Or would he tell the truth, and reveal their hiding places?

Asha fought the panic welling up within her, urging her to jump out of the pile of garbage and run for her life. She remained still, knowing her future depended on Milo's answer.

"I did not see them go that way," Milo said, no wavering in his voice. "But can you see them here? There are only two roads. Maybe you should split up and each go down one. What other way could they go?"

Asha wanted to cry. To cheer. To dash out and hug Milo until he could not breathe.

The men argued with one another about which way to go, then Asha heard their footsteps, running. The noises faded away.

Silence.

Asha waited. And waited. Even after she felt certain they must be gone, she could not gather up the courage to leave her safe hiding place, no matter how horrid it was.

"*Didi*, you come out now." It was Milo's voice.

Full of relief, Asha clambered out of the garbage pile. It took several tries, as the shifting mound of trash kept pulling her back into its foul grasp.

"Milo, can you help me out?" Asha asked, reaching out her hand for assistance.

Milo did not move from his stance several yards away. "Sorry, *Didi*. You nice lady, but you stink so bad. I stay here."

Asha laughed. She did not even care. "Milo, you were our knight in shining armor tonight."

Milo looked down at his arm. "It is not shining in the night. Sometimes you say very strange things, Asha *Didi*," he said, his head bobbing in confusion as Asha continued to smile. He did know one good English phrase to use. "I save the day, yes?" he asked proudly.

"Yes." Asha wanted to hug him, but instead put her heart into her smile. "You saved the day."

The other three warily crept from their own hiding places. The four stood looking at one another, covered in filth, free from their captors, but now held captive by their own stench.

The other three jumped in surprise when Asha giggled. She could not help herself. The relief was so great, and the sight of them all truly amusing.

The others, not used to smiling, much less laughing, stood in befuddled silence. They stared as Asha's giggle turned into a laugh.

Milo laughed also. "No pretty looking girls you are now!" he said in broken English. "All ugly with yucky garbage smell! Ha ha!"

The smallest hint of a smile appeared on Rani's face. The other two stared in awe, then finally, a moment of gladness seemed to break through for they, too, smiled.

For Asha, that moment was worth everything.

Milo signaled, and soon his father appeared, rickshaw in tow. His eyes covered the trash piles, then the four women. Asha wanted to laugh again. Oh, the joy of being free!

Though all four girls could fit into the one rickshaw if they squeezed tight, Asha did not want to leave Milo's father with a rickshaw that would smell for days after he dropped them off. Not to mention it would be slow going with their combined weight.

She suggested they instead take an auto. It would be much faster, and maybe some of the smell would be carried away through the open doorways as they rode.

Milo's father tried not to show his relief as he left to find one. Milo followed, sending back a quick smile before he, too, slipped away into the crowded street in front of the hotel.

Twenty minutes later, a tiny vehicle full of girls stopped at a familiar gate. Asha could not contain her cry of grateful relief at arriving safely at the compound. They still had much to do that night, taking the women to safety outside the city. But her part was finished. She had fulfilled her task. The women were on their way to freedom.

"Thank You, God," Asha whispered. She had never said a more sincere prayer.

CHAPTER THIRTY-EIGHT

The gate swung wide and Asha rushed inside, a woman coming home. The three girls followed much more slowly, cautiously, uncertain of their new surroundings.

A familiar figure rose from the swingset. Had he been waiting there the entire time? Waiting for her?

Asha's heart filled as Mark ran toward her. As if he did not notice anything about her appearance or smell, he ran right up to envelope Asha in a tight hug, telling her he had been on his knees since she left, praying for her safety.

Asha looked up with her heart in her eyes. She wanted to wrap her arms around him and never leave the security of his embrace.

But her embarrassment over how she must look, and especially how she smelled, propelled Asha into action.

She backed several steps away. The smell filled the space between them. Mark spoke with a grin. "I can't wait to hear how you managed to end up so . . . so intriguingly . . . um . . ."

"Covered in garbage?" Asha helped him out.

His grin warmed her to her toes. She could not help smiling back. "I promise to tell you all about it, after I get a shower." She emphasized the word "after," which brought another smile to his face.

Out of the corner of her eye, Asha noticed her three charges huddled together like children. "I'm so sorry," she said, approaching and telling them with soft words that the foreigner was not to be feared. That he was the one who had planned and organized their rescue.

"He is a follower of the God who loves women?" Rani asked, her eyes on Mark.

Asha looked back at Mark. She smiled. "Yes, he is." She turned back to her new friends. "And he is the best man I know."

Stacy Richardson appeared, walking toward them at a brisk pace. "I saw you from the window," she said in Bengali. Then she switched to English. "These poor girls look as frightened and uncertain as a new batch of orphans. Why don't you let me take care of them?"

When Stacy smiled knowingly, then held her nose, Asha felt her face redden. "You look like you could use some cleaning up yourself," she said.

Stacy bustled off the three young women, after several reassurances from Asha that they were safe now, and had nothing to fear from anyone on the compound.

Once they were on their way to Stacy's house to get cleaned up and dressed for their trip out of the city, Asha turned back to Mark. He was still standing there, looking at her as if she were beautiful, seemingly unaware of how horrid she smelled. And she could only imagine how awful she looked.

"I, uh, think I'll just go take a shower."

He looked at her tenderly, then stepped back to let her go, telling her she did well.

"You don't even know what happened yet," she countered.

"No," he admitted. "But I know you did well."

She faltered beneath his gaze. How much better this was than sneaking out on her own, trying to do things in her own power. Tonight, she felt like she had come home. Like she belonged.

Then a slight breeze brought her smell in full force back to her consciousness. Wrinkling her nose, Asha excused herself with a forceful, "I have *got* to get this filth off me."

Mark's laughter followed her. Then he stopped laughing and said, "And please change your clothes and take off all that jewelry and junk. You're driving me crazy dressed like that."

She smiled back over her shoulder, flattered in some indefinable way to know that it had gotten to him.

The clock displayed two a.m. by the time Asha finally scrubbed herself free of the smell. She wondered how the other girls were faring. Dressing in her most comfortable cotton salwar kameez, Asha dried her shoulder-length hair and applied some lip gloss to her lips, now dried out from the heavy cheap lipstick she had been wearing.

She exited the Main Building, shutting the door quietly behind her, wishing she could be sleeping like most of the other inhabitants there on the compound. Stifling a yawn, she went in search of her three rescued friends, finding them freshly showered and each wearing a clean outfit of Stacy's, sitting on the front porch steps of Stacy's home.

Asha was about to finally ask what the two girls' names were when they all heard an engine roar to life nearby. She saw the girls stand as one, ready to run into the shelter of the building.

Turning, Asha saw that it was the Land Rover, with Mark in the driver's seat, pulling out from under the awning near the compound gate.

Stacy came out the front door just as Asha was reassuring Rani and the two other girls that everything was fine. "They're all feeling understandably jittery," she said in her clear, direct manner. "When I told them Mark was taking them to a village outside the city where they would stay safely until they could contact their families, they kind of panicked. I guess too many men have promised to take them someplace safe and they found out the opposite was true. They kept asking me if you were going with them."

Asha stifled another yawn as Mark, leaving the engine running, ran up to the group. "Ready, everybody?"

"But I thought you were going to go with them to the village," Asha reminded Stacy.

"Well, I was, and I still plan to, but it looks like they aren't going to feel safe unless you come along, too."

Asha was so tired, but Stacy did not leave much room for argument. How could she refuse, knowing her three friends would be fearful if she did not go?

"Okay, I'll go," she said in Bengali, noting the relief that came at her words. Mark stood behind her left shoulder. She turned to him with yet another yawn. "I can't believe how tired I am. And look at them." She gestured toward the three young women. "They don't seem the least bit tired. You'd think they stayed up all night regularly or something."

Hearing her own words, Asha cringed. "Oh dear." She covered her mouth, thankful they had not heard her comment. "I guess they do, don't they?" Fatigue had left her emotions raw and she felt tears coming. "Oh, Mark, how will they live with all those memories?"

"It will take time," Mark said softly. "But with God, all things are possible."

"They look so young," she said in English.

Stacy passed by, answering, "They are. The taller one is sixteen, like Rani. The little one is only fourteen."

"Fourteen?" Asha's eyes spilled over. "Fourteen."

The youngest of the group—Shanta was her name, Stacy told her—looked up and saw Asha's tears. She approached. "You are crying," she said in softly accented Bengali. "Why?"

All eyes turned to Asha. What should she say? Hoping it would not offend, Asha said truthfully, "I am crying for you. For all the evil that has been done to you."

Young eyes, so filled with the evils of the world, widened in disbelief. Her voice came out in a whisper. "No one has ever cried for me before."

Asha's tears dropped from her chin, unnoticed. She touched her new young friend on the arm. "Oh, I think God has."

This seemed to have a great affect. The girl spoke again. "She," she said, gesturing toward Rani, "said that you know a

God who loves women, who even loves prostitutes. Will you tell me about Him?"

The fatigue ran off her like water, and Asha was suddenly glad she had agreed to go with the girls. She had much more important things to do than sleep. She needed to take this young girl's hand, and walk with her to the foot of Heaven, to introduce her to her Best Friend.

Mark drove for several hours. They left the city. Its smells and its nightmares. All four of the girls, Asha included, marveled as the sun rose over deep green fields and lush trees and growing plains of rice.

The farther they got from the city, the more nature reigned, and the more at peace they all felt. The dangers fell behind, and as the sun announced the coming day, one by one, each fell asleep without fear. For three of the passengers, it had been the first time to sleep peacefully in months.

Mark looked across at Asha. She had curled up in the passenger seat next to him, her head resting against the window. His heart had soared as he listened to her telling the girls about God rescuing Rahab, about Jesus forgiving the condemned woman, about God changing her own life. Now, as she slept beside him, he dared to ask God if she could, indeed, be the one for him.

His father did not seem to mind the idea, Mark thought with a smile. And his grandmother already loved her. He thought of his mother. What would his mother have thought of Asha? He imagined introducing them and watching them interact. A sorrow took root in his heart that such would never be, and suddenly he realized that he would very much have liked to have Asha know his mother. They would have become good friends.

"What deep subject are you contemplating over there, sir?"

Mark turned to see the object of his thoughts awake and watching him with interest.

"How long have you been awake?" he asked, thinking how comfortable it was to be near her like this.

She stretched, catlike. He was not surprised that he found the motion very appealing.

"Not long." She yawned, looking out at the passing landscape. "I never would have imagined there was so much beauty so close by."

"Well, we have been driving for hours, you know," he reminded her.

"I know. But I guess, being in the city all the time, I sort of forgot that places like this existed. It's so . . . peaceful." She sighed with drowsy contentment. "How much longer before we're there?"

He chuckled. "I thought you were enjoying the peaceful scenery."

"I am." She smiled. "But I will say that this isn't the most comfortable place I've ever slept. Please tell me that wherever we're going has a room where I can get at least three hours of sleep in one chunk."

"No problem there. We should arrive in less than half an hour, and sleep for all of you will be the first thing on the agenda."

"Mmmm," Asha said, and Mark thought it sounded like a cat purring. "Sounds wonderful."

She curled up again and within minutes was asleep once more. Mark felt his heart open wide and welcome her in.

Then his face fell and his heart constricted. In a few short days, she would be flying back to America. Back to her hometown, back to her own world, back to that James guy she talked about.

What was he going to do when she left?

And the thought that hurt even deeper, what if she never came back?

CHAPTER THIRTY-NINE

Asha felt as if she had gone back in time. Beyond the telephone poles and wires lining the road, the landscape that stretched before her had probably looked the same for the past thousand years. Rice fields patched the view into a quilt of vibrant summer green, dotted here and there with tiny bamboo huts.

She took in as much fresh air as her lungs could hold. How could anyone choose the city over this?

The others had piled out of the Land Rover and were looking around in much the same awe that Asha felt. She saw Shanta, the youngest, fighting tears. "I thought I would never see rice fields again." Her voice was young and vulnerable. "I thought I would be trapped in that place for the rest of my life."

Almost as if she could not help it, the girl threw her arms around Asha and hugged her fiercely. "Thank you," was all she could say.

A tiny seed of hope within Asha uncurled and stretched toward the sun. An idea, strong and beautiful and warm filled her. Was this what God wanted her to do with her life? Rescue young girls from slavery and give them back their lives?

Her musings were interrupted as Mark directed them all down a worn dirt path toward a patch of small buildings. Most were made of mud, their thick walls sturdier and cleaner than

Asha would have expected. She touched one wall. The surface was surprisingly cool.

A woman appeared, her pale blue sari drifting behind her in the breeze as she exited one of the buildings to their left. The sun was behind her, setting her in an angelic glow. Her smile was welcoming and kind, her words clearly chosen to put them all at ease.

"Welcome to my home," she said, her voice gentle. She spoke in Bengali. "God has given this place to me that I may share it with you. Please consider it your own home until God provides you with another."

As the woman led the three rescued girls inside and began showing them around, Asha held back at the door. She felt rather than heard Mark walk up behind her. His voice low behind her ear sent shivers across her shoulders.

He leaned his weight onto his hand, now against the door frame where she stood. "The woman who lives here calls herself Rahab. It is a fitting name. She was a prostitute, and her husband . . ." He trailed off and Asha turned to him, curiosity piqued.

"What about her husband?"

Mark smiled down at her. "Well, it's a great story. I'd better wait and let them tell it."

Asha knew Mark was well aware of how much she hated waiting. "You know that irks my soul when you do that," she said and he laughed, ushering her inside with the others.

The woman was explaining the different buildings. "Oh dear," she said. "I'm getting ahead of myself. I always get so excited when new people come."

She called a name, and a young woman appeared, smiling shyly. Asha watched as the woman named Rahab asked the younger girl if she could get some tea for them all. The girl responding quickly and eagerly.

Rahab smiled at the retreating form. "We call her Rebekah, for she has a gift for serving others with a willing heart."

"What was her name before?" one of the girls asked.

"Her name before and her life before no longer exist to us," Rahab said with an easy smile. "When she came here, she left her old life behind. And when she became a child of God, she became a new person. New person. New life. New name."

Rebekah returned with a tray laden with tiny teacups on saucers. Asha could smell the Indian spices that had been cooked into the milky *chai* tea. Her stomach began to growl, reminding her she had not eaten since supper the night before.

As they drank the hot tea and each chose an offered *samosa* snack, the woman introduced herself to the girls. At the mention of her name, all three sat upright.

"Is this not the same name as the woman in the Bible—the woman God rescued?" Rani asked the question on all three girls' minds.

Their hostess was impressed. "Yes, it is the same name. I gave myself this name, because I was once a prostitute and God sent a man to rescue me. He is now my husband."

Asha smiled as the three girls unconsciously edged forward in their seats.

Rahab explained. "A man came to my room one day. He was different from all the others. He paid for my time, but he did not want my body. He sat in the corner, away from my bed, and he told me about Jesus. He told me I could be free. I could have a new life. Be a new person."

Her eyes were wistful. "I did not believe him. I was certain there was no hope for me. Not after what I had become."

Again unconsciously, three heads bobbed in agreement. "He came every week. I tried to send him away. I tried to hate him. I even tried to tempt him. He kept offering me hope, and I had given up on hope long before."

Her smile was full of love. "But he was like Jesus, and he just kept coming. He did not listen to my words. He saw into my heart. And one day, I realized that I had begun to change. I had started praying to God and asking for His help. I began to hate what I did, and my disgust for it and for myself only grew. Finally, one time when the man came again, I was ready. I begged him to tell me how I could be forgiven, how I could be free. Even if I never escaped the brothel, I wanted to be free in my soul."

At that moment, a man entered the room and Rahab's story momentarily stopped. He was not attractive in a physical sense, but the look of love that flamed to life in Rahab's eyes when she saw him made him somehow appear tall and handsome and strong.

He sent a brief, welcoming smile to all present, then his eyes returned to his wife. "She is my pearl," he said with pride, not embarrassed in the least that all present knew of her past. "Life has hurt her deeply, but God used the hurt and the difficulties to make her into a treasure beyond price."

Asha felt tears. She felt no qualms or concerns about leaving her new friends here; it was easy to see they would be loved and cared for, and they would have a beautiful example of true freedom to watch every day.

Rahab's gentle voice filled the room once more. "Jesus gave me a new life, one without fear and without . . ." For the first time her voice faltered. "Without people treating me as . . ." She looked at her new young friends. Her smile was pained. "Well, you know of what I speak."

Again, three heads nodded, the gesture now accompanied by tears. Asha was watching their walls crumble, like the walls of Jericho. Freedom, true freedom, was on the horizon for them all.

"So now that Jesus has given me life, I wish to give it back to Him. My husband and I, we are the caretakers of this place. I call it 'The Scarlet Cord,' after the red rope the spies told Rahab to put in the window. It was that sign that would show her faith in God, and would protect her when the walls fell down all around her."

"Here, we ourselves are a sign of faith and hope, even as our past lives crumble around us. Sometimes I feel I will fall and be destroyed with it, but each time I am reminded of my past, God rescues me again with His love and promises of forgiveness. I am free now, and my greatest wish for you is that you will know true freedom, too."

Her smile lit the entire room with peace. Asha could see her three friends absorbing it, basking in the hope she offered.

"And also," Rahab added, standing and walking toward the window where she fingered a beautifully embroidered curtain hanging there, "in this place, we will teach you how to make beautiful garments and other products to sell, so you may gain independence and earn your livelihood. That is, unless your families desire your return, of course."

A subtle tug on Asha's *orna* brought her focus back to Mark, now standing behind her. His slight head tilt summoned her to follow him into the kitchen, where he explained, "This place is funded by gifts from people in America. It is a great ministry, but sometimes the finances get really tight."

Rahab's husband joined them, hearing the tail end of Mark's words. "It would be wonderful," he offered in addition, "if God were to call someone to full-time ministry here. There is so much to do, so much more than we can do on our own. Very few of the women are welcomed back into their families, and we just don't have places to send them. We could rescue so many more women if we had places where they could work and earn money to sustain themselves. It is my prayer that God will send more laborers so we can rescue more girls. There are so many who are just waiting for a chance to be free."

Asha felt Mark's eyes on her. A still, small voice whispered in her ear, but it was hard to hear over the hammering of her own heart, and the distraction of Mark's eyes. Could God perhaps be wanting her to be the one to help this ministry grow? She could not imagine anything more fulfilling.

The man smiled and returned to his other guests. Mark and Asha stood still, neither speaking, his eyes on her and her eyes on the floor. She could not bear to look at him. If she did, Asha was certain her heart would overtake her and she would forget to seek God entirely.

Mark watched the emotions play across Asha's face. He wondered what she was thinking, but dared not pressure her. He had no right to take God's place and tell Asha where she belonged or what she should do with her life.

The temptation was strong. He wanted to give her all the reasons why it just made sense for her to consider India for her future. But a voice inside brought to his attention that reason really had nothing to do with his desire for her to return.

Mark needed to pray. And he needed to do it away from the temptation standing right next to him.

He excused himself and left the building, taking refuge in the Land Rover from the sun's relentless heat, and the even more relentless pounding his emotions took every time he looked at a certain woman.

When they left later that day, after everyone had a much needed rest, Mark found himself gritting his teeth. He and Asha were the only ones in the vehicle. Stacy had opted to stay for several days so she could help the girls contact their families to see if they would be welcomed back home. Asha had wanted to remain as well, but there was not enough time. She would be leaving India soon. Leaving him.

He had watched her as she said goodbye to the two rescued girls, then to Rani. Asha had cried. His heart had ached to hear her tell Rahab that, whether by prayer or by money or by returning someday, she was going to stay involved.

Now the ache grew and resonated across his chest. He had decided to let it be, to let her return home without any pressure from him. Then, if God sent her back to India, then he could tell her what was on his heart. That she was on his heart, and she kept taking more and more spaces in it. He was beginning to fear she would take the whole thing and not even realize it.

Better not to risk. Better to wait. At least that is what Mark kept telling himself. But as the miles passed and the silence between them grew thick with words unsaid, the cadence kept repeating inside him, a rhythm he could not ignore.

He tried small talk. They discussed the upcoming visit to see Ruth. Who would be taking Asha to the airport. Where she would have layovers on her way home. Asha mentioned she would be glad to see her parents again, but would be sad to be leaving behind all the people in India she had come to love.

Was he one of them? Mark's jaw tightened as he clamped his mouth shut. His knuckles whitened on the steering wheel.

The rice fields passed behind and the city engulfed them once again into its colorful, loud cacophony of sound and sight. They were less than a mile from the compound when Mark suddenly pulled the Land Rover to the side of the road. The moment he stopped, beggars and hawkers surrounded the vehicle.

Mark closed all the windows, sealing them inside. He ignored the men and women banging on the doors and windows with their wares for sell. He did not see anything but Asha, who was looking over at him, eyes full of questions.

Mark took a deep breath. He rested one arm up on the steering wheel, turning his body to face her.

"Asha," he started, hearing his voice and hating how solemn it sounded. She was looking at him, wide-eyed, as if he were the principal and she in deep trouble. He thought of reassuring her that he was not going to say anything bad, but then decided it would be better to just say what he needed to say and be done with it.

He took a deep breath again. *This should not be so hard.* Then again, why would laying the heart bare before another human being ever be easy? He only had one heart. He did not like the idea of it being crushed.

"Asha," he tried again. Her head tilted. Just the hint of a smile spurred him on. In a rush, he said, "I—you—we—"

Well, that about summed up what he wanted. But it did not exactly communicate. Mark sighed, focused, regrouped his thoughts, then let his heart talk for him.

"You have completely shaken up my world. I never expected to like that, but I find myself wanting to find you, to talk to you, just to see what unpredictable thing you'll say or do next. I hate it that you're leaving and I wish I could ask you to stay. I know I can't. I know you have to do what God wants you to do, but . . . I'll be asking Him, if it's His will, that maybe He'll send you back."

He stopped talking and waited for her response. Asha's beautiful brown eyes had gone huge. She put a hand on her heart, but said nothing. She closed her eyes. What was she thinking?

Asha put a hand to her heart, trying to contain it inside her chest. For a moment, the look in his eyes was too much to bear, and she closed her eyes, holding her heart, waiting for the flood of emotions to pass enough so that she could speak.

Large, strong fingers twined over and around the hand she had left lying between them on the seat. When she opened her eyes, the love she saw took her breath away.

"Would you pray about it, too?" Mark said. Asha felt her hand clench into a fist. His wrapped tight around it. "I know I belong here in India. If there's any chance at all that you belong here, too . . ."

His eyes. Oh, his eyes.

"I'll wait," he said finally. "However long it takes."

Asha could not speak. She could not move.

The slightest smile turned up the corners of his lips. Beggars and vendors still pounded outside, but neither were aware. "It's never happened to me before, but I'm pretty sure I'm falling hard for you." Then he smiled, the wide, full smile she loved so much. "And considering how traumatic this whole experience has been, I'd rather not do it again if I don't have to." His eyes teased her lovingly.

Asha opened her mouth to speak, but no words came. She looked around and remembered where they were, and that they were surrounded by curious, prying eyes. She withdrew her hand, joining it to the other at her heart, holding tight to keep them from trembling. "Do you have any idea what you just did to my heart?" she whispered.

His smile started at his lips and burst through his eyes. "Something good, I hope." His eyes traveled over her face, stopping at her lips. Asha held her breath.

Then abruptly, to Asha's complete surprise, he started the engine of the Land Rover and began to slowly edge it back toward the road, the cluster of people surrounding the vehicle moving with it, still calling and thrusting everything from bags of chips to plastic bowls and cooking pots up against the windows.

"Sorry," he said as they pulled away from the crowd and the vehicle regained speed. "I just remembered that we were out in the middle of the city, and if I didn't do something quick, I was going to kiss you and ruin your reputation forever." His voice was teasing, but his eyes glanced over her face again with regret.

Asha was already feeling lightheaded. She laughed nervously, but when, for a fraction of a second, he focused on her lips again, her body melted into the seat and she quieted. Resting her head back, she watched him navigate through the busy city streets. He avoided a herd of goats and another herd of sheep, and nudged through an intersection with no traffic lights while motorcyclists and rickshaws flowed like fish all around them.

When the compound gate opened, Mark glanced at her one more time. When he looked at her like that, she felt beautiful. She wanted to say so. To tell him everything that was on her heart.

She opened her mouth to speak, but Mark's voice filled the space instead. He was looking forward now, into the compound. "Something's not right."

Asha's eyes followed his gaze. The compound gate was open. The guard was there. Everything seemed normal.

Then she saw the police. And Milo's father. And Milo.

"Oh, no," Asha breathed out. What had happened? Was Milo's father in some kind of trouble?

Then a thought came to mind that jarred her to her toes.

Were the police there looking for Rani and the others?

Had they somehow found out about Milo's involvement in their escape, or his father's?

And if they asked her and Mark where the girls were, what could they say?

"If they start asking questions," Mark's voice was low and urgent as he touched her hand briefly, "just let me take care of it, okay?"

She nodded in glad acquiescence. For once, Asha had no desire whatsoever to dig her fingers into the situation at hand.

CHAPTER FORTY

*Un*nease knotted Asha's stomach. She stayed behind Mark, hoping no one would notice she was even there. What had they already told the police? Had anyone mentioned that she herself had left the evening before dressed as a woman of the streets?

Mark's father strode toward them. His features were grim, which frightened Asha even more than the presence of the police. It must be truly bad if John Stephens was not smiling.

"Son, I'm glad you're back," Mr. Stephens said, putting his arm around Mark and leading him toward the group. Asha followed and heard him say, "You remember that stuff that went missing awhile back from the storage shed? And the tools that we never could find?"

Mark nodded. Asha was having a hard time keeping up with the conversation. What did that have to do with the police, and Milo's father?

"Well, we found out this morning after you left that none of those things just went missing. They were stolen, along with several other things your grandma was missing. She assumed she was just getting old and starting to forget where she'd left things." At this he did chuckle slightly, but a sadness quickly sobered him again. He pointed with his chin toward the guard, who Asha suddenly realized was standing between two policemen.

"Looks like he's been stealing from us for months." John Stephens' face was grieved. "He had a connection with a rickshaw driver. The guard would steal our stuff, and the rickshaw *wallah* would take it and sell it on the black market. I bet he was making a pretty little penny on the side."

Mark sighed in disappointment, but Asha's sigh was pure relief. This did not have anything to do with the girls running away last night. *Thank God.*

John Stephens sighed also. "We told the police we won't press charges, but he definitely can't work here anymore. I feel just terrible about the whole thing. I hired that guy ten years ago when he was just a kid. I thought we could trust him."

"How did you find out?"

The question seemed to perk Mark's father out of his somber mood. "Now that's an interesting turn of events. Seems the rickshaw guy in cahoots with the guard got into some trouble himself and couldn't come around anymore. So the guard started working on Milo's dad here."

Asha turned her gaze to where Milo's father stood, leaning one leg up on his rickshaw. Milo had taken a seat in the rickshaw, watching the scene with interest.

"Milo's dad pretended to be in on the whole scheme, see? The guard had set it up to deliver some stolen stuff last night. When you and the little lady here came out so late, he got nervous and didn't know quite what to do. And then," and here Mr. Stephens did start chuckling again, "when he saw our little friend here all trumped up like a hussy . . ."

Asha blushed to the roots of her hair.

"The guard actually snuck outside the gate . . ."

Asha remembered. That was when Mark had kissed her. She had not given a single thought as to why the guard needed to go out and speak with Milo's father. The man could have climbed the wall and done a jig on it and she would not have noticed. Some undercover missionary she was.

"He told Milo's father that Asha here was young and pretty, and if he took her to the right people," he put his fingers up into quotation marks, "he could get a nice high price for her."

Mr. Stephens started to laugh, but one look at the fury on his son's face shut down the mirth completely. "You're right, Son. There's nothing funny about that." He put a fatherly hand on Asha's shoulder. "Thank God He was watching over you last night. Had it been any other rickshaw driver, you would have been in more danger than you could have imagined."

His hand patted her shoulder. "I'm glad you got back safe and sound, and the other girls got out. Horrible business, the whole thing is. Just horrible."

Shaking his head as if ridding it of all bad thoughts, John Stephens spoke again. "So, early today, the guard takes a load of our stuff—our stuff!—and gives it to Milo's father to sell. Milo's dad brings it back to me, with the police in tow. What a morning!"

Asha left Mark with Mr. Stephens and walked to where Milo and his father waited. "Thank you," she said humbly in Bengali. "My life was in your hands last night, and you . . . well, thank you."

The man gave a slight head tilt, acknowledging her gratitude. Milo, less inhibited, grinned down at her from the rickshaw seat. "We do good, yes, *Didi*? My dad saves the day!"

"He certainly did." Mark came to join them. They all turned to watch as the policemen accompanied the wayward guard off the compound.

Mark turned back to Milo's father. "Sir, you have been honest and just, when it would have been easy to be the opposite. We would like a man like you to be the guard on our compound. Would you consider the job?"

The man—Asha wondered if he had any name other than "Milo's father"—stood to attention, his eyes full of disbelief. He began speaking rapidly. Mark responded. They talked back and forth so quickly, Asha could not keep up.

Milo slid off the rickshaw to stand beside her. "This job he is offering, very good. Pays double what he gets as rickshaw driver. And no hurting back and hurting feet. Very easy job."

Milo turned to listen again, and his eyes lit up. "And there is small house here for the guard to live. Oh, *Didi*, this is like God raining down the good things on us! No more my father has to stay in dirty and poor place like before. Can stay here. With good people."

Asha nearly cried when Milo slipped a small hand in hers. "If my father say yes, if he stay here, I stay here, too. Is good place. I can live with my father, and go visit my friends when I want. Is all just right, yes?"

She hugged him. "Yes, Milo, it is all just right."

Milo looked up at her. "Asha *Didi*, you will stay also? Is good place. Good people. And Mr. Mark, he is looking at you like the men in the Bollywood films before they are singing romantic love songs."

Asha wanted to laugh, imagining Mark singing to her. *He would never.*

To Asha's embarrassment, Mark and Milo's father had finished their conversation, so Mark had heard Milo's words. He saw her look of utter disbelief, and with an impish grin put a hand to his heart and began to sing a popular Bollywood song.

John Stephens had just returned from closing the gate behind the policemen and the former guard. His eyebrows shot up. Had they not been attached, Asha was certain they would have flown right off his head, he was so surprised.

Milo grabbed his crutch from where it leaned against the rickshaw and began dancing around in a circle, singing along. Asha laughed, feeling her face redden as Mark grinned over at her.

"I've never been serenaded before," she said.

His grin was self-conscious. "I don't think that would really count."

John Stephens just shook his head in disbelief and continued on his way back to his house.

Milo finished the song alone, skipping around his father's rickshaw with joy. When the song was over, he came again to Asha's side and asked once more if she would stay. Asha hugged him again, this time full of regret. "I wish I could, Milo." Her words were for the child, but nearby a man was also listening.

Asha's eyes held Mark's. "I wish I could stay," she said again. "But I have to go back and finish my last year of college."

"No need for college." Milo waved her off. "You can learn what you need right here."

Asha smiled. "It is true I have learned more during my two months here than I think I have in my whole life," she said. "But I need to go back and get some training for what I think God wants me to do. If He gives me a job to do, I should learn to do it very well, yes?" she asked, using his way of speaking.

He pondered this for a moment, then the smile was back again. "Okay, you go," he said, giving his permission imperiously. She bit her lip to keep from laughing. "But I will be asking the God to bring you back again."

Asha looked up and found Mark's eyes still watching her. Not letting her go. "Yes, Milo," she said with feeling. "You pray that the God will bring me back again."

CHAPTER FORTY-ONE

Asha managed to find her seat on the plane and get her bags into the overhead compartment before she started crying. *You started this trip crying, and now you're finishing it crying.* She was thoroughly annoyed with herself.

Slim fingers brushed the tears away. She squeezed into her seat next to the window, stuffing her purse between her feet.

She tried thinking about how great it was going to be to see her parents again, her friends, and her beloved North Carolina mountains. But memories of the past week kept crowding all other thoughts out. Going with the orphan children to visit Ruth one last time. Saying goodbye to Milo. Her last rickshaw ride with Eleanor Stephens to buy souvenirs for her family. The warm sendoff from the missionary team, and their invitation to return someday.

And Mark. Asha's mind saw the banyan tree, the swingset, the dark alley where he held her.

She saw his eyes as they had said goodbye that morning. How awkward he looked when he asked if he could write to her regularly. The soft, gentle kiss he gave her before she had to walk away.

Asha felt the tears falling again. Frustrated at her own weakness, she reached into her purse and dug around in various sections until she found her small travel packet of tissues.

She had to tug and pull to release the small packet from its very secure place in the outside zipper pouch of her purse. When she finally succeeded in pulling the pack out, an envelope burst out with it and fell between her feet to the airplane floor. She reached between her knees to pick it up, bumping her head on the seat in front of her.

Once in her grasp, Asha flipped the envelope over. It had her name on it. Written in a distinctly male handwriting.

Heart speeding up, Asha ripped the envelope open. She pulled out a small card.

Inside it was a picture. Asha looked at it and laughed out loud, then covered her mouth quickly with her hand as several passengers turned to stare.

Where in the world did he get this? Eleanor Stephens must have been watching from the window. Or perhaps one of the other missionaries had just happened to have their camera out at just that moment. Red crept into her cheeks. She wondered how many people had been watching that day.

Milo was in the forefront of the photo, his face filled with glee, his crutch swinging in the air. Behind him, his father's rickshaw made a colorful backdrop to the scene. Asha stood to the left, her hand covering her mouth but not hiding the smile in her eyes. And on the right, looking completely ridiculous, was Mark, hand on his heart, mouth open as he belted out a love song in Hindi.

She turned the photo over to see if he had written anything on the back. He had. "The words to that song say 'You make me into a crazy man.' Now you have proof."

A laugh bubbled up inside her, but she restrained it to merely a giggle, not wanting to have to explain the photo to a curious neighbor or two. She tucked it securely back into the envelope, then pulled it back out to look at it again. Though she would show everyone at home her own large collection of photos from her trip, this one she would keep for herself. Her own secret memory.

The pilot's voice droned from the speakers throughout the airplane. Then the stewardess did her routine of showing various emergency procedures.

Asha neither heard nor noticed as she opened the card and became completely absorbed in the words held in her hand.

> *Dear Asha,*
> *Remember the time we sat under the banyan tree and you told me that the meaning of your name was "Hope"? Well, I looked it up last night. It does mean "Hope" in the Sanskrit language. But I also looked up what it means in English, or American. Under that label, there were three meanings: "wish, desire, hope".*
> *For the people of India, your Sanskrit name is perfect. But for me, the American meaning is who you are, for all three of those meanings are how I feel about you.*
> *The orphan kids are going to miss you a lot.*
> *I know I already do.*
> *Write soon.*
> *Love,*
> *Mark*

She read the words several times as the plane taxied down the runway and lifted into the air. India fell away below her, and Asha dropped her head back against the seat, wondering how much of herself was being left behind with it.

A soft whisper of a smile reflected in the airplane window. Asha stared at her reflection. She looked the same, but she knew she would be returning home a different person.

God had taken away things she thought were important and replaced them with things that really mattered. She would never look at the world the same again.

Or at least she hoped not.

Drowsiness lulled Asha as the plane settled high in the sky and the seatbelt light went off. She closed her eyes and imagined returning to India, rescuing more girls, helping develop a program for The Scarlet Cord. Most of all she imagined walking back through the compound gate to find Mark standing there, arms open, waiting for her.

She sighed, but the sigh was not one of sadness. Hope had taken root. It would be nurtured and nourished, and, if God willed, in His time it would blossom into something truly beautiful.

Whatever happened, Asha knew that she, and Mark, and the future—all were in God's hands.

And it was a beautiful place to be.

And they shall rebuild the old ruins,

They shall raise up the former desolations . . . .

Instead of your shame

You shall have double honor . . . .

Everlasting joy shall be theirs.

For I, the Lord, love justice.

Isaiah 61:4,7,8

CREATING CIRCLES OF PROTECTION
IN THE NAME OF CHRIST.

Women At Risk
INTERNATIONAL

"Every 2-4 years the world looks away from a victim count on the scale of Hitler's Holocaust." Women in this world of ours face nothing short of a hidden gendercide.
—The Economist

800,000 people are illegally trafficked against their will every year...70% of the women are sold into sexual slavery chained to beds of horror.
—US State Department

THE NEW SLAVERY...HUMAN TRAFFICKING IS THE FASTEST GROWING SEGMENT OF ORGANIZED CRIME. 100,000 ARE TRAFFICKED INSIDE AMERICA.
—FBI

HOW CAN YOU HELP RESCUE WOMEN AND CHILDREN?

Excerpt from

STOLEN CHILD

BOOK TWO OF THE STOLEN SERIES

$\mathcal{M}$ark hung up the phone, stunned. He sat, then stood. He paced, then sat down again.

She was gone. She was in danger.

And he was stuck in the capital city, a six-hour bus ride away. What was he going to do?

He had called Cindy Stewart the moment he arrived at the guest house in Dhaka. Her voice was strained, and she had gotten straight to the point. The Bengali man she had sent to the village where Asha was visiting her family had found Asha's home, but Asha was not there. Not in the village at all.

"I don't want to concern you unnecessarily," she said, "especially since your flight got canceled because of the cyclone . . ."

A sliver of fear climbed up Mark's spine.

"What are you trying to say?"

The nurse was silent for interminable seconds. When she did speak, her words shot through him. "There are rumors that the neighboring village across the way is planning to attack the Christian village . . ."

Heart pounding now, Mark's mind scanned through the possible dangers to Asha. She was in the Muslim village, not the Christian one. No, the man said she was gone. Gone where? Did someone take her to safety? Or—Mark's heart stopped. Was she in the Christian village for some reason?

"What—" Mark's voice betrayed him. He cleared his throat and tried again. "You said all this has happened before. What happened the last time?"

Again, silence. Then the soft voice spoke. "They burned the village to the ground. They beat the pastor and several others.

They didn't beat anyone to death, but two people did die in the fires."

Now it was Mark's turn to remain silent. His mind was pacing between panic and prayer.

He had to rescue her. But he couldn't. He was trapped by the weather of all things.

With little else to say, Mark quickly ended the phone call. He had not yet unpacked; had not even taken his one backpack to his room before making the phone call.

Now, unable to imagine enduring an entire night of not knowing, he grabbed his backpack from the floor where it leaned against the chair leg, jotted a quick note to explain his departure, then left.

He quickly summoned a taxi. "To the bus station, please," he said, his voice filled with urgency. "As fast as you can go."

Surely there was a bus somewhere in the city that drove through the night. If there was one, he was going to be on it.

Cyclone or no cyclone, Mark was going to find the woman he loved.

READER CLUB/DISCUSSION QUESTIONS
PART ONE: Chapter 1-10

1. Who is your favorite character so far? Why?

2. What would be the hardest part of a missions trip for you?
   a. Leaving family?
   b. Leaving your familiar setting?
   c. Difficult cultural rules?
   d. Germs?

3. Asha's parents struggle sharing their real feelings. How does your family express feelings? Too little? Too much? Not at all? How did that affect you growing up?

4. Asha's impulsive nature gets her into trouble. Can you think of a time you jumped into action too soon? What happened?

5. Asha and Mark start off on the wrong foot. How do you tend to react when you are tired and frustrated? Does your way clash with the way someone close to you reacts? How could James 1:19 help in such situations?

6. On page 82, Mark says it's easy to see things clearly when you come from the outside, but harder to see into what is familiar and normal in your own world. Do you agree? Have you ever caught yourself judging by your own perspective and perhaps later finding it to be incorrect?

7. Sparks keep flying between Asha and Mark. By the end of this section, what kind of box (or label) has Asha put Mark into? What box has Mark put Asha into?

Just for Fun: Fact or Fiction? (Answers on page 297)
   1. Is the compound a real place in Kolkata?
   2. Is Milo based on a real child?
   3. Do the people living on the river really use the water for washing, cooking, bathing, etc?

READER CLUB/DISCUSSION QUESTIONS
PART TWO: Chapter 11-22

1.   So far, which character do you relate to most? Why?

2.   Would you enjoy experiencing a new culture, like trying new foods? Why or why not?

3.   How did you feel the first time you heard about human trafficking? If you had been Asha, how would you have reacted to the pink note's words, "I was stolen. Will you help me?"

4.   Why do you think Asha feels so strongly that it is her responsibility to rescue the trafficked girl?

5.   Do you tend to act on your feelings, like Asha, or on reason, like Mark? Each way has its weaknesses and strengths. Do you think it is good to always go with your natural tendencies, or do you think each type needs balancing/tempering?

6.   Can you think of someone opposite you, who God may have sent into your life to balance you?

7.   Do you think Asha's decision to meet Rani secretly is wise? What would you do?

8.   Has reading Rani's story changed your idea about prostitutes? How? Do we tend to look at people in categories rather than as individuals? How does Jesus see people?

9.   Did Ruth's story surprise you? Do you think there may be people around you who have equally surprising stories? Are you the type they would feel secure enough with to share their past?

Just for Fun: Fact or Fiction? (Answers on page 297)
     1.   Is hospitality really as important as Chapter 10 implied?
     2.   Do women get trafficked like Rani did?
     3.   Are the market and sari shop based on real places near the red-light district?

READER CLUB/DISCUSSION QUESTIONS
PART THREE: Chapter 23-34

1. Thinking of the horrors of human trafficking can be overwhelming and lead to despair. How does the promise in Jeremiah 29:13 give comfort?

2. What do you think about Rani's question, "What good is it to be rescued from something terrible, if you're not rescued to something good?" Is it enough to fix someone's bad circumstances, or do people need more than that?

3. Do you think it would be difficult to develop a romantic relationship in such a restrictive culture? Would there be any benefits to a relationship with so many boundaries?

4. Do you think Mark knows Asha better than James did? Why or why not?

5. At this point, what do you think Asha still has to learn? About herself? About ministry?

6. When Asha's secret comes out, it damages her relationships—with Mark and the other missionaries. How does withholding the truth hurt ourselves and others? Do you think it is ever right to keep secrets or "rearrange" the truth? What if a friend asks you, "Does this dress make me look fat?" =)

7. Asha learns the hard way that good intentions do not make a wrong a right. Have you ever told yourself your actions were okay because _____, only to find in the end that God will not bless disobedience, no matter how well-intentioned?

Just for Fun: Fact or Fiction? (Answers on page 297)
    1. Is the largest banyan tree really in Kolkata?
    2. Do men work even in women's clothing shops?
    3. Is the pig market a real place, and separate from the regular market?

READER CLUB/DISCUSSION QUESTIONS
PART FOUR: Chapter 35-41

1. Asha wanted to find significance by rescuing Rani. Do you ever feel the pull to get involved in ministry to prove something to others, to God, or even to yourself?

2. Where are you most tempted to find your worth?
    a. Your looks?
    b. Your accomplishments?
    c. Your possessions?
    d. Your relationships?
    e. Your abilities?
    f. Other? _____

3. Where do you think God wants us to find our worth? Can you think of any Scriptures about how God views us that could be used with someone struggling with their sense of worth?

4. Have you ever had to humble yourself and ask forgiveness like Asha did? How did you feel beforehand? How did you feel afterward? Do you think there is an emotional blessing/freedom that comes with obedience?

5. In a crisis, how do you tend to diffuse tension? Are you annoyed with people like John Stephens, who try to joke it away?

6. If you were to be involved in rescuing trafficked women, would you prefer being involved through:
    a. The actual rescues?
    b. Planning and overseeing?
    c. Praying?
    d. Giving money?
    e. Raising awareness?
    f. Working at a safe house?

7. Do you think Asha will return to India? To Mark?

8. Every person has a story to tell. What does your story—your own unique history, experiences, sufferings—tell others about Jesus?

Just for Fun: Fact or Fiction? (Answers on page 297)
    1. Are there really idols that "guard" shops and homes?
    2. Is Rani's rescue a true story?
    3. Is there really a Scarlet Cord?

FACT OR FICTION: ANSWERS FROM THE AUTHOR

PART ONE:

1. Is the compound a real place in Kolkata?
Fiction—this was made up.

2. Is Milo based on a real child?
Fact—he is actually based on two children, one a real street kid with only one foot who used a crutch (that ice cream shop scene was based on a real event that happened) and another little boy named Milo whose personality I just fell in love with.

3. Do the people living on the river really use the water for washing, cooking, bathing, etc?
Fact—and yes, they use it for a bathroom too!

PART TWO:

1. Is hospitality really as important as Chapter 10 implied?
Fact—the story of the expensive Coke was based on a real event. I had forgotten my water, my mouth was on fire, and they brought out a liter of Coke for me to drink. It was so humbling.

2. Do women get trafficked like Rani did?
Fact—unfortunately, this is a common method of trafficking.

3. Are the market and sari shop based on real places near the red-light district?
Fiction—though I'm sure there are plenty of markets near the red-light district, this particular section came from my imagination.

PART THREE:

1. Is the largest banyan tree really in Kolkata?
Fact—it is, and I've seen it. It's so cool!

2. Do men work even in women's clothing shops?
Fact—and it is quite amusing watching them model saris for you.

3. Is the pig market a real place, and separate from the regular market?
Fiction and Fact—this particular market is made up, but in Muslim areas, pork would never be permitted near any other food, so it would be in a separate place for non-Muslims.

PART FOUR:

1. Are there really idols that "guard" shops and homes?
Fact—in Hindu areas, this is a common sight.

2. Is Rani's rescue a true story?
Fiction—I did not want to endanger any real work, so made the rescue entirely fictional.

3. Is there really a Scarlet Cord?
Fiction—unfortunately, at present, I know of no safe house for girls freed from the red-light districts in Kolkata. Let's pray one in!

ACKNOWLEDGEMENTS

I owe thanks to so many dear family and friends, without whom this book would never had made it this far.

Thanks to Mom for asking, "If you could write about anything, what would you write about?" That one question started the idea for this book.

Thanks to the Calvary Baptist Church ladies in Norwalk, OH, who read the initial manuscript and found my typos and grammatical errors. Your encouragement to get the book published meant a lot to me. A special thanks to Katie Cade for helping get the word out!

I also want to thank Rachel Hozey for her great editing. This book is so much better thanks to you.

Thanks Kierston and Julia for my great first website.

Thanks to Women At Risk International for rescuing women and children all over the world and for sharing that passion with me.

Most important, I thank the Lord Jesus. This book is Yours. Please use it to rescue others and bring them to Yourself.

Lastly, thanks to Brian, my husband, who listened to me read every single word of this book aloud, made sure my guy paragraphs actually sounded like a guy, and has believed in me enough to help make this dream happen.

ABOUT THE AUTHOR

Kimberly Rae has lived in Bangladesh, Uganda, Kosovo, and Indonesia. She has rafted the Nile River, hiked the hills at the base of Mount Everest, and stood on the equator in two continents, but health problems now keep her in the U.S. She currently writes from her home in Lenoir, North Carolina, where she lives with her husband and two young children.

Rae has been published over 300 times and has work in 5 languages. All three books in the Stolen Series—*Stolen Woman, Stolen Child,* and *Stolen Future*—are Amazon Bestsellers. Kimberly is currently writing a new series, taking up where the Stolen Series left off, for teen and pre-teen girls. "I want to present trafficking in an age-appropriate way within an exciting story that teens and their parents will like," says Rae. Sign up for Kimberly's newsletter to keep up with new releases and get special discounts, or contact the author at www.kimberlyrae.com.

www.kimberlyrae.com
Facebook Page: Human Trafficking Stolen Woman
Twitter: @KimberlyRaeBook

38013487R00182

Made in the USA
Middletown, DE
13 December 2016